read

Murder
at the
High School Reunion

Steve Demaree

Steve Demaree
To God Be The Glory!

Steve Demaree

This book is dedicated to the two people I love the most and whose love I deserve the least, my wife Nell and my daughter Kelly. May God continue to bless me with their presence in my life.

This book is also dedicated to all my friends on Facebook. If you are not yet a Facebook friend, send me a request to become friends.

May each of them and each of you enjoy this book.

Books by Steve Demaree

Dekker Cozy Mystery Series

52 Steps to Murder
Murder in the Winter
Murder in the Library
Murder at Breakfast?
Murder at the High School Reunion
Murder at the Art & Craft Fair
Murder in Gatlinburg
Murder at the Book Fair
Murder on a Blind Date
A Body on the Porch
Two Bodies in the Backyard
A Body under the Christmas Tree
Murder on Halloween
A Valentine Murder
A Body on April Fool's Day
A Body in the Woods
A Puzzling Murder

Off the Beaten Path Mystery Series

Murder in the Dark
Murder Among Friends
A Bridge to Murder
A Smoky Mountain Mystery

Stand Alone Mysteries

A Body in the Trunk

Aylesford Place Series

Pink Flamingoed
Neighborhood Hi Jinx
Croquet, Anyone?
Scavenger Hunt

Other Fiction

Stories From the Heart

Non-Fiction

Lexington & Me
Reflecting Upon God's Word

1

Lou and I stepped from the Blue Moon Diner, where I had had a scrumptious breakfast and Lou had picked at something on his plate that didn't look very appetizing to me. I closed the door and looked up to see our friend and fellow officer with the Hilldale Police Department, Lt. George Michaelson, pull up behind Lightning, my yellow VW bug. George got out of that gun-metal gray tank of his and walked toward us.

"Well, Cy, Lou, did you hear the bad news?"

"Rosie just told us. But how did you know?"

"Oh, didn't you know? I work for the police department now."

"Well, I knew they'd been paying you for over thirty years, but I had no idea that you'd started doing something to earn that money."

"Well, if anyone should know about drawing money without earning it, it'd be you, Cy. So, what do you think of the news?"

"Well, we probably won't know anything for sure for a month, and then we'll just have to deal with it best we can."

"A month? You think it'll take us that long to find them?"

"Find who, what? What are you talking about, George?"

"I thought you said you knew. What are you talking about, Cy?"

"The bad news, of course. You yourself asked me if we'd heard it, although I can't figure out how you'd know. You never eat here. Besides, it won't matter to you if the place closes."

"The school isn't going to close, Cy."

"School? What school, and what does any school have to do with whether or not the Blue Moon closes."

"So, that's your bad news?"

"Yeah. The owner is thinking of closing down for a month, taking a vacation, and trying to decide whether or not to reopen. I don't think the place has been the same since they lost Lou's business."

I was referring to the fact that my feeble friend has been dieting for way too long.

"Evidently your bad news is different. So, let's hear it."

"Well, sorry to heap more bad news on you, but you might have to go back to work."

"You mean you're thinking about killing someone?"

Lou is Sgt. Lou Murdock, and I am Lt. Cy Dekker, and he and I make up the entire homicide department of the Hilldale Police Department. Since Lou and I have passed fifty years of age and thirty years of service to the police department, and Hilldale doesn't have to use as much crime scene tape as New York City does, we worked out a deal with the department where we'll work only when there is a murder to solve. The rest of the time we draw our retirement checks, which are a little less than the paychecks we were receiving when we worked out this deal.

"So, I guess the two of you haven't heard?"

"Evidently not, but I've got a feeling that we're about to."

"I can always wait and let you find out when someone leaves the bodies on your doorstep."

"Just spill it, George."

"Okay, here's what we know. The county high school class had their twenty-year reunion the weekend before last. Word is that a couple of those who attended haven't been accounted for since."

"Anybody we'd know?"

George, like Lou and I, attended the Hilldale city schools. Hilldale High was and still is larger than the county high school, a school where only those who live out away from town attend. Since that has always been the case, we didn't know a lot of the county kids growing up. Plus, we are over ten years older than those who attended this reunion.

"One of them was some guy who caused a lot of problems back when he was in high school, but he's been gone from here a long time. The other one, Betty Gail Spencer, lives here and is married. The funny thing is her husband didn't report her missing. No one knew she didn't go home from the reunion until she didn't show up at the shoe factory on Monday morning. We checked with her husband. He doesn't seem to know or care where she is."

"Sounds like if we find the bodies, it won't take Lou and me long to solve this one."

"You know better than that, Cy. The simple ones always take longer."

"You've got that right. So, where did they disappear from? And is anyone looking into this?"

"The reunion was at the high school. We sent an officer out to the school. It was locked. No one was there. We checked. Both the principal and the custodian were away on vacation, so we had to get a key from the county to check out the place. The officer walked through the building and checked around the outside of the school, but he didn't find anything. Then, that officer was sent to check with whoever was in charge of the reunion, but that didn't lead to anything, either. So far there's no evidence of foul play. Some people think the two of them ran away together. Anyway, those of us in the department aren't so sure. We've even got a pool going on what day the bodies will be found."

"And you're going to keep the bodies hidden until it's the day you chose?"

"Well, I've got to, Cy. After all, I don't make your kind of money."

I knew exactly that George makes the same amount I do or the amount I made when I worked full time, plus he has a wife who works and contributes money to the bank account.

"Well, when we get the call, I'll hunt you down as soon as I interrogate the husband."

"I'm looking forward to it, Cy. Listen, I've got to go. One of us has to work."

We bid George goodbye and watched him get back into his tank and drive away. I turned to look at Lou who'd been silent ever since we walked out of the Blue Moon. Poor guy probably didn't have enough strength to say much, and more than likely he wanted to wait until he had something important to say. As if on cue, Lou opened his mouth.

"You're thinking about something, Cy."

"Just wondering who we have to see in order to put my five dollars in the pot. If we're going to have to solve this thing, I want to get a little something extra out of it."

Lou laughed as he opened his billfold and took out his five dollars.

All in good time. First, I had an idea.

"Lou, we don't have anything pressing today. How'd you like to take a drive out to the county high school, see if we can spot anything suspicious?"

"And if we find the bodies, move them until my day or yours, just in case someone else has already found and hidden them?"

"I don't know about touching them. As long as they've been missing, they must smell a bunch."

"What if the coyotes have already found them?"

"I guess we just hope that we can find a finger, so we can bring it back for prints. Of course, from what I understand, all the coyotes in this county are of the two-legged variety."

Our back and forth repartee was starting to get a little gross. It was time to change the subject.

"So, Lou, what do you think?"

"You that anxious to go back to work, Cy?"

"Well, I did finish reading that Carolyn Hart book last night, and I figured out who did it, which means my perceptive powers are at work. And I haven't started another book yet. Any reason you don't want to take a look?"

Lou gave me a look that told me he was game if I was. It was going to be another hot July day, but it was still early, and we could drive out to the school, look around, and get back in plenty of time to eat lunch and then take a nap during the hottest part of the day.

As I mulled this over in my head, it sounded like a reasonable plan, but then things don't always work out the way we plan them. Maybe we should have waited until someone found the bodies.

2

George had already told us that the principal, teachers, cafeteria workers, and the custodian were enjoying their summer vacations, so I knew whatever we learned, we would learn on our own. Lou and I arrived at the county high school and parked in the lot, which was to the right of the school. I looked around, spotted no bodies, or signs, or flashing lights leading me to where the bodies were. I wasn't quite sure what to look for, but I carefully hoisted myself from the confines of Lightning and walked slowly to the road to get a good look at the front of the school. I'd only been in the building a couple of times, and that was many years ago, so it wasn't like doing this would allow me to relive memories. Even this part of the county was unfamiliar to me. Up to this point, it had been off-limits to murderers, and I had no other reason to venture out that way.

What immediately came to mind is how much smaller the school was than Hilldale High. This two-story red brick school didn't seem to spread out much farther than I do when I sit down. Looking from the road, it seemed to be in reasonable repair, at least on the outside. While the school was still being used each day, fifty or more years after its inaugural year, I doubted if more than two hundred students invaded the building each year, which meant that each grade consisted of fifty or fewer students.

Another look around the exterior of the school produced no more bodies than my first glimpse, so I motioned to Lou and the two of us headed to the most likely place to dispose of bodies, the Thornapple River, which flowed behind the school. Even though it was early in the day, the short jaunt to the river brought beads of sweat out onto my forehead. I cleaned them off with the back of my hand the best I could. I'm not a handkerchief kind of guy, and I didn't have anything else available to wipe them away. If it were winter, I could've used my coat sleeve, but then if it were winter, I doubt if I'd be sweating.

Lou and I looked out upon the river, small as far as rivers go, but not someplace where you could walk across if you knew where the rocks were. I had no idea how deep it was, and I had no inclination to find out. I did, however, want to see if I could find any evidence of two bodies being dragged to the river. Of course, if that had been the case, more than likely all evidence would have been erased in those two weeks since it happened.

I was vaguely familiar with the school. Over the years I had had a couple of friends who attended County back in the day, so I knew about the river landing of sorts. While County has few students, unlike the number of students that attend Hilldale, some of those students live in remote regions of the county, and a few of them can get to school easier using the river, rather than the road. At least that was the way it was back when I was in school when the river was much wider and deeper, and it flowed uphill both ways, and you had to navigate the rapids in order to get anywhere. At least, that's what I was told by my friends who used the river for transportation. They told me that sometimes there were as many as six rowboats tied to a tree branch all day, while those who navigated the river each day were inside trying hard to learn or keep from it.

I looked. Things must have changed over the years. I didn't see any nearby tree branches, at least not near the landing, but there were a couple of small bushes. I wanted to see how much things had changed since the last time I was there, back when I was a mere shell of my current self. I walked over to the bank. I wasn't surprised that the area two feet below where students moored their boats was still there, but was surprised to see a rowboat down below, tied up to one of those bushes. The fact that I saw no bloodstains in or on the rowboat should have been enough to tell me to mind my own business and turn around, that there was no reason to investigate further, but I wondered how much more I could learn from that small, flat space of ground between where I stood and where the rowboat was bobbing up and down on the water. Actually, it wasn't doing a lot of bobbing. Maybe it was tired.

Momentarily, I forgot about how hard it is to stop a good size man in motion, and I looked for a place to step down onto the dirt below. I have no idea what kept my feet from ripping through the bottom of the rowboat, or what kept me in a fairly upright position. Obviously, the boat was sturdier than I expected it to be, but my luck was short-lived. At about the same time Lou hollered, I realized that the shore on the opposite side was looking closer than it did before. Slowly, I turned around and realized why. While Lou wasn't waving goodbye, the distance between us had widened.

The look on Lou's face told me he didn't know whether to panic or laugh. I knew which one. It wasn't his carcass out in that runaway rowboat. Lou collected himself before I did.

"Start paddling, Cy!"

Remembering that I never learned how to swim and that I didn't want to capsize, I turned slowly to look for the oars. Rowboats are not ocean liners. It didn't take me long to realize that my rowboat had no paddles, oars, or twigs to help me change directions. I wondered what I'd do when my vessel hit the bank on the other side, the side away from Lou and Lightning.

I didn't wonder for long, because my slight movements had changed the boat's direction and I was slowly being transported downstream.

"Stick your arms in the water, see if you can steer."

I felt like telling my friend where he could stick his arms, and then I realized that he was trying to help. I eased my body down into the boat and managed to do so with the boat still upright. I hadn't heard anything about alligators in the Thornapple River, so I leaned over and dipped my arms into the water until my lips were almost kissing the rotting wood. Not only couldn't I touch the bottom of the river, but I couldn't do anything to change the direction my flimsy vehicle was headed.

I turned to look at Lou, who was shouting encouragement. I wasn't sure if he was concerned about my well being or was afraid that I'd locked Lightning and had put the keys in my pocket. At that point, I wasn't sure if I locked her or not.

I continued to look at Lou, who was running behind the school, trying his best to keep up with me. I lost sight of him just as he tripped over a tree root and went splat. By the time he'd gotten up, I'd traveled a few more nautical miles and trees blocked my view of the school.

With Lou no longer in sight and no GPS on board, I turned to face my dilemma. I wish I'd paid more attention when our teachers taught us about local geography. I had no idea if the Thornapple River went over Cumberland Falls or Niagara Falls, or if I'd soon be shooting the rapids. The best I could remember, it eventually ran into a larger body of water, which wasn't the outcome I coveted. Briefly, I envisioned running into Thor Heyerdahl and the Kon Tiki somewhere in the south Atlantic. Then I vaguely remembered that Heyerdahl had died and figured anything I'd run into in the Atlantic would probably be larger than the Kon Tiki. I tried to remain optimistic and thought of how large the Atlantic is and that there is a lot more water than sailing vessels. Then, the thought of all that water made me hope that all of this was a dream and I was merely in my bathtub at home. I pinched myself and realized that that wasn't the case and started to look for a way out of my predicament before I reached the Atlantic.

I looked left and right, looking for someone to come to my aid. I saw no houses, no civilization. Where was a Wal-Mart when you wanted one? There wasn't even a McDonald's where I could order something to go. My only hope was that the area was so remote that I would soon run into strange people filming an episode of Survivor. I'd never seen Survivor. I had no idea if they had filmed in our area already. I had seen *Deliverance,* and I wanted no part of deranged-looking men accompanied by a couple of guys on banjos.

At one point it looked like my schooner had drifted a couple of inches closer to land. I had no idea what time it was but figured it had been at least fifteen minutes since I'd ventured farther than I should have. The only good things were that I hadn't spotted any bodies sticking out of the water and that that so-called boat of mine hadn't started leaking. I didn't see any sharks, either. And there was one other bit of good news. While I could tell that it was getting hotter, the tree branches that hung out over the river kept the sun from beating down upon me. It also kept God from sending me manna to help me keep up my strength, but then I knew if God wanted me to eat He'd find a way to get food to me. I just wasn't sure if I was ready to try squirrel or some of those other things that go scampering out in the wilderness. I hoped I wasn't out there long. I didn't want to start looking like Lou.

Lou. I hadn't thought of him in a few minutes. I hoped the fall hadn't knocked him unconscious. Even if so, I figured he'd find someone or someone would find him before I found Friday. More than likely Friday was still hanging out with Robinson Crusoe, anyway. And there was no possibility of finding Dr. Livingstone until I crossed the Atlantic because best I could remember, Stanley found him in Africa.

I'd become so absorbed in thinking about Lou that I'd failed to notice that my luck was changing. No, I wasn't about to encounter alligators, crocodiles, piranha, the dreaded waterfalls, or Gilligan. The kindling on which I was ensconced had drawn nearer to the shore. If I dove from where I was, I would've been able to drown myself a mere two feet from land. Instead, I blew on the outside of the boat and hoped for the best. It worked. A mere thirty minutes later, castaway time, the bottom of my skiff scraped against the top of Mt. Ararat. I had no raven or dove to cast out, but it didn't matter. I could see that the floodwaters had receded, and since I saw no cannibals or boiling pots, I took one giant step for mankind. Evidently, it wasn't enough of a giant step. My right foot slid back down the muddy slope and into the water. I lunged for dry land, hit my knee against the boat, and baptized a second foot. I found something to grab on to and pulled myself up onto dry land. It was then that I had a small inkling of what Columbus felt like, those many centuries ago.

It was at least a couple of minutes until I realized that the dry land on which I stood was on the other side of the river, which incidentally was in the next county, for whatever that was worth. I cupped my hand to my ear. I heard no chants or dueling banjos. I heard no "I'm over here, Cy," either. My journey was not yet over. And I didn't see Waldo. I didn't even wonder if he had a change of clothes.

3

There was no way I wanted to walk barefoot, so I sat down, poured the water out of my shoes, took off my socks and wrung them out the best I could, then put everything back on. Thirty minutes later, I'd managed to lift myself to my feet and scanned the wilderness. Wherever I had landed, it was an uninhabited planet. If I wanted to find some strange little green or red men who could take me to their leader, I'd need to go looking for them. Evidently,, no one had seen my landing and had come to investigate.

I sloshed on, hoping to soon find civilization. The next county over was almost as remote as the waterway I'd recently navigated. That meant my chances of finding someone with a still and a gun were good, provided I wandered deep into the trees, which I didn't plan to do. I took stock of my provisions. I found a large rock and emptied the contents from my pockets onto that rock. I had my keys, enough money to buy food if I found someplace that sold it, and eleven Hershey kisses. I had no idea how many months it would be until I was found, so I had no choice but to ration my kisses. I started by eating only two of them. I only had to open the first one to see that I wasn't the only thing that had melted in the heat. Not wanting to miss a morsel, I scraped my teeth across the foil and then used my tongue to rescue anything I'd missed.

The hot sun caused my mind to wander. I wondered about those two missing people. If I ran into them, I wanted them still to be alive, and if they were, I wanted them to have rations. If I had to share my Hershey kisses with them, it meant that I'd already eaten at least half of my ration. My stomach wouldn't understand if I starved it. I needed to find my way back to civilization.

I figured my best chance of finding civilization was to find a road. My best chance of finding a road would be to walk in the opposite direction of the river. I'd gone only a short distance when I realized that the trees that hovered over me while I was on the water hadn't continued to keep the sun off me. It was much hotter than the air-conditioned confines I'm used to. In a short time, I'd managed to sweat off a couple of ounces.

It took me only a couple of days to find a road. It wasn't yellow or brick, but I hoped it would lead me back to my recliner. I stood by the road and took stock of my situation. Not wanting to waste a lot of time, I took off in the direction that was closer to Hilldale. At least it was somewhat the same direction from which my watercraft had floated me. I hoped it was only a matter of minutes until a vehicle passed by.

It didn't take me long to realize that someone must have posted detour signs on each end of whatever road it was on which I found myself. I continued walking, walking farther than I wanted to walk in my lifetime. It was beginning to look like my socks would dry out before I encountered another human being.

After somewhere around a mile or so, or two or three days' travels, I spotted a driveway that led a house, well back off the road. Judging from the sun that beat down upon me, I gathered that it was close to noon, and anyone knows that all country people come in out of the fields at noon to eat lunch, to gain enough sustenance to go back out and work in the fields some more. That wasn't the life I wanted for myself, but if I found myself staring at someone who lived this type of life, there was no way I was going to quibble with how he or she chose to live. I would simply stand there, look pitiful, and hope that this person would invite me to dinner.

I arrived at the farmhouse and listened. I heard no one starting up a chainsaw, nor did I spot anyone wearing a hockey mask, so I stepped up onto the porch and walked over to the door. I knocked gently, not wanting to alienate anyone. When my first knock aroused no one, I knocked more loudly and garnered the same result. It was then I remembered how a lot of country people enter and exit using their back door. I walked around back and knocked on the door. A few seconds later, I looked around for the bell, the one the wife rings to let her husband know that it's time to come in from the fields and chow down. I found the bell and rang it as if Quasimodo were deaf. This brought some hound dog that must have been sleeping and caused him to start nipping at my soggy socks. I think only the smell shunned him away.

I waited a reasonable amount of time for someone to arrive from the hinter fields, and when no one did and I realized that it wasn't a Saturday. I figured the poor people had to give up farming and get a job in town. I only wished they could have held out for a couple more weeks. I popped a Hershey kiss into my mouth, a kiss that held up better than the others, and gained enough strength to start my trek back out to the road.

On what seemed like the morning and the evening of the second day, I found myself within one hundred yards or so of the road. I looked up and saw a car motoring down the country road. I hollered, waved my hands back and forth, jumped up and down, and as a last resort, ran toward the vehicle. On my way, I huffed and puffed, but I didn't blow any houses down.

I arrived at the road about the same time as the abovementioned vehicle reached the next time zone. The sun must have been really beating down by this time, and it had affected me so much that the car actually looked like a police car, one of ours, even though this wasn't our county. Even more than that, the passenger looked a lot like my friend Lou, the one who suffered a concussion at the school, mere days before I arrived at my present location.

I looked up and down the road. There were no trains, planes, or automobiles, so it was time to make a decision. I could sit down beside the road and hope that humans found me before buzzards did and that those humans were law-abiding citizens. Or I could ease on down the road. In a weak moment, much against my better judgment, I eased.

A hundred or so miles down the road, or a few centuries later according to the Mayan calendar, I took stock of my situation and realized I was down to one Hershey kiss. If I were to survive, it was up to God to turn it into a loaf of bread and a fish. It was then that my hallucinations increased because I heard a sound that strangely resembled a motorized vehicle. Just in case it was real, I turned, not wanting to be run over merely because I didn't get out of the way in time. Again the vehicle looked like a police car, and again the smiling face in the passenger seat looked like my trusted friend Lou. He and the driver seemed to be singing. The car pulled up and stopped beside me.

"Row, row, row, your boat, gently down the stream; Merrily, merrily, merrily, merrily, life is but a dream."

I looked around for a second vehicle, one whose occupants were not having fun at my expense. When I saw none, I made do with what I had.

Weary from my forty years in the wilderness and not thinking clearly, my not-so-pleasant voice shouted, "Where have you been?" It was then I looked at the driver, who strangely resembled Heather Ambrose, the woman of my dreams, the prettiest young thing the police department has to offer.

"Cy, are you okay?"

Since the question appeared to emanate from the woman of my dreams, I refrained from the gruff answer I would have given anyone else at that moment.

"Well, it hasn't exactly been my best day."

"So, Lou was telling me. You poor thing."

With that, she sprang from the car and hurried around to where I was barely standing. She threw her arms around me and gave me a hug and a kiss on the cheek. It was enough to make me want to locate the owner of the rowboat to find out when it would be available for rent again. After all, the rowboat was large enough for two people.

In a matter of seconds, my thoughts changed to how I could arrange for Lou to get back to town and Heather and me to be stranded together. It was then that her words brought me back to reality.

"You two have really had it rough today."

"I was being banged against the rocks by the rapids, but I don't remember Lou being in the boat."

"Yeah, but Lou got shot at, and almost run over."

I looked at my partner in crime, who nodded. Surely Lou wouldn't have made up some story just to get Heather's sympathy. Only I would have done that.

"It's true, Cy. When I got up off the ground I saw that you'd disappeared around the bend, so I tried to figure out what to do. I ran to Tweetie," (Lou sometimes calls Lightning Tweetie), "saw that it was locked, and the keys were nowhere to be found. Since neither of us has a cell phone, I figured the only thing to do was head out to the road and flag down the next motorist. It was almost fifteen minutes before someone came along. I saw this old lady driving a truck, and I started waving my hands frantically, trying to flag her down. When I saw her speed up, instead of slow down, I reached for my badge to let her know that I'm a cop. Evidently, she thought I was going for a gun; because she almost clipped me as she sped by, hit the brakes hard and spun the truck around to where it was facing me, then reached for the shotgun mounted behind her. I'd barely dived behind the edge of the building when the first blast of that shotgun came uncomfortably close to the only body I'll have for the rest of my life.

"About this time, another car came along, saw the gunfire, almost clipped me trying to turn around as quickly as possible, and headed off in the direction from which he'd come. Luckily, this person called headquarters, and they sent Heather. When she got there, after we'd enjoyed a leisurely lunch, just kidding, Cy, she called in and reported what had gone on. Someone downtown decided to postpone dragging the river for your body and sent out an officer with a small boat and a trolling motor. A few minutes later, he reported that your rowboat had run aground a mile or so down the river, on the opposite bank. Do you realize how far we had to go before we could find a place to cross over to this side? We've been driving back and forth looking for you."

Lou's words weren't as comforting as Heather's arms and lips, but I appreciated his concern. When he finished sharing his dilemma with me, Heather suggested that I get in so she could drive us back to Lightning. Momentarily, I pictured Heather and me alone there, with Lou still knocked out from his concussion, but then I remembered that I was old enough to be Heather's father and that I was the one who encouraged her to take up with Officer Davis.

When I realized that Lou wasn't going to get out and give me his portion of the front seat, I hopped in the back, where the prisoners are transported to jail. We'd gone only a quarter of a mile when dispatch called Heather. A teenage boy had called in to report that someone had stolen his rowboat. He added that while that had happened before, it had never happened since he'd started hiding the oars. Since the boat was stolen from near the county high school, they wanted to know if there was any connection between the theft and her present assignment. Heather confirmed that there was, and I got on the radio to tell them where the boy could find his rowboat.

Lightning seemed excited to see me when we returned to the school, where Heather dropped us off. As it turned out, Lou hadn't eaten either, so we dashed off to the Blue Moon for a very late lunch. The ordeal had lasted so long that my socks were dry by the time we arrived.

4

I was so worn out and starved that I didn't do much the rest of the day except eat and sleep. Of course, some people say that's all I do anyway. They don't realize how much reading I do.

I was hoping for a return back to mundaneness, but that wasn't going to happen. In some ways, the next day was worse, because the next day I had to do something I dreaded each time it happened. Not only did I have to walk despite all the aches and pains I had in places that I didn't know existed, but it was the day when I had to drag myself in for my every-six-month physical, listen to Doc complain about the sorry shape I was in, and then convince him to pass me again. Only this time it was different. This time Doc was more obstinate than I was.

"Cy, do you realize that you've gained weight?"

"Your scales must be off."

"Nope, and they're the same scales I use each time I need to check your weight or weigh some livestock. Only this time, instead of the much-too-heavy three-hundred-three pounds you usually weigh, you weigh in at three-eleven. Cy, that's just too much. I'm not going to pass you."

"Oh, come on, Doc."

"I'll tell you what I'll do, Cy. I'll give you two weeks to get down to two-hundred-ninety-nine pounds. Until then, you're not to do any work. And I guess you've heard about those two missing people from the high school reunion. Most people think they're dead. Cy, if we find the bodies and you don't have the weight off yet, you're off the case. Use Lou as a measuring stick. It took him forever, but see how much better he looks now. Do you want him to have to solve a case without you? Maybe George will have to help him. And I understand that some people have been telling Heather she ought to put in a request for a transfer to homicide when you and Lou retire. What if she and Lou decide to team up because you're not in shape to handle the work?"

"Doc, I've been doing this work for over thirty years!"

"And you're getting older. If you don't get the weight off and get your body in better shape, you might not be with us much longer. I don't want to attend your funeral, Cy. Now, do what I tell you. I'll see you in two weeks."

"But, Doc."

"I'll see you in two weeks. In the meantime, change your eating habits and start exercising. You know what to do. Now, do it."

"So, Doc, did you put your five dollars in the pot, the one about when they find those dead bodies?"

"I did. I have next Tuesday."

"There are so many people in on this thing the best I could get is the Tuesday two weeks after you. Lou's got the day after me."

"Well, maybe if one of you wins, you'll have enough time to get your weight off and solve the case."

I mumbled something in response and walked out of Doc's office a defeated man. I knew he meant business this time. I didn't know which would be tougher, exercising or changing my eating habits, but I knew I had to do both of them, and I had to start that day, not the next.

+++

I'd gone alone for my physical. Lou was at his place, doing other things. That meant that I could go ahead and plan my attack. I wasn't sure whether to tell Lou or not, but I'd thought of this scenario many times. If it ever came to my having to do some type of exercise, I knew what my choice would be.

I'd weighed my options. Going walking or jogging in my neighborhood wasn't an option. I lived next door to the world's worst neighbor, Heloise Humphert. She was always hitting on me, wanting me to cohabitate. If I left the house, she and that little dog of hers would follow me, and even headphones wouldn't save me from that grating voice of hers. So, walking in my neighborhood was out. So was walking at the mall. What if someone saw me, knew that I was a cop? Imagine if someone started spreading the rumor that some cop was in such sorry shape that all the old people were passing him. They might start asking for my job, saying it belongs to someone younger, someone in better shape. Well, it probably does, but right now there's no one in Hilldale qualified to do what I've done for over thirty years. So, walking at the mall was out. For the same reason, as well as the fact that I'm not sure I could live through all that exercise, was joining a gym. That's not for me.

There was only one route for me to go, exercising inside my home. I'd break any exercise bike, and I couldn't stand hopping up on a treadmill and going nowhere. No, the exercise would have to be fun. I'd either buy a Wii, Wii Fit Plus, and some of the Wii sports games, and/or a dance game, or some video I could pause or turn off and on until I could keep up with those doing the same exercises. I had to choose, Wii Fit Plus or Richard Simmons and *Sweatin'*

To The Oldies? I wasn't sure if I could stand looking at Richard Simmons. I had to do what Lou is doing.

I wouldn't waste any time. I'd go to the mall, buy some kind of system, and hire someone under the age of thirty to hook it up for me.

+++

I called Lou, made some excuse as to why I couldn't meet him for lunch that day, and then headed for the mall to seek out some expert about what I might need to get Doc off my back. I spent fifteen minutes listening to some guy who might not have been old enough to vote. Since he seemed to know all about the Wii, I listened to him and took his advice.

I arrived home and called, Mark, my yard boy, to see if he would come over and hook up my system for me. I swore him to secrecy. He arrived and had everything up and going in no time at all. He insisted on staying and helping me design my own Mii, the cartoon character which would be me on the screen. I was treading on dangerous ground. I'm sure Lou has a Mii for his system, but I didn't want any of the guys downtown asking to see my Mii. I could imagine what George, or Frank, the medical examiner, would have to say about that.

Mark wanted to make sure I could navigate my system, so he inserted the discs for first Wii Sports, then Wii Sports Resort, and walked me through some of the games. The next thirty minutes went by quickly.

Next, Mark slid in the disc for the Wii Fit Plus. I found my Mii, and it was time for me to weigh. Mark turned his head while I listened to a cartoon character tell me I was obese. I already knew that. I wanted someone to tell me how proud it was of me for mounting that stupid board. I noticed that the Wii showed me that I weighed three pounds less than Doc's scale said I did. More than likely,

Doc's scale is a little heavy, but it could be that I lost a little weight on my trip to the mall, or it was a delayed reaction to my trek through the wilderness.

I was already vaguely familiar with the Wii and the Wii Fit, and the Wii Fit Plus is an updated version of the original Wii Fit, with a few more bells and whistles. I got conned into trying the original at Lou's apartment one time, in front of our dates, Betty and Thelma Lou. I remembered that it wasn't as bad as I made it out to be. But this time was different. This time I knew that I couldn't get by doing only one exercise, and doing it only one time. Doc meant business.

I thanked Mark for his help and paid him for his time. He didn't want to take my money, but I convinced him that he'd saved me days of frustration. I watched Mark walk out the door and down the steps. I made sure that no one was hiding in the bushes and then walked over to begin my pain and agony. As I mounted the board, I focused on seeing the look on Doc's face when I weighed in two weeks.

Mark told me that the Basic Step exercise would be one of the easier ones to start with. All I had to do was step up onto and back off of the board without stubbing my toe while trying to do this in rhythm. I did four repetitions before I was sure I was dying. After a break, until I could breathe normally again, I mounted the board a second time. I tried hula hooping, basic stepping, and something else. One of them twice. I wanted to weigh, to see if I'd gotten down to two-ninety-nine. I wasn't sure if I could live through a second workout on the Wii Fit.

It was then that I remembered I can lose weight easier by watching what I eat, rather than sweating it off. It was time to go to the computer to see what I could Google about weight loss. Three hours later, I was a changed man. Changed because I wasn't quite as confused as *before* I got on the computer. Actually, I studied several ways to lose weight and decided to follow what made the most sense to

me. I learned how much to eat, and what to eat. I thought
I was going to have to eat some kind of foul-tasting cereal
and foods that didn't look like food. Instead, I found out I
could eat bacon and eggs for breakfast, just not the whole
larder.

I ran across a formula that told me how much I could
eat and still lose weight. I could begin by eating twenty-
four-hundred calories a day and still lose weight. After I'd
lost a considerable amount of weight, I might have to cut
back a little.

I studied to find out how much meat to eat at one meal,
which was considerably less than I was used to eating. I
read that if I ate the right percentage of protein each day,
it would satisfy my hunger, and keep me from being
hungry all the time and pigging out like I had been used to
doing at every meal. I learned that sugar, soft drinks, and
processed foods were my biggest enemies. Did that mean I
had to wave goodbye to those two desserts I ate at every
meal? I figured it did. I also learned that there were books
and calculators that would let me know how many of each
thing was in every food. I even learned that there were
websites I could go to to find out how many calories and
grams of fat there were in foods at chain restaurants. I
hadn't been in the habit of eating at chain restaurants, but
this was good to know, anyway.

I got so engrossed in studying nutrition and ways to
lose weight that by the time I looked at my watch, it was
5:00. There was no way I could avoid Lou for the rest of
my life. It was time to call him, to let him in on my secret.

5

"Lou, it's Cy."

"It's about time you called me."

"Lou, I need to talk to you."

"Oh, no! You've got cancer."

"Not unless you know something I don't."

"So, you have to have open-heart surgery."

"Have you been talking to someone?"

"Actually, I have. I called Doc. I knew your physical was today, and you canceled lunch on me, so I called him to see what's wrong with you."

"And what did he tell you?"

"He wouldn't tell me anything. You know that doctor-patient confidentiality thing. So, I guess you'll have to tell me. What've you got?"

"I got a Wii, Lou."

"Cy, I think we've got a bad connection. It sounded like you said you have a Wii. All kidding aside, what's wrong with you?"

"Well, I was a little out of breath after ten minutes."

"You mean you, the guy who swore never to get near a Wii again, the guy who didn't want me to talk about Wiiing, went out and bought a Wii. Did you lose a bet, or take up drinking?"

31

"Neither. I went to see Doc. He told me that I'd gained eight pounds, and if I don't lose twelve pounds in two weeks I'm through, and you'll be working with Heather."

"He did, huh? So, how'd you like to go out and pig out at our favorite buffet tonight?"

"Not funny."

"I thought it was. Okay, you win. I'll settle for seeing Heather after hours."

"What about Thelma Lou?"

"Okay, I'll see one of them on the days we don't have to solve someone's murder and the other one at night. How's that?"

The silence on my end told Lou that I was serious about losing weight, and then going after Heather, who was almost one hundred years my junior.

"Cy, this is a big moment. I'll tell you how big. Why don't I come over to your place?"

"Could you wait a while? Heather's on her way over now."

"In your dreams. I'll be there in fifteen minutes. I'll become your trainer and make a new man out of you."

I hung up, quite surprised. Lou never backed his red, 1957 Chevy out of the driveway for anything other than an emergency or a double date. He preferred riding shotgun unless we were taking Betty and Thelma Lou out to eat. Thelma Lou was his love interest and had been for a while. Betty and I were merely company for each other. I was still in love with my Eunice, who died of cancer many years ago, and Betty still loved Hugh, who died a few years ago.

+++

Lou came popping in ten minutes later, a smile all over his face.

"So, Cy, let me show you how to make a Mii."

"I already have a Mii."

"I mean your likeness for the Wii."

"I mean that, too."

"I should've known. There's no way you could hook this up yourself, so whoever hooked it up for you, showed you how to use it, and created a Mii for you."

"You think you're so smart."

"So, who did it, Mark, your yard boy?"

"How'd you know it was Mark?"

"Well, I didn't think you'd invite your next-door neighbor over, and surely you wouldn't let anyone else on the force know you bought a Wii. And you don't know anyone else."

"What about the people at church?"

"You wouldn't know which one to ask. Say, Cy, when did you get a computer?"

"I've had that a while. I can Google, too."

"What's Google?"

"Lou, you teach me about Wiiing and I'll teach you how to use a computer. You need to buy one, you know. It's time for you to come out of the dark ages."

I showed Lou my plan of attack, what I planned to eat. He thought it looked better than the stuff he was eating, but since he'd lost almost fifty pounds, he wasn't sure whether to change or not.

After we discussed food for a while, Lou and I Wiied. Old Smart Aleck twisted and turned, stepped on and stepped off my board for twenty minutes. I could do only ten minutes. Of course Lou needed to create a Mii before he started. After a while, we ordered pizza, a thin-crust veggie one, and both of us ate only two pieces. I wasn't sure how Rosie would react the next morning when Lou and I showed up at the Blue Moon and I ordered two eggs, two pieces of bacon, broccoli, and a medium-size green apple. At least the Blue Moon wouldn't continue to be a temptation. The next day, Friday, would be the last day the Blue Moon would be open for a while, and maybe the last time, period. We'd eat breakfast there, linger a while, and then Lou and I would head to the grocery. It would be hard learning how to cook. I usually ate out or opened a package or a can of something. I assumed I would curtail eating out, and packaged and canned foods were some of the biggest no-noes on my new menu plan.

+++

I went to the grocery after we left the Blue Moon. Lou helped me, so I managed to find everything in a little over four hours. We unloaded my purchases into the refrigerator and my pantry. I was tired, so we went out for lunch and dinner. I'd already decided that it would be easier to begin my new diet with breakfast.

The next morning, I opted for a couple of hardboiled eggs, two pieces of bacon, a cup of broccoli, and a pear. I thought I could figure out how to prepare the pear. I even had an idea for the broccoli and the bacon, but I had no idea about the eggs. Oh, I knew I needed to put them in water and boil them. I just didn't know how long to cook them. While I didn't know how to fix them, I knew someone at Google would, so I rushed to the computer. It was a good thing I did. My guess was to stick the eggs in boiling water and let them boil on high for three minutes. Google, on the other hand, recommended that I add them to cold water, bring the eggs to a boil on medium heat in a covered pan, then turn the burner down to simmer and let them simmer for fourteen minutes. Google even told me how to extract said eggs from the shell without losing half my egg or eating some of the shells. Believe it or not, I managed to do that without much of a problem. Still, all of this work was harder than telling Rosie what I wanted to eat each morning.

6

On the third day, I realized that I needed to navigate the Wii, see what all there was for me to do, then get serious about doing it. This wasn't quite as dumb as stepping into that rowboat, but it was in the same neighborhood. At least I could step off the board anytime I wanted, without drowning or getting muddy in the process. And I didn't have to worry about how I was going to get home. I was already home, and as far as I knew, no one was peering through my window, laughing at my feeble attempt to improve my stature.

I learned that the Wii Fit Plus had four types of exercises; yoga, strength, aerobic, and balance. From what I could tell, the yoga exercises help my flexibility, the strength exercises strengthen my muscles, the aerobic exercises help me get the fat off, and the balance exercises help me to improve my balance. Supposedly, all the exercises are important, but I planned to spend the bulk of my exercise time doing aerobic exercises since Doc didn't tell me that I needed to be more flexible or balanced, or that I wasn't strong enough. I'm sure he would have if he had some way of measuring those areas so that he could tell me I wasn't up to the department's standards.

I soon learned that I could kill myself quite easily attempting some of the yoga exercises, or die much quicker trying some of the strength exercises or doing aerobics for longer than my body deemed possible at that moment. Still, I had to push myself. I didn't want to look out my front window someday and see Heather driving by with Lou smiling beside her.

+++

Each morning, after I arose and went to the bathroom to rid myself of every ounce of weight that I could, I trotted to the Wii Fit board filled with trepidation, afraid that I had lost no weight and that a picture of Doc would appear, telling me that I was failing to do what he had mandated. Instead, each morning, shortly after I weighed, Lou called to see about my progress. I had disciplined myself enough that most mornings I was able to share some good news with Lou.

+++

Somehow I managed to make it through the first two weeks. Cooking, and eating what I'd cooked, was hard, but not nearly as hard as those Wii exercises. Some of them I wouldn't recommend to anyone over the age of thirty, particularly those Strength Training exercises. Some of the Yoga exercises were much tougher than anything I could do. At the end of each exercise, the Wii gave me a point total based on how good of a job I'd done on that exercise, and most of the time the Wii was tougher than the Ukrainian judge at the Olympics. I'd yet to score many points on any of them, but at least I did score some points on most of them. I was best at some of the Aerobic exercises and had improved considerably on some of the Balance exercises. And at some point each day, when I'd had enough of Wii Fit but wanted to exercise some more, I'd slip out that disc and put one of the sports discs in. While I had never been much of a sportsman, I actually enjoyed some of the sports games. Of course, most of them didn't burn off as many calories as the aerobic exercises. One that did was boxing, but one day I did a little more boxing than I should have and my arms were sore the next day.

7

For most of our adult lives, Lou and I have had the same hobbies. I love watching old TV comedies. My favorite two shows were and are *I Love Lucy* and *Hogan's Heroes*. Lou surprised me one year with a DVD player and the entire first year of *I Love Lucy* on DVD. Over time, I acquired all the episodes available from both shows, as well as some episodes of other of my favorite classic comedies.

Lou, on the other hand, has been a puzzle guy. Lou's always been puzzling to me, but his hobbies include both types of puzzles; crossword, and jigsaw, plus some other types of puzzles found in books, like logic problems. Most of the time Lou has spent at home, he could be found working some type of puzzle or reading a classic novel. Until Wii Fit entered our lives, neither of us attempted any exercise greater than the effort it took us to get out of bed each day, which on some days was quite an effort.

When Lou and I entered semi-retirement, we added another hobby, only this time both of us added the same hobby. Both of us have always been fascinated with solving things, so when we learned that there was a bookstore in Hilldale devoted strictly to mysteries, Lou and I headed over to Scene of the Crime to check it out, and we returned home with thinner wallets.

Because both of us left the store with an armload of books, we became as big of a hit there as we were at the Blue Moon Diner. Myrtle Evans, the elderly owner of Scene of the Crime, smiled when she learned that her newest customers were big spenders. As we returned to replenish our stock by picking up new titles to try, she learned a little about us and what our tastes were like, but we never let on that we were police detectives. Anyone who knows anything about mysteries knows that there are many types of mysteries, and many mystery fans prefer one type of mystery to another. While whodunits were our favorites, we ventured out from time to time and tried other types of mystery authors. This was easy to do at Scene of the Crime because each section and room identified the type of mysteries it held.

It had been several weeks since Lou and I had finished our most recent murder investigation. That amount of time off had given us ample time to pare down our stack of unread books. When I mentioned this to Lou, he was as eager as I was to go shopping.

We opened the door of Scene of the Crime, causing the bell to ring and Myrtle Evans to look up from where she sat on her stool behind the counter. I could almost see the drool dripping from her mouth and the dollar signs registering in her head.

"I've been expecting you, boys."

"We're getting that predictable?"

"Well, let's just say that the other day, during one of our slow times, I thought of the two of you and figured you'd be back in soon. I took the liberty to choose some titles for you."

She got up off the stool and searched the shelf behind her, where she had put two, large, shopping bags full of books. One at a time she lifted the bags up onto the counter. They weighed more than something a woman her age should have lifted, but she had both bags on the counter before either of us could assist her.

"Now, if you boys don't want any of these books, I understand, and if there are any more you want, feel free to look as you usually do."

"You've always steered us in the right direction before, Mrs. E. I'm fine with these if Lou is."

Lou and I always bought the same books, and we read them in the same order. Since we read at roughly the same pace, it gave us an opportunity to talk about each book as we read it, much like we do with each murder investigation as it goes forward.

Lou nodded to me that he was fine with her selections if I was, so I turned to Mrs. Evans.

"No, Mrs. E., you've always steered us right before. These will be fine. Just tell us how much we owe you."

"I included a book from some of your favorite authors, plus I added books by a couple of authors you haven't tried yet, ones I think you'll like. Let's see, that comes to $287.54 each." To some people that might sound like a lot of money, but all of the books were hardbacks, and a couple of them were early editions of books written a long time ago.

Lou and I paid but lingered a while talking books with Mrs. Evans, and a couple of customers who came in that we'd met before. It was fifteen minutes before we grabbed our books and headed for home. Well, I took Lou home, then went home and plopped down at the dining room table. I usually opt for someplace comfier, but I wanted a flat surface to lay the books on.

Neither Lou nor I bothered to look at any of the books while we were still in the store. I was excited to see what new treasures I owned. I reached into the bag and plucked the first book, *A Little Class on Murder* by Carolyn Hart. I'd read some of the others from Hart's *Death on Demand* series, and thoroughly enjoyed them, so I was glad to have another one.

Each time I bought another bagful of books, my routine was the same. When I got home, I took out one book at a time, glanced at it for a moment, and then put it aside. After I'd removed all the books from the bag, I'd sit down in the chair and read the dust jacket to see what the book was about. Then, I'd call Lou and one of us would suggest which offering to read first.

I reached back into the bag and pulled out another title. This too was a Carolyn Hart mystery, but one from her *Henrie O* series. Death on Demand was the name of a bookstore devoted solely to mysteries, much like Scene of the Crime, but in the *Death on Demand* series, the bookstore owner, a young woman, finds herself trying to solve a murder that takes place on the resort island where she lives, an island much like Hilton Head. Henrie O., on the other hand, is an elderly woman who gets mixed up in murder and may have to travel to do so. My new Henri O. title was *Death on Lovers' Lane*.

I continued to reach into the bag and pull out another selection until the bag was empty. When I finished, I found out that Mrs. Evans had included books by my two favorite authors of contemporary British mysteries, Martha Grimes and P.D. James, as well as a British author new to me, Jill McGown. I looked forward to reading *The Anodyne Necklace* by Grimes, *Unnatural Causes* by James, and *A Perfect Match* by McGown.

Other contemporary selections included *Murder With Peacocks* by Donna Andrews, an author new to me, *The Camel Club* by David Baldacci, an author I'd heard of but had yet to read, *Loves Music, Loves To Dance* by Mary Higgins Clark, *Tell No One* by Harlan Coben, *The Firm* by John Grisham, and *A Diet To Die For* by Joan Hess. I laughed when I read that title. My newfound commitment to losing weight made it a fitting time to read that book.

Mrs. Evans didn't forget to include some of the great classic authors, as she added *The Mysterious Affair at Styles* by Agatha Christie, *The Case of the Curious Bride* by Erle Stanley Gardner, *Patient in Room 18* by Mignon Eberhart, and *The Bishop Murder Case* by S.S. Van Dine.

I counted the books, fourteen in all. I planned to get busy reading and read as many books as I could before those bodies were discovered, provided there were any bodies to discover.

I sat down and read the dust jacket or back cover of each book. All of them sounded great. If only I could lose weight reading. Since Lou got a head start on me, I was sure he was anxiously awaiting my call.

"Did you make it through all of yours yet, Lou?"

"No, Cy, I was waiting to start reading until after you called."

"Smart aleck. I know you haven't started reading yet, but do you have any idea where we should start?"

"Well, just so you remember what your top priority is, why don't we start with that Joan Hess book? I remember how much we liked that other book of hers we read.

"It sure was funny, and from what I can tell, this Donna Andrews book is supposed to be funny, too."

"Looks like we've got a good variety."

Both of us were eager to get to our books, and since we'd decided which book to begin with, we said our goodbyes.

+++

Our books were the only things that kept the next few days from being difficult for us. Lou and I were used to being together every day. Before we retired, I picked him up each day and the two of us went about the city's business, one murder at a time. When there were no murders to investigate, we still rode around together, did whatever we needed to do to earn our keep, and ate all three meals together. When Doc ordered me to lose weight or desist, Lou suggested that each of us eat at home. He knew that I had a far better chance of losing weight if I stayed at home, and he knew that I wanted to remain a cop as long as he did.

It was two days later when I called Lou. I'd finished reading *A Diet To Die For* that morning. When I got ahold of Lou I found out that he'd finished the book the night before. We spent ten or fifteen minutes talking about the book, catching up on our Wii exercises, and deciding which book to read next. We opted for *A Perfect Match*. Both of us had almost finished our second book of the week by the time I picked up Lou for church on Sunday morning.

We didn't see each other the next week, but we talked once a day on the phone, discussing the book we were reading and how much weight both of us had lost. It was much the same the following week. I didn't see Lou until I picked him up for church. If we kept our noses to the grindstone, both of us could finish our fourth book of the last two weeks before that Sunday was over. As it turned out, it was a good thing we did.

8

The next morning, Monday, the phone rang just as I was getting ready to leave to see Doc. According to my Wii scales, I had lost enough weight to satisfy him. I hoped his scales agreed with mine.

I picked up the phone.

"I don't have time to talk. I have to get to the doctor."

"It's me, Cy. I just want you to know you need to be ready to go back to work."

Each day we worked on a case, Lou had a thought, which was ultimately helpful in our solving the case. I called them Lou's messages from God.

"You got a message?"

"I think so. At least I received a thought that said, 'North To Alaska.'"

"That was a Johnny Horton song, wasn't it? I don't want to go to Alaska, and I have no desire to become a singer, either."

"I agree with you on both counts. I'm sure that soon we'll know what the message means. Just between you and me, I don't think that someone shipped those bodies to Alaska."

We cut out the riffraff. I now had a second reason to get to Doc and get the weigh-in over with.

+++

I arrived at Doc's office. My new weight surprised him. I'd lost thirteen pounds. At two-hundred-ninety-eight pounds, I was a new man or at least a slightly smaller version of the old one. As it turned out, it was good that I lost the weight and received Doc's blessing. Well, I didn't exactly receive Doc's blessing. He asked me to come back once a month and weigh in. As long as I'd lost weight each time, he'd allow me to keep my job. And keep my job I did. Mere minutes after I left Doc's office, I received a message that the county high school custodian had returned from his vacation. He'd opened the walk-in freezer and found the two missing persons. Not exactly Alaska, but a good hint, anyway.

+++

I called Lou and then headed to his place. He was ready when I arrived. He ran out the door, jumped in the car, and acted like he wanted to kiss me.

"Cy, I'm so glad to see you."

"Lou, we saw each other yesterday. Remember? Church?"

"I know, but it's hard getting used to not being with you each day."

"You had me worried there for a minute. I thought I was going to have to draw my gun to keep you from kissing me."

"Not on your life, Red Ryder, and don't try anything with me, either."

"Don't worry!"

+++

Frank Harris, the medical examiner, was heading to the front door of the school when Lou and I arrived. I'd planned on Wiiing before I left the house. I knew that those two frozen bodies wouldn't mind if I did, but I decided to work in my exercise regimen later. I tooted the horn at Frank, who turned around, waved, and waited for Lou and me.

"Lou, it looks like I'm seeing less and less of you, but about the same amount of Cy."

I knew Frank meant weight when he said that, and not how often he saw either of us, because if he saw one of us he saw the other. I smiled. When a man is used to weighing three-hundred-three pounds and has lost down to two-ninety-eight, not even his own mother would notice the difference. Some people have trouble telling that someone who has lost fifty pounds has lost weight, provided that person is well overweight, which is what most of my world thinks I am.

"It's good to see you, too, Frank. I assume you haven't had anything to do for a while, so this will give you something to do."

"Unlike you, Cy, who only has to work after someone has been murdered, I'm called in for many kinds of death. However, it is good to see you," Frank uttered, as he reached out and patted me on the back.

"Listen, Frank, can we postpone finding the bodies until tomorrow?"

"And why do you want to do that, Cy?"

"Well, I got in that pot too, and my day is tomorrow. Why don't we keep them nice and cold until then?"

"Well, there are three reasons why I don't think that's a good idea. First of all, the custodian already found the bodies. He might not take too kindly to keeping these bodies for another day. And what if he talked? It would give the police department a black eye."

"I don't know how you count, Frank. Was that one, two, or all three reasons?"

"Let's call it two. The other reason is it wouldn't be fair to the person who won the pool."

"I won't tell if you don't tell, Frank."

"Now, Cy, you're not telling me that you would cheat a fellow officer, are you?"

"No, Frank, but it's harder to lose when you come close. By the way, how much was the pot and who won?"

"It came to $270."

"That much? Who won?"

"I stopped by and picked up the money on the way out here."

"And how many days have you had this guy hide the bodies?"

"Remember, Cy, he just got back from vacation this morning."

Rather than waste the rest of the morning sweating in the sweltering heat, Frank and I dispensed of pleasantries, and he and Lou followed me into the school. We were met at the front door by an average-looking, sandy-haired man dressed in khakis, with a white patch on his shirt, with blue writing that said his name was Walter. I guessed that the man was somewhere in his late forties.

"I'm Lt. Dekker. This is Sgt. Murdock, and the medical examiner Mr. Harris. Are you the man who found the bodies?"

"I'm afraid so. I've been on vacation since the night of the reunion, just got back to work today. Sometimes, when I'm here by myself, I go a few days without opening the walk-in 'refrigerator or freezer, but it's hot today. I kept working up a sweat and forgot to fill up the ice trays in that old, small 'refrigerator. When I went over and unlocked the big freezer, I opened it and found...well, follow me, you'll see."

"Did you recognize the two people?"

"To be honest with you, I didn't look at them real close, but I doubt if they're anyone I know. I went outside, checked all the doors and windows to see if anyone had broken in, and didn't find nothing. I just got back in before you pulled in. Could it be that these two have been here since the reunion?"

"I assume you've read about the two people who turned up missing after the reunion."

"Can't say as I have. See, I've been out of town, visiting my daughter and her family. Just got back to town Saturday night, didn't go nowhere yesterday. Does that mean you have a good idea who they might be?"

"We think so. Was it a man and a woman?"

"Like I said, I didn't check. But come to think of it, I think one of them was wearing a dress. Anyways, I panicked for a minute, didn't know what to do. Then, I locked the freezer back in case someone came in, though I didn't expect no one. I called the principal but just got a message. He might be out of town, too. He's not expected to be back 'til next week. Anyways, I called you guys, then went and walked around the school to see if I could spot where somebody got in the school while I was gone. Nothing."

We talked as we walked. We turned right, walked down the hall and turned left into a large kitchen. A walk-in refrigerator and freezer stood against the right-hand wall. The custodian walked over to the wall, just past the two units, and stopped just before he got to a door that was on the back right side of the building. He removed a key from a nail, made sure he had the right one and unlocked the padlock on the freezer.

He took off the lock and opened the door, then stood back so we could see. There were two people lying face down in the freezer, huddled together. The two were facing away from the door, but I noticed right away that the one on the right was wearing a dress, and had shapely legs that certainly didn't belong to any man. We encountered no smell but noticed both frozen people had skin that had a slight red tint to it. Luckily, Lou and I wouldn't be around when the bodies were no longer frozen.

None of the three of us recognized the victims, so I motioned for the custodian to step in and see if he knew either of them. He did so and then shook his head, indicating that both people were strangers to him. Somewhat shaken, he stepped back out of the freezer as soon as he could.

Lou and I let Frank look over the victims first. To give him privacy, the two of us ushered the custodian out of the kitchen and asked him for someplace we could sit and talk. He led us to his office, near where we came in. As we were about to enter his office, which was more of a glorified closet, the SOC crew arrived. I gave them directions to the kitchen, then joined Lou and the custodian in his small workspace.

I motioned for Walter to take a seat. I took the only other chair. Walter told Lou he could find a chair in the cafeteria across the hall. Since Lou wasn't some dumb sergeant, he brought back a chair, rather than sit in one in the cafeteria. I waited for Lou to return before I began to see what the custodian could tell me.

"The name on your shirt says 'Walter.' Are you Walter?"

"Yep. That's me, Walter Gillis. I'm the custodian here, been here three years now."

"And were you here the night of the reunion?"

"Yep. I left on vacation the next day. I was anxious to get away to see my daughter and grandkids, but I knowed I couldn't run them people out of the school until 1:00. They was allowed to stay until then."

"About how many people attended the reunion?"

"I don't know. I was told there would be somewheres between thirty and fifty."

49

"Did you know any of them?"

"I don't think so. I didn't really pay no attention to none of them except'n for Miss Calvert. She's the one who booked the place. She had a couple of other women show up just after she did, but I didn't know neither of 'em. I pretty much keep to myself. Better that way. That way nobody can accuse you of nothing."

"I assume you were the first one at the school. Did you work all day on that day?"

"Nope, during the summer I come in one or two days a week to keep up with the dust. That day, I got here a little before 4:00. Got inside just before the storm hit. It was pretty bad out this way. Like I said, Miss Calvert was the first one of them to get here. She showed up somewheres around 5:00, not long after the storm passed outa here."

"Tell me about that night. Did the group stay in one place?"

"Well, it depends on what you call stay in one place. I was told they'd be touring the school at first. They came and asked me if I would unlock some of the classroom doors so they could go in and sit in the same seats they sit in when they went here. The school told me they might want to do that, that it was okay, but I had to stay with 'em, make sure they don't cart nothing off. Luckily, there wasn't a lot of them to watch. I told 'em 'fine' but I had to lock all the doors agin before they ate dinner. So, at 6:45 I started relocking all the doors. I had to look in each room, make sure everythang was all right and nobody was in there, then lock the door. After that, their to-do was in the cafeteria, but after a while, I could hear some of 'em comin' out to wander the halls, use the facilities, or go outside and smoke. Ain't nobody allowed to smoke in the school. They's real strict about that. They's also real strict about drinking. I told the lady there was to be no drinking, but I could tell some of them sneaked some stuff in. It led to a few arguments among some of the party-goers, but as long as nobody done no damage to the school I wasn't stepping in. They don't pay me enough to break up arguments. Anyways, it wasn't none of my business."

"Anything else happen that might stand out?"

"Well, after a while, probably around 10:00 or 11:00, this here guy shows up, wanting to know where his wife is. I was in the restroom at the time, but when I came out and seen a crowd just outside the cafeteria, I walked up to see what was going on. That Calvert woman came up just before I did, and she said she could handle it. I told her if'n it got out of hand I was calling the police. That seemed to calm everybody down somewhat, so I took my friend Earl to my office so we could visit. I hadn't seen him in a while."

"Wait, wait a minute. Who's Earl, and where did he come in?"

"He came in with the guy who was looking for his wife. Turns out that the storm we had that day knocked over a tree and blocked the road out where this here guy lives. Well, somebody called this guy from here, told him his wife was running around with some drunk and he'd better come and get her, take her away. This here guy knew that Earl had a boat, and they could get to the school by way of the river, so that's what he did, called Earl. Earl's a really good guy, always willing to help out somebody."

The thought of the school and the river made my mind wander. I envisioned the two people floating down the river, without a paddle, hollering for help. Lou nudged me to bring me back to the moment at hand.

"Did that guy find his wife?"

"Not here he didn't. At least not as far as I can tell. A while later, he come in here, knocked on the door, and thanked Earl for bringing him. He told Earl that he had another way to get home. That was the last I saw of him."

"So, you had your office door shut?"

Steve Demaree

"Not all the way. It was open a crack. That way people knowed I was in here, and I could hear if something really got out of hand."

"So, what happened after that?"

"Earl and me sat here a few minutes, talking. I could tell he missed the place, so I give him a chance to revisit the old days. See, Earl was the janitor here before I was. I worked with him the last year he was here. We got to be good friends, and he showed me the ropes. Anyway, we walked over to the cafeteria, made sure there wasn't nothin' going on that shouldn't be, then Earl and me walked the halls and he looked over the place he used to clean. Nobody could make a school shine like Earl could. We'd pass some room and Earl'd tell me a story about somebody. After a while, we come back down here, made sure everthang was okay. Course I assumed that it was, 'cause we didn't hear nothing and the school's not all that big."

"And was everything okay?"

"It seemed to be. Earl said he'd better get and headed out to his boat. I walked out with him, watched him until his boat got outa sight. Oh, when I came back down here, I seen some of them people leaving, and others had already gone, but some stayed right on up until 1:00."

"Did you check everything before you left, make sure that everyone had left the building?"

"No, Earl and me checked all the rooms while we was upstairs. All the doors was locked. Did you go to school here, Lieutenant?"

"No, I grew up here, but I went to the city schools."

"Well, you might not know this. There's only a couple of classrooms downstairs, woodshop, and art. The rest of the downstairs is the gym, the cafeteria, the principal's office, the guidance counselor, things like that."

"Did you go here, Walter?"

"No, I growed up somewheres else. I ain't been here but four years now. I worked a year filling in for whoever was sick or on vacation, or if they needed more help somewhere for some reason. They knowed that Earl was going to retire in another year, so they sent me over to help him since he wasn't getting no younger, they give him a chance to teach me the ropes, so I wouldn't have to learn everthing the hard way."

"So, tell me about how things ended that night?"

"I went in the cafeteria, reminded everyone that it was 1:00. There was only a handful of 'em left, though most of 'em had only been gone a few minutes. They packed up their stuff, while I checked the other two doors, to make sure they was locked. That's when I found out that someone had been in the kitchen and unlocked the outside door. That was the first I knowed about that. I opened the door and looked out, but didn't see no one. So, I locked up and walked out with Miss Calvert, pulled out right behind her."

"Is the back door key where someone could get ahold of it?"

"Not any of that bunch. Not without being lucky. The only one that wasn't behind a locked door somewheres was either with the principal or up there."

He pointed to keys hanging on the wall behind him.

"Was it marked 'kitchen door?'"

"It was, but I'm pretty sure nobody was in my office."

"How easy would it be for someone to unlock the back door from the inside?"

"Real easy. You just turn the thingamajig inside the knob sideways."

"So, whoever unlocked that door would have had to have unlocked it from the inside?"

"Yep, but after that, someone could have used that door as many times as they wanted."

"Let's get back to when you left. Were there any cars in the parking lot when you left?"

"Nope, but I already noticed that when I looked out the back door. If there had been, I wouldn't have left without checking things out again. The parking lot was empty. I went home, got as much sleep as I could, then took off to see my daughter. She was expecting me around about 4:00 Sunday afternoon."

"One more question. Was the freezer locked the night of the reunion, and if so, where was the key?"

"Yep, it was, and the key was right on the hook where it always is. You remember me taking a key down and unlocking it for you a few minutes ago?"

I nodded.

"Well, that's where it always is."

"And the key was marked 'Freezer?'"

"Right."

I thanked Walter for his help, and Lou and I got up to rejoin Frank.

+++

"As far as I can tell, Cy, these people died in this freezer, but I won't know for sure until after I perform the autopsies."

"You think they've been here since the night of the reunion?"

"There's no way to tell for sure, but my guess is 'yes'. The man had a driver's license on him, the woman had no ID. He was James Russell Conkwright, Jr. of Illinois."

"You mean Big Russ's son."

"One and the same, and one of the biggest juvenile offenders as long as his daddy could buy off the judge. Big Russ even got him off from a possible murder charge. That's when he left town. And not long before that, there were rumors that he got drunk and shot someone. Of course, that could never be substantiated."

"I didn't know about the shooting incident, but I remember the wreck. He was driving drunk. The girl with him died."

"I think that's what ultimately killed Big Russ, too. For the most part, he was a good man, but that son of his was nothing like him."

"Looks like somebody didn't like it when that son came back, either. Now, all we have to do is figure out who the woman lying beside him is and where she fits in."

"I think it's safe to say we'll be able to find a lot of people who didn't like Junior, and each of them will have a different motive. I'm glad you're the ones tackling this case, and not me. I'll just let you know how they died. Plus, we'll call in the husband whose wife was missing, find out if she's still missing, and if so, have him come in to see if this is her."

"Maybe he'll be our first suspect."

"Could be, Cy, but I doubt if he's your last."

I turned from Frank and walked over to the print crew, who seemed to be finishing up.

"Find anything that might help us?"

"We've got plenty of smudges, most of those we won't be able to do anything with. But we did lift some prints from the door of the freezer like someone had gripped it before opening it, and a full set of prints, as if someone had leaned against it. Also, we have another set of prints from the wall, near where the keys were hanging. Other than that, we didn't find anything in the rest of the kitchen. I'd say during the school year, finding anything would be nearly impossible, but with school out, and the place being cleaned since the school was used, this could be something. Of course, they could be the custodian's prints, or whoever opened the door and found these people. We'll let you know as soon as we have anything."

+++

I drove back into town, dropped Lou at his place, and then drove home to fix lunch. How weird that sounded. It was hard enough adjusting to fixing my own meals when I had nothing else to do. Now I had to do it and solve a murder, too.

I'd forgotten all about the mid-morning snack I was supposed to eat on my new diet. I brushed that aside and fixed myself a burger with no bun, and a salad. I poured a mixture of lemon juice, olive oil, and some herbs over the salad. It reminded me of those see-through dressings I can't stand, but I had to try this, at least long enough to get Doc off my back. I ate and thought about starting a new book, but I wasn't sure how busy we'd be with this case. I'd give it a couple of days and then check with Lou, see what he thought we should do. Instead of reading, I Wiied for a few minutes. After that, I was ready for a nap.

I was sure that Frank would know the woman's identity the next day. If she was the woman we thought she was, I had another person to question. It would make for a full day; the Calvert woman, the retired custodian, and the husband. I was sure there would be others. It was beginning to look like things would soon be back to normal, minus the meals we were used to eating at the Blue Moon. The Blue Moon. I wondered what Rosie was doing. I wondered if the owner had decided whether or not to reopen. And I wondered that if the diner reopened, would Lou and I be among its customers. Doc had given me an ultimatum. Could I eat at the Blue Moon and still lose weight? If so, I'd have to change what I ate there. It was too much to think about with a couple of new murders facing us.

9

I began the next morning by eating a breakfast of two eggs, two pieces of bacon, a bowl of oatmeal with some cinnamon sprinkled on top, and an apple. While it settled, I read my daily devotionals and my Bible.

I had just finished when the phone rang. I knew that only a few people had my number, so I answered the phone, pretending to be upset.

"Which one of you rapscallions is trying to ruin my day?"

"The one with all the bodies."

"So, Frank, you have something for me already?"

"I do. I know how you're itching to get out of the house. I want to give you a chance to get some exercise."

"So, what did you learn?"

"They're both dead."

"So, they did that cryo thing, and didn't have anyone there to unfreeze them?"

"Go take a shower."

"I plan to, just as soon as I exercise."

"Cy, the only exercise you ever do is lifting yourself from your bed each morning."

Boy, will Frank be surprised when he sees the new me.

"Well, it's the only way I can get out of bed, that one-half of a sit-up thing. You have a better idea."

"No, since you don't have a crane in your bedroom, but I do know a little more about our dead people than you do."

"Who told you I don't have a crane in my bedroom? How do you think I've been getting up the last few years?"

"I figured your next-door neighbor came over and helped you up."

"If she did, I'd be in quarantine."

"You should be anyway. Cy, I've got work to do. Do you want to know about these people, or not?"

"If I say, or not, does that mean I can go back to bed?"

"Yeah, but I'd say you'd lose your job over it."

"Well, then, shoot."

"Well, first of all, it's simple. To use layman's terms, they froze to death in the freezer."

"What do you professionals call it? Hyperventilating?"

"No, Cy, that's something else. Now, are you going to let me finish?"

"Go ahead, but remember to use words we peons can understand."

"They hadn't been hit over the head with a blunt instrument, although Conkwright did have some lacerations on the front of his face as if he'd fallen down on the sidewalk. Actually, it was more like he'd been pushed from behind, but that didn't have anything to do with the way he died. It didn't even knock him out. Also, the victims hadn't been moved since they died. However, we found fingerprints on the door that belong to both of the deceased, and there were smears on the wall, near where the 'Freezer' key hung, that we think belonged to the deceased male. Both of the deceased had been drinking, the male enough that he was drunk, the female had had a few, too."

"So, do you think they were so inebriated that they walked into the freezer, shut the door, and froze to death?"

"And used some kind of rope trick to lock the padlock and put the key back?"

"They could have put the key back themselves, and the custodian could have seen the padlock unlocked, and locked it back. But someone, whether it was the custodian or not, had to padlock the door after they entered the freezer. Anyway, I'll ask the custodian if he locked the freezer when he locked the back door. Anything else you have for me?"

"Just that the freezer door doesn't close automatically. I tried it. You have to push it to. Oh, and the husband, a guy by the name of Duck Spencer, came in and identified his wife. He seemed upset with her death but irate that she was found with Jimmy Conkwright. I have his address, plus the address of the woman who booked the place if you want to talk to either of them."

"Wow! You're doing two jobs now."

"Yeah, but only getting paid for half of one."

I wrote down the addresses Frank gave me, hung up my phone, then picked up the phone again and called the school. With these newfangled phones, there's no hanging up, but my phone is almost as old as I am, so it must be hung up each time I end a call. It's so old it has a rotary dial.

I called the school and talked to Walter. He said he couldn't remember unlocking or locking the freezer that night. He also said that someone got ahold of the principal and he was on his way back from vacation a few days early.

I hung up, called Lou, told him what I knew. Since it was still early, I told him I'd Wii and shower before I picked him up. After hearing a "Good for you," from him, I hung up. I wasn't sure if Lou was glad I was going to Wii or shower. Probably both. Since Lou is an early riser, I assumed that he'd already done both.

+++

Lou opened the door to Lightning, sat down and buckled himself.

"Jennifer Garner."

"No, Cy Dekker, and you are..."

"I mean Jennifer Garner were the words I received this morning."

"Well, who in the world is Jennifer Garner? Is God trying to fix you up with someone?"

"No, I think He thinks I'm best suited for Thelma Lou."

"I don't know if you're best suited for anyone, but if there is someone for you, it's Thelma Lou."

"Maybe this Garner dame is someone God wants to fix you up with."

"And maybe she was someone who was at the reunion who saw someone close and lock the freezer door. We'll see if anyone knows her. If not, I'll Google her when I get home. Maybe she was the homecoming queen at County."

Lou's thoughts for the day appeared to be God's subtle influence in helping us solve each case. Occasionally, the clues were easy to figure out, but sometimes they were tough. This was a tough one for me. All I know is that each time someone is murdered Lou always gets a thought that has something to do with the murder. I call them his messages from God, even though Lou hears no voice.

I thought about who this mystery woman was until Lou changed the subject to the Wii, a word I used to detest. He inquired about what exercises I'd done that morning, and how much weight I'd lost. I actually beamed when I told him I'd lost another four-tenths of a pound. Had the Wii or my new diet taken over my brain?

+++

It was only our second day on this case, so I had to tug hard on the wheel to keep Lightning from turning toward the Blue Moon after I picked up Lou.

"According to Frank, Rose Ellen Calvert works at the library. They've been open for a few minutes. What say we drop by the library and pay her a visit?"

"As you wish Ol' Getting Skinny One."

"Remember not to say anything to anyone else."

"Oh, from what I heard, the guys downtown already know about it."

"They don't know about my new eating regimen and my Wii Fit, do they?"

"I don't think so. I know I haven't said anything."

+++

We arrived at the library. I hoped they had someplace where we could talk to Rose Ellen Calvert without everyone hearing what I had to say. Maybe someplace in the library where I wouldn't have to be quiet, and no one would know what we talked about. As it turned out, it didn't matter. Miss Calvert was off that day, so I perused my notes and found her home address. She lived just around the corner from the library.

I drove around the corner and parked. We could have walked from the library, but I prefer to get my exercise in the air-conditioned confines of my home. We pulled up in front of a modest brick home, got out of the car, looked at the house, and wondered if someone was looking back at us. I went up to the door and knocked. A few seconds later, a plain-looking woman answered the door. She was on the slender side, and on second glance, you could tell that she could have looked a lot better if she had done something with herself, like change her hairstyle and wear some make-up. But then who am I to tell people how they should look? Still, I couldn't help but think that if she would change her wardrobe, fix her hair differently, wear some makeup, and trade her ugly looking glasses for a pair of contacts, she might have been worth looking at, even if she still didn't come up to Wonder Woman status.

"Are you Miss Calvert, Miss Rose Ellen Calvert?"

"That's right, and you are...?"

"I'm Lt. Dekker. This is Sgt. Murdock. We're with the Hilldale Police Department."

"Are you collecting for the policeman's ball or something?"

I wanted to tell her I collect only for the Cy Dekker fund, but I refrained, and gave her a simple "no."

"Have I done something wrong, Lieutenant?"

"I don't know. Do you have a book overdue at the library?"

"I happen to work at the library. I would never have an overdue book."

"I know that, about your working at the library, I mean. We stopped by there first and found out that this is your day off."

"But I still don't understand why you want to see me."

"It's about the high school reunion."

"Oh, I see. Does this have to do with Jimmy Conkwright and Betty Gail Spencer?"

"Why do you ask?"

"Well, everyone knows that they've been missing since that night. Did you find them? Are they dead? I mean they left drunk. Were they in a wreck? Of course, if they were, it looks like someone would have found Jimmy's car by now unless they crashed into the river. Is that what happened?"

"I'm afraid not, Miss Calvert. May we step in for a few minutes? I want to see what you can tell me about that night."

"Sure, I'm sorry. Where are my manners?"

I wondered why the woman guessed that we were there about Conkwright and Mrs. Spencer, and why she guessed that Conkwright's car had crashed into the river. It was possible that only one person knew where Conkwright's car is. Could it be that that one person is Rose Ellen Calvert?

Just inside the front door, past a small coat closet, was the living room. The librarian motioned for us to have a seat. I waited until she too had sat down before I questioned her anymore.

"Miss Calvert, we're trying to put together all that happened that night. I'd like for you to tell us everything that happened, beginning with when you arrived at the school."

"You act as if they were murdered. They weren't murdered were they? Where did you find them, anyway?"

"We'll get to that in a moment. Now, just start at the beginning, as if you were giving a book report."

She smiled, nervously, and then began.

"Well, I arrived at the school just before 5:00. For a while, I thought I would have to drive out there in the storm, but it quit raining at my house a little after 4:30. Evidently, it quit at the school just before I got there. I saw all kinds of leaves and downed tree branches as I drove out. Luckily, there was nothing blocking the road. When I got there, the janitor was there. He let me in. A couple of people were coming to help me set up.

"The festivities began with a tour of our old school. Someone suggested that we walk down the halls where we once walked, relive old memories, and go in some our of old classrooms if that was allowed."

"And did you do that?"

"We did. Only about half of the group showed up for that, but that was fine with me. Some of the guys started bragging about some of the things they did in high school, and some of the ex-cheerleaders started talking about what fun it was to be a cheerleader, and when we went into one of our old classrooms, someone said, 'Let's find our old

63

seats,' so we did. Some people remembered where they sat, others guessed. The guys sat down and slouched like they used to do, and one by one we started reliving memories, telling stories about each teacher or someone in the class. Most of the others liked doing that better than I did.

"I excused myself at 6:30. The janitor was up there to keep an eye on things, and he said he would lock up. When I left, he was leaning against a wall halfway down the hall, so as not to disturb us. See, we were to begin with dinner at 7:00. The dinner was being catered, and I wanted to be downstairs when the caterer arrived. She arrived on time, and went about her job."

I made a note that the janitor had neglected to tell me anything about a caterer, but then he was upstairs when the caterer arrived.

"Go on."

"Well, there's not much to tell, early on. Nothing seemed out of sorts. Well, nothing until Jimmy Conkwright arrived. Jim Bob Gibbons went over to Jimmy, and I overheard him say, 'No funny stuff tonight, Jimmy.' Jimmy just nodded and smiled. I knew Jimmy had a reputation for drinking, so I looked him over good. I couldn't see where he had a bottle of anything on him. At least not then.

"Well, it wasn't ten minutes before Jimmy started hitting on some of the women. It didn't matter if their husbands were there, or not. A couple of times Jim Bob had to break up a fight, just before it was about to start."

"Can you remember who was about to fight with Conkwright?"

"Once it was Billy Korlein. The other time it was George Justice. Both April Korlein and Sandy Justice used to be cheerleaders, back when we were in school. Jimmy went over and said something about them still looking good and asked them if they would do a cheer just for him. I remember Billy saying something about Jimmy hadn't changed a bit."

"So, what happened next?"

"Well, Jim Bob seemed to calm everyone down and directed Jimmy to a chair at a table on the other side of the room."

"Was that the end of Jimmy's flirtations?"

"Well, it was for a while. Then, Betty Gail Spencer came in. Everyone noticed that her husband wasn't with her, especially Jimmy. He went over and rubbed up against her and she smiled. George walked over and asked her where Duck was. Duck is her husband. It's a nickname. Anyway, she said Duck decided not to come. After dinner, Jimmy and Betty Gail left the cafeteria. I think they went to his car. Anyway, when they came back in, several minutes later, they both smelled of alcohol. Jim Bob said something else to Jimmy, but Jimmy just laughed."

"And then what happened?"

"Well, shortly after the caterer packed up and left, someone whipped out a CD player and put some CDs on to play, ones popular when we were in high school. Jimmy got up and started dancing with Betty Gail. Lieutenant, he was dancing much too close. Billy Korlein said something about her being a married woman. This made Jimmy mad and he stumbled over and grabbed April Korlein and tried to get her to get up and dance with him. Well, the guys got together and shoved Jimmy out the door. A couple of minutes later, Betty Gail walked out looking for him."

"When you say out the door, do you mean the cafeteria door or the front door?"

"Well, the cafeteria door for sure, but I think the front door, too."

"I'm sure Betty Gail Spencer noticed all this. How long after she went looking for him did they come back to the cafeteria?"

"Neither of them came back. As soon as Betty Gail walked out after Jimmy, George Justice got on his cell phone and called Duck, told him what was going on. Then, Jim Bob, Billy, and George went out looking for Jimmy and Betty Gail."

"How long after Justice called Spencer did the guys leave the cafeteria?"

"Well, I'd say that George was on the phone with Duck at least five minutes, and maybe they waited another five minutes to see if Betty Gail came back before they huddled together and decided to see if they could find her."

"When the guys went looking for them, do you know if they were together, or did they split up?"

"All of them were gone a few minutes. I'm not sure how long. I don't think they came back at the same time. No, I know they didn't. After they all came back in someone mumbled something about Betty Gail nursing Jimmy's wounds and that the two of them had gone into hiding somewhere. Anyway, they waited for Duck to get there."

"And did Betty Gail Spencer's husband show up?"

"He did, and there was some other guy there, too. I think it was our old janitor, Mr. Spickard. It had been years since I've seen Mr. Spickard, so I'm not sure it was him, but it looked something like him."

"Was Mr. Spickard the janitor when you went to school here?"

"Yes."

"So, tell me about what happened before Mr. Spencer showed up?"

"Well, a couple of times George's phone rang. I think it was Duck, but I'm not sure. Anyway, after it rang the second time, George went over and stood by the door. A couple of minutes later, Duck came in. The entrance to the cafeteria is almost directly in line with the front door, and not more than twenty feet away, so it was easy for George to see Duck and vice versa.

"Anyway, Duck asked if George knew where they went, and George said no. Duck said he didn't see them out in the parking lot. They were about to go look for them again, with Duck along, when the janitor and the man I think is Mr. Spickard came out of the men's restroom, talking and laughing, and patting each other on the back. They came over when they saw everyone standing out in the hall, near the cafeteria. They tried to calm us down a little, and then went into the janitor's office together. A while later, after the guys came back one at a time from looking for the missing couple, the janitor and Mr. Spickard came to check on us. When they saw things were relatively calm, they walked off down the hall together. I think this was after Duck walked out in a huff. I could tell he was upset, and rightly so."

"Anything else happen?"

"Nothing out of line. A little at a time, people starting leaving. Most left a little after midnight, but a few of us were still here when things ended at 1:00. We carried things out, the janitor walked out as I did, and he followed me out of the parking lot."

"Did you notice if there were any cars left when you walked out?"

"I did because I was curious as to whether Jimmy and Betty Gail had left, and if they left in one car or two."

"And what did you see?"

"Evidently they left in separate cars because there were no cars in the lot."

"And did you pass any cars on the way back to town?"

"Not on the road the school is on, and not at all until I got most of the way to town."

"Miss Calvert, you mentioned that Jimmy had a reputation for drinking. Do you remember any instances of drinking or bad behavior on his part when you were in school?"

67

"Lots. If it wasn't for his dad, Jimmy would have been expelled, and maybe put in jail. The last straw was when he was out driving drunk with some girl in the car, and Jimmy rounded a corner too fast and hit a tree. The girl was killed instantly. At least, she was dead when the ambulance arrived. Jimmy had stumbled off somewhere, but everyone knew that it was his car, because he drove the only red Corvette in town. Someone said there was a red Corvette in the parking lot at the reunion, and since none of us have one, we figured it had to be Jimmy's car."

"Do you know the name of the girl who was killed?"

"Miriam Van Meter. I didn't know her well. She was only a freshman when I was a senior. I think that was part of the reason Jimmy hit on her. That and the fact that she did whatever it took to be liked. She didn't talk much about herself, and I think a lot of what she said was a lie. She claimed to live with Mrs. Edwards, said she was her niece. Lola Cartwright told me that she didn't know if she was Mrs. Edwards' niece or not, but she'd been to Mrs. Edward's house and never saw Miriam there. All I know is that she was one of those kids who came to school by rowboat, and she always managed to try to be the last kid leaving school, so no one could tell where she was headed. She was strange. By the way, Mrs. Edwards' house was nowhere near the river, but then I guess Miriam never thought about that. While Miriam arrived by rowboat most of the time, I lived close enough to ride my bicycle, that's how I got to school unless the weather was bad. There wasn't a lot of traffic on that road in those days, so it wasn't dangerous to ride a bike to school. Of course, there still isn't very much traffic on that road."

"Did you go to the funeral?"

"Miriam's? No, I didn't really know her that well, even though we attended a small school. Most of the girls didn't like her anyway since she was always flirting with the boys."

"Back to the night of the reunion. Who left the cafeteria after the last time you saw Jimmy and Betty Gail?"

"Well, the guys I mentioned. And if you include trips to the restroom when you want to know who left the cafeteria, I'd say most of us. I know I had to go once after that. Some of the other ladies did, too."

"Miss Calvert, did you or anyone else take anything out of the kitchen refrigerator or freezer at any time during the night?"

"I know I didn't. I don't think anyone else did either. Why, is something missing?"

"Not that I know of. I'm just curious. So, not even the caterer?"

"The caterer was in and out, but as far as I know, neither she nor her helper went to the kitchen. There's actually a door that leads from the kitchen to the cafeteria. I don't think anyone used that door all night. Everyone was in and out of the main door. Now that doesn't mean that no one was in the kitchen. It could be that one of the guys was in there when they were looking for Jimmy and Betty Gail, but I don't know that for sure."

"Miss Calvert, does the name Jennifer Garner mean anything to you?"

"No. I'm pretty sure she wasn't anyone who went to school with us. Being a small school, I remember most of their names. Besides, I worked in the school library back then, so I had to learn everyone's name. Is this Garner person someone who lives around here?"

"I don't know. Her name just came up in conjunction with our investigation."

"Well, I'm sorry. I can't help you."

"One more thing. Did anyone wear gloves that night?"

"Of course not, Lieutenant. No one wears gloves in the summer."

I thanked her for her time, told her I'd be back if I thought of anything else. That last remark didn't seem to please her, but she didn't say anything.

I did notice her looking at Lou from time to time. I wasn't sure what that was all about. Maybe she thought he was cute. Maybe she wondered why he never opened his mouth. Whatever it was, it didn't matter. Whatever Rose Ellen Calvert thought of Lou, it had no bearing on our case.

10

Lou and I walked down the steps back to Lightning. We got in, sat down, and looked at each other.

"Well, what do you think, Lou?"

"It seems like a lot of people had the opportunity to lock them in the freezer, only someone would've had to have been brave to do so, with all those people in and out of the cafeteria. It would have been easier to kill them outside unless someone else was outside."

"We'll find out, but I bet some of those guys were outside looking for them. Besides, it's much easier to shut a door on someone inside of a freezer than it is to chase two people down and conk them on the head, even if they are drunk."

"And from what you said Frank said no one was conked on the head. It doesn't sound like whoever did this planned it out ahead of time. At least if they did, I doubt if anyone planned to lure Jimmy and/or Betty Gail to the freezer and lock them in. Nor can I see anyone leaving a trail of bread crumbs, or more likely, beer bottles."

"I'd say you're right, Lou. But evidently whoever did it didn't mind killing both of them, even if he or she had a grudge against only one of them."

71

"Unless that person didn't realize that there were two people in the freezer."

"Oh, I'm sure whoever did it knew what he or she was doing."

+++

Lou and I sat discussing the case for a few minutes. I looked at my watch to see what time it was. It was getting close to lunchtime. I'd missed my midmorning snack again. At that rate, I might turn out to be the skinniest cop on the force. Yeah, right!

Since the next person on our list, Duck Spencer, lived way out in the country, I dropped Lou at his place, then ran home and fixed my lunch. I told Lou I'd pick him up at 1:30, and we'd go visit suspect number two.

A couple of minutes after I started Lightning and took off, we got a call on the police radio, something that seldom happens. One of the missing cars had been found. When the bodies were found inside the school, the department started looking for the cars again. Finding the first one was easy. It was parked right beside Betty Gail Spencer's house. It took a little longer to find Jimmy's car, and the main reason they found it so easily is that they started searching at the scene of the crime. They pulled Jimmy's car from the river. It went in a few feet from where I initiated my boat ride. The back end was smashed in. It could have happened when the car hit the bank on the way to the river, but my money was on the fact that someone else's car helped it find its way to the river. Maybe the murderer didn't want the janitor double-checking the school to see why one of the vehicles was still there. I'm sure that if whoever did it suffered any damage to his or her vehicle, that person had gotten it fixed by now. Still, body shops keep records of the work they do. Maybe this thing would be as simple as finding whose vehicle had been repaired recently and arresting the owner for murder.

+++

I fixed a quick lunch and packed a small cooler with afternoon snacks. I almost whistled when I stepped out the door to go pick up Lou and corner a couple more suspects. I sat the cooler down and had my back turned as I was shutting the door when I felt something tugging on my pant leg. Before I could look down, I heard something that sounded like fingernails on a chalkboard.

"Oh, Cyrus, she remembers you."

I stumbled when I turned around and faced my next-door neighbor from the dark side because something was still attached to my pant leg. I stumbled again, backward this time, when I realized my next-door neighbor was mere inches from my face. I thudded against the door that I'd shut too quickly. I regained my footing before I spoke.

"Miss Humphert, there are laws against vermin invading other people's property."

"Cyrus, you know Twinkle Toes didn't mean anything. She was just showing her love for you."

"I was talking about you, Miss Humphert."

"Well, Cyrus, you know I love you, too," she said as she invaded my space even more.

It was then that the woman and her small companion noticed my cooler. I picked it up before either of them could drool on it.

"Oh, Cyrus, you packed us a lunch. How wonderful! And it's such a small lunch. I guess I know what you want to do."

"I've been giving you hints for years now. It's about time you caught my drift."

"So, where are we going?"

"I found a nice little place for you. It's right on the river, and it has the cutest little rowboat. I'll let you step into the boat first, and then I'll drill the hole."

"Oh, you sly rascal, you. You want to give me CPR."

"I can't think of many things I'd like to give you, Miss Humphert, but CPR isn't one of them."

I could see that she was momentarily distracted, so I swung the cooler around and knocked her off balance enough that I was able to duck under her arm and get around her. My problem was that I failed to notice that when Muffy realized she couldn't have whatever was in my cooler, she wrapped her teeth around my pant leg again. I thanked my workouts on the Wii for my ability to stay on my feet as I whisked the rapscallion away with my free foot and stumbled down the steps away from the dastardly duo.

"Oh, Cyrus. I didn't know you could dance like that. Why don't you come on over to my house and we can make music together? Maybe we can get on *Dancing With The Stars?*"

"I'd love for you to see stars, but I'm afraid if I did anything to make it possible, I might lose my job."

"That'd be great! That would give us more time together."

"Miss Humphert, the last time I was around you this long I ended up going back to the doctor twice a week for two months to get another shot so I could get over whatever it was you gave me."

"Just come over to my place and I'll make sure it takes even longer for you to get over me."

"I'd love to get over you, maybe by about twenty feet, and then we could play Drop the Anvil. I'd go first. In the meantime, I've got work to do. Why don't you and Muffy go practice your dance steps? By the way, I'd love to see you on that show. How many weeks would you be gone?"

With that, I wheeled and turned in my best time ever in the forty-yard dash, just under one minute. Before she could move, I was in Lightning and backing out of my driveway. Maybe the Wii could help me in ways I'd never envisioned. But I still wasn't sure how I could use it to get rid of a neighbor.

+++

I allowed Lou his laughs as I asked him if my face was broken out and then told him why I asked.

"Cy, you should apologize to that woman, maybe give her a gift."

"What did you have in mind? A rope and a hood, a bouquet of poison ivy, or an electric fence and a collar?"

Lou laughed again, but then Lou didn't have to live next door to her. He didn't always have to be on the lookout, in case of an ambush. I did.

+++

Although I'd never spent much time out on Thornapple River Road, I knew how to get there. There are two roads leading north out of Hilldale, one northeast, and one northwest. The northeastern road was the one I took that morning. I drove five miles, crossed the bridge over the Thornapple River, and immediately took the road to the right. Unlike the road out of town, Thornapple River Road is narrow, and not a lot of people live out that way. But when the county high school was built many years ago, not a lot of people lived anywhere, but more people lived at that end of the county so that location was chosen for the high school.

Today, the majority of the people live at the end of the road nearer the main road. The right side of the road, the side the river is on, is relatively flat. There's a steep incline on the left side, but there are a few houses on the left side of the road. Those are harder to see driving by because all

75

of those homes are well above the road. Still, in winter, everyone who lives up there can look through the barren trees and see the river. The rest of the year, the trees give them privacy. Because the right side of the road is flat, our drive became a scenic one, consisting of seeing an occasional home, then a view of the river, which at times was only twenty feet or so from the road we traveled. The road, like the river, was serpentine at times, which prevented me from checking out the scenery too closely, but it straightened out shortly before we arrived at the high school.

We passed the high school without checking to see if there were any more bodies on the premises. I noticed a truck and two cars there. When we met Frank at the school, there was only one vehicle there other than mine and Frank's, so I knew that the truck belonged to the janitor. I assumed the cars belonged to the principal and his secretary, who were back at work with the beginning of school a mere two weeks away. Of course, they could have merely been there for the day, to see what repercussions there were from the bodies being found. Since the janitor wasn't there every day yet, and the principal was still in the middle of his vacation, maybe the school would be vacant again the next day.

Flat Rock Road veered off to the left a couple of miles past the school, and because both Duck Spencer and Earl Spickard, the retired custodian, lived on Flat Rock Road, Lightning, Lou, and I veered, too. The rock might have been flat, but the road wasn't. At least not in the beginning. Lightning sped upward, propelling Lou and me against the back of our seats, much like the first climb of a rollercoaster. After a steep, thirty-foot incline, the road leveled out and crossed over the top of Thornapple River Road, and went back and forth across the river, until someone had decided to keep it on the Thornapple River Road side of the river.

There weren't a lot of houses on the road, so I didn't have to slow down often to see if the house we were nearing was Duck Spencer's place. We passed a place where a tree had fallen and someone had used a chainsaw to cut it into smaller chunks. I assumed this was the tree that fell the night of the reunion, the one that prevented Duck Spencer from driving to the school.

About a half of a mile later we neared a mailbox whose number matched the address I had down for Duck Spencer. The land was flat, and from the looks of the place and my limited knowledge of measurements, I guessed his property to be about an acre. There was a barn-like structure out back to the right of the vinyl-siding covered house, and that was where I found Duck Spencer, tall, slender, but muscular, with long, straight, medium brown hair, and a little grease on his clothes and in his hair. He walked up as we propelled ourselves from Lightning's clutches.

"Can I help you?"

"You can if you're Duck Spencer."

"Then I guess I can help you. What can I do for you gentlemen? Got a car needing fixing?"

"No, my car's fine. I'm Lt. Dekker. This is Sgt. Murdock. We're here about your wife's death."

"I guess you didn't hear. I already went and identified her. It was her all right. She didn't look none too good."

"Not too many people do when they're dead. I'm not sure if they look better or worse if they've been frozen."

"Is that what happened to her?"

"You didn't know?"

"Come to think of it, the guy might have said something. So how'd she get in that mess?"

"That's what we're trying to find out."

"Then I'd say your best bet would be to talk to some of them people who was with her that night."

"I understand you were there that night."

"Just a few minutes, but I never seen *her*."

"How many minutes?"

"Oh, I dunno, maybe fifteen or twenty minutes. Me and some of the other guys looked for her, but when we didn't find her after a while I left."

"How'd you get to the school that night?"

"I'd say you probably already know that. A guy up the road used to be the janitor there. This here road was blocked from the storm, so I checked with him and he took me in his boat."

"I assume you're talking about Earl Spickard."

"I figure you already know who it was."

"Did Mr. Spickard go with you when you looked for your wife?"

"Naw, it was some of them who went to school with her. It was one of them that called me and told me she was acting up with some guy."

"Was it George Justice who called you?"

"Yeah, my man George."

"And did he tell you which guy she was acting up with?"

"Yeah, but then I figured she would hook up with that slimeball when she was so hot to trot to get out of here that night. He was no account in school."

"So, did you go to school with them?"

"Yeah, but I quit before twelfth grade, got me a job."

"So, you knew that Jimmy Conkwright was going to be there?"

"Naw, but it didn't surprise me none, him being someone who was always causing trouble, ever chance he got. With that there Internet, he probably heard about the reunion, either that or Jim Bob Gibbons told him about it."

"Who else went with you when you went looking for your wife?"

"It was just the four of us, me, George, Jim Bob, and Billy Korlein."

"And did you stay together, or split up and look for her in different places?"

"Together, mostly."

"What kind of work do you do now, Mr. Spencer?"

"I got my own business. I'm in the auto body business."

"That means you fix wrecked vehicles. You wouldn't happen to have fixed one recently with a dented front end, would you?"

Duck Spencer grinned.

"Well, as a matter of fact, I did have one just a week or two ago that was dinged a little in the front."

"Whose car was it?"

"Well, can't say as I remember right now."

"Mr. Spencer, I can requisition your books."

"Does that mean look at 'em? If so, won't do you no good. I didn't charge for this one. A favor for a friend, you might say."

"Could it be that this friend is the one who locked your wife and Jimmy Conkwright in the freezer?"

"Is that what happened? Naw, it wasn't nothing like that."

"Mr. Spencer, I can't say that you look all broken up over your wife's death."

"I can't say that I'm happy she's gone. I loved her at one time, still do, but she just got too high falutin', started goin' out at night, never telling me where she went."

"Was that when you starting hitting her?"

"If that woman had any bruises on her, it was that good for nothing. I didn't do it. I never laid a hand on that woman, even though there were times I wanted to."

"So, tell me, Mr. Spencer. How did you get home that night?"

He grinned again.

"When we walked up from the riverbank, I seen her truck over in the parking lot. I had keys to it too, and I already decided that if she didn't come home with me, I was taking her wheels and hightailing it out of there."

"But wasn't the tree still blocking the road when you got home?"

"Yep, but I'd already figured I'd park the truck there and walk the rest of the way. It was worth it, just to take away her wheels."

"Tell me why you didn't go with your wife that night."

"I was going to, at first. Then, the more I thought about those high and mighty people being there, holding it over me because they graduated, an' I didn't. That afternoon, I just told her that I wasn't going. She threw a hissy fit and stormed outa here. Got outa here just before the storm hit, a long time before the reunion. I don't know where she went. Like I said, I didn't know that rich boy was going to be there. The only rich boy in our school and he used all his money to make all the girls chase after him. I figured he was long gone from here. Nobody seen him in years."

"Mr. Spencer, why didn't you report your wife missing when she didn't show up that night?"

"I figured she was still with him."

"But you never reported her at all. It was some of her co-workers that reported it when she didn't show up for work on Monday."

"I was wondering who it was. I shoulda knowed it was them people. They liked her, but I think she behaved better at work. She even started drinking. I don't hold for no drinking."

"When did you first suspect that maybe your wife was dead?"

"Not until they called me. I just figured she'd run off with that no-good rich guy, and if she wanted him instead of me, that was all right with me."

"Did you know a girl named Miriam Van Meter?"

"Don't think so."

"Think close now. She was the girl who died one night when she was out with Jimmy Conkwright and he ran into a tree."

"Oh, was that her name? Naw, I didn't know her. See, she came the year after I quit."

"So, tell me, not a lot of guys are nicknamed Duck. How'd you get your nickname?"

"Got it in school. I was quite a fighter back in the day. I'd make somebody mad and he'd take a swing at me, and I'd duck before he could hit me. Then, I'd pop him one under the chin. If I caught him low enough, some of those guys couldn't talk for a few minutes. I popped that rich boy one time. He turned me in and got me 'expelled, and he's the one who started it. His money got him whatever he wanted, but no more. But I guess it did get him a good burial."

"So, you know that he died, too?"

"I didn't until I went to 'identify my wife. After that, I heard people talking."

One more thing, Mr. Spencer. Does the name Jennifer Garner mean anything to you?"

"Nope. Does she have something to do with this?"

"She might. I just wanted to know if you know her."

"Sorry, name doesn't ring a bell. I know I never done no work for her, though. If you run into her, and she happens to need some bodywork sometime, tell her to give me a call. I work cheap. I'm here most of the time. You'd be surprised how many people drive all the way out here to have their bodywork done. I do a good job, see."

Especially if someone needs to keep the bodywork quiet, someone who might get that work done for free.

I'd probably have more questions for Spencer, but I couldn't think of any more at that time. So, I left my thoughts about Spencer's bodywork, thanked him for his time, and Lou and I walked away.

81

11

From the house numbers and the fact that Duck Spencer had sought out Earl Spickard on the night of the reunion, I figured that Spickard didn't live too far from Spencer, and I was right. But right after we left Spencer's place, in a wooded area that bordered his property, I spotted a roadside park with a picnic table. I pulled over, reached over the seat and grabbed the cooler as I got out. I'd brought enough food for Lou, too, and since Lou and I were suddenly eating the same food again, we could snack together.

"So, what do you think, Lou?" I asked as I opened the cooler.

"I think I'm proud of you, Cy. I didn't know you had it in you."

"I don't mean that. What do you think about our grieving widower?"

Lou reached into the cooler, selected a hard-boiled egg, and plucked it from its confines. He must have grabbed it by one end, and too hard, because the egg sprang from his hand and spurted into the air. Lou circled under it and managed to cradle it in his hands when gravity took over.

"Good catch, Lou!"

He smiled, took a bite out of the egg as if to teach it a lesson.

I learned from Lou's mistake and carefully removed the other egg from the cooler.

After Lou had downed his egg, he looked up and answered my question.

"Cy, I have no idea if this guy's our murderer or not. I don't want to put all my eggs in Col. Mustard's basket before I meet Professor Plum. Let's just say that he's not exactly heartbroken that his wife's no longer with us. Still, he seems more the type to pummel the two of them to death than to sneak up and lock them in the freezer. That seems more like something a woman would do."

"Remember, he said he never beat her. Maybe he's not a pummeling type of guy. Of course, it's obvious he had no use for Jimmy Conkwright, but then we have yet to meet any members of Jimmy's fan club. Still, could Jimmy's presence make Duck Spencer act out of character?"

"Well, if he was telling the truth, he didn't know Conkwright was coming, although he did find out before he left home that Conkwright was there in case he wanted to plan something if he caught Conkwright with his wife."

"Tomorrow, we may stop by the shoe factory where Spencer's wife worked and see what anybody there has to say about how Spencer treated his wife."

Lou and I mulled over what we'd learned, as we divvied up the four celery sticks, the four carrot sticks, the four cherry tomatoes, and the ten green olives. There were times when Lou and I would have considered hitting the olives with the vegetable sticks, but at that moment our minds were on the case. Besides, the cracked paint of the picnic table and the dust that had taken up residence there put a damper on things.

"Do you think he took his wife's truck because he knew that she'd never need it again?"

"I don't know, but I hope we soon find out. It's possible that Spencer could have done it, paid someone to do it, or fixed someone's car or truck after he or she used it to push Conkwright's car into the drink. I wish we knew if his wife and Conkwright were locked in the freezer before or after Spencer got there."

"Yeah, I'd love to know when Spencer first knew or suspected that his wife was dead. Somehow I don't think he was telling us the truth."

We paused again from exercising our brains and lifted out our dessert. What used to be two pieces of pie each had transformed into two little green apples, one each. Rather than accost suspect number three with apple juice all over our chins, I returned to Lightning and extracted enough paper towels to make both of us look presentable.

I noticed Lou was looking at me, so I took a moment for levity and acted out some of the steps from the Wii Fit exercise, as well as a hula hoop rendition or two. I regained my senses when I attempted to do the tree exercise from the yoga workout, and almost fell and made a calculation on the Richter Scale. Lou applauded my two successes and laughed when I almost fell.

I knew that it was time to leave, time to interrogate our next suspect.

+++

Lightning seemed to know where she was going, but evidently not. A couple of minutes later, we hit a dead end. There wasn't a house or mailbox anywhere. I looked at Lou. Both of us were stumped. I looked at the address again. Supposedly, Earl Spickard lived somewhere on this road, but when I asked Lou if we passed any houses or mailboxes on our way there, he said "no." There was nothing to do except backtrack. I drove even slower this time. Lou checked the right side of the road. I checked the left. Before I knew it, we were back at Spencer's place. I had no choice but to turn in.

"Something else on your mind, Lieutenant?"

"I'm having trouble finding Earl Spickard's place."

Spencer laughed.

"It's sorta hard to find. There ain't no drive that goes back to it. Just go to the end of the road, park whatever that thing is you're driving, then head through the trees on the right. Eventually, you'll get there."

I thanked Spencer again and we left.

I did as Duck Spencer told me. I pulled over at the dead end. Lou and I got out, saw where there was enough of a break in the trees to allow us to walk down an unmarked path, and we walked in that direction. We were about to give up when Lou spotted what looked like a cabin in the distance. It looked lived in, but we saw no car or truck anywhere. I knocked and we waited for someone to answer. The whole thing didn't look like more than one large room, so I doubted if it would take Spickard long to answer the knock. When no one answered, I knocked again. Still no answer.

"Let's try out back."

When still we hadn't located anyone, I did what I was taught to do in the country. I hollered.

"Anybody home!"

"Down here!" came a call from the distance.

Lou and I did our best to gauge from where the response came and took off in that direction. A minute or so later, we located an older man, fishing. His hair was turning white, as was the stubble on his face, which told me he hadn't shaved in a couple of days.

"You Earl Spickard?"

"Yep. Who might you be?"

"Well, I might be just about anyone, but I'm Lt. Dekker of the Hilldale Police Department and this is Sgt. Murdock."

Spickard started to laugh at my first statement, then stopped when he found out we were the police. He looked puzzled.

"I'm trying to read that look on your face."

"Oh, that. It's just that I'm surprised to see you for a couple of reasons."

"Oh, why's that?"

"Well, I'm surprised anybody from the police department can find this place, plus I can't imagine why the police would come calling on me."

I decided to be honest with him.

"Well, I have to admit, I did need some help finding you. As to why we're here, we have some questions about the night you took Duck Spencer to the high school."

"Didn't nothing happen to Duck, did it? I would've been happy to bring him home, too."

"No, nothing happened to him. As a matter of fact, he's the one who told me how to find you. I couldn't find you the first time I tried."

Spickard laughed again.

"My place is hard to find. I like it that way."

"So, where's your mailbox?"

"It's up there someplace. The mailman knows where it's at. Don't get much mail no how so having the thing is a waste of time."

"So, tell me about what you did that night."

"Everything, or just the part where I took Duck?"

"I don't care about what you did before he got here. Just start with when he knocked on your door."

"Well, he comes a running up toward the house. I sees him comin' and heard him, too. He was out of breath. I say, 'What's wrong, Duck? Something wrong with Betty Gail. Betty Gail's Duck's wife."

"He says, 'Yeah, there's a lot wrong with Betty Gail. She's at that high school reunion with that no good Jimmy Conkwright.'"

"And did you know Jimmy Conkwright?"

I noticed that Spickard's demeanor changed.

"You bet I knowed him. He was a mean son of a gun, only stayed outa jail 'cause of his rich daddy."

"How did you know him?"

"See, I use to be the janitor at that school 'til I retired. He went to school there when I was there. I didn't know most of them by name, but I knowed him. I was hoping he'd do something so they could put him away."

"From what I understand, he might have. Did you know Miriam Van Meter?"

"Can't say that that name rings a bell."

"She was the one who was killed when Conkwright was driving drunk one night."

Spickard tried to wipe his tear before I could catch him. No such luck.

"No, I never knowed no one by that name. I remember about him killing some girl, though. His daddy got him off from that, too. If'n I remember right, she was just a freshman. Too young to know to stay away from the likes of him."

"It seems that way. Let's get back to the night of the reunion. Why did Duck Spencer tell you he needed a ride?"

"Well, we'd had a storm out this way earlier. Duck said a tree blowed over and blocked the road. Said he couldn't get through that way."

"And he knew you had a boat?"

"That's right."

"So, you offered to take him to the school."

"Seems like you already know everything."

"Just a little bit. What did Spencer have to say on the way up the river?"

"Not a lot. I could tell he was in a hurry to get to the school, said something about teaching her a lesson. I didn't know at the time what he meant, but I did later."

"Oh, what did he mean?"

"Well, I don't know this for gospel, but I think Duck took her truck. I just know he didn't need me to bring him home. I wondered how she'd act when she walked out and found out that her truck was gone. I still don't know. I'll have to go down sometime and ask Duck."

"So, pick up where you left off and tell me what happened when you got to school."

"Well, just as soon as we hit the bank, ol' Duck hopped outa the boat and took off running for the school. He was already inside when I got there."

"So, you went into the school, too?"

"Yep, like I said, I used to be the janitor there, and the last year I was there the man who's janitor now started working there. We became good friends. Very good friends. If either of us needed something the other one would help him any way he could."

"You're talking about Walter Gillis."

"That's right. I walked in the door and there was Duck standing and talking to some people. I'm not sure who all, but I thank they was people who went to school there when I was there. I recognized faces, but not too many names. Anyways, I knowed my way around, so I walked in the door, looked in at the place that they called my office when I was there, and seen Walter wasn't in there, so I went on down to use the facilities. I ran into Walter in there. He was in one stall. I was in another. We come out at the same time, seen who each other was, and patted each other on the back. He was so glad to see me. It'd been a few weeks since we'd seen each other. Anyway, we walked out of the restroom, passed the others, who was about to go stomping off somewhere and went into Walter's office. The two of us sat there a while talking, and I got to itching to see the old home place again, so we got up and walked through the school. Walter checked with some lady before we took off to make sure everthing was okay."

"Would you know Jimmy Conkwright if you saw him?"

"I'm not sure. I 'spect so. If so, I never laid eyes on him that night, but I heard he was there."

"What about Betty Gail Spencer?"

"I never seen her neither, but I knowed her. I think Duck's right. The last time I seen her she seemed like a different person."

"In what way?"

"Kinda wild like."

"How many times did you see Duck Spencer after you got to the school?"

"Just once that I can recollect. He stopped by, leaned in the office and told me he didn't need a ride home. He smiled as he said it. I said, 'Are you sure?' and he said, 'Oh, yeah, as long as the truck starts.' It weren't long after that that I up and left. I really enjoyed spending some time with my friend Walter. He made me promise that I'd get back to see him sometime soon."

"Did you see anyone out in the hall while you were at the school?"

"I didn't pay no attention to that, but yeah, I guess I seen some of 'em. They were all hepped up to find Duck's woman."

"When you saw them, were they alone or with someone?"

"Is there something you're not telling me, Lieutenant?"

"Answer my question and I'll answer yours."

"Same answer. Some of 'em was by theirselves."

"Mr. Spickard, Betty Gail Spencer was murdered at the school that night."

"You don't say. Well, I'd say your man is that good for nothing Jimmy Conkwright. You probably won't need to look no farther."

"I think we will."

"Oh, why's that? Did he buy hisself one a them alibis?"

"You might say that. See, he was murdered, too."

89

"You don't say. Well, that's the best news I heard in a long time. When you find out who done it, maybe we can have a parade for the guy."

"It looks like I'm going to have to look a little longer to find someone who's grieving about poor Jimmy Conkwright."

"No, Lieutenant, I think you're gonna have to look a lot longer. I never met nobody who didn't hate his guts."

"What about Betty Gail Spencer? Did people hate her guts, too?"

"I don't know about her, but I'd say that most people'd just say that all she needed was a good butt whipping. Duck woulda never done that, though. He worshiped the ground she walked on. Course, he was mighty put out with her that night. Too bad she got mixed up with that good for nothing Conkwright again, 'though unless she'd seen him somewhere and Duck didn't know nothing about it, she got messed up before she seen that good for nothing again. I don't know what got into her."

"Mr. Spickard does the name Jennifer Garner mean anything to you."

"Nope. Is she supposed to live out this way somewheres?"

"I'm not sure. Her name just came up in our investigation."

"Well, like I told you before, I pretty much keep to myself. Sometimes, the only time I see someone is when I go to town to pick up things I need. Course I do see Duck once a month or so. He comes by to check on me, make sure I'm doing all right. Sometimes he picks up what I need, saves me a trip. Other than him, not too many people live out this way. I like it like that."

I thanked Earl Spickard for his time, and he told me to come back anytime and we'd see if the fish were biting.

"I'm usually here someplace."

I thanked him again, and Lou and I turned to head back to civilization. We only hoped Lightning hadn't gotten tired and left without us.

12

We got back to Lightning and took inventory of where we were. So far we'd talked with Walter Gillis, the current janitor at the county high school; Rose Ellen Calvert, the woman who coordinated the high school reunion; Duck Spencer, the murdered woman's husband; and Earl Spickard, the retired janitor. For sure, I planned to talk to Jim Bob Gibbons, Billy and April Korlein, and George and Sandy Justice, to get their take on who was where and when that night. If only someone would confess, or all but one person would agree on what went on.

I looked at my watch and was surprised it was already after 4:30. While everyone who attended the county high school lived out in the country when they were in high school, only one of my remaining suspects still lived in the country. That one was Jim Bob Gibbons. From what I could tell, he was closer to Jimmy Conkwright than any of the others. I wondered if his take on that night would agree with what the others had to say. It wouldn't take me long to find out. While Gibbons still lived out in the country, he lived in a different part of the county. I hoped that by the time I got to his house, he'd be home from work.

+++

I found Gibbons' house easier than I found the old man's. It was a small, red brick, and it looked like he might have had a couple of acres of land surrounding it. I pulled into the drive, got out and went up and knocked, but no one answered. I was contemplating what to do when a four-by-four pulled into the driveway. Out jumped a man nearing forty, which was the right age for Gibbons. He had on jeans, an Army green T-shirt, and boots. He was slender, sandy-haired, and clean-shaven.

"This is private property. What do you want?"

"You Jim Bob Gibbons?"

"You got cop written all over you, even though you're driving some kind of sissy car. Listen, I don't care what she says. I didn't touch that woman."

"Which woman is that?"

"Emma Mae Parsons. Ain't that what you're here about?"

"Afraid not."

"So, you ain't no cop?"

"No, I'm a cop, all right. I'm Lt. Dekker. This is Sgt. Murdock. We'd like to ask you a few questions. This is if you're Jim Bob Gibbons."

"What's this all about?"

"Are you Jim Bob Gibbons?"

"Yeah, yeah, I'm Jim Bob. Now, what's all this about?"

"It's about the night of the high school reunion."

When I said that, Gibbons seemed to relax.

"Oh, is that all? What 'happened? Did Jimmy Conkwright go and get hisself in a buncha trouble? Surely, he's not trying to get me to bail his sorry you know what outa jail. He's got more money than Carter's got liver pills."

"Not anymore."

"You kidding me. Jimmy lost all 'is money. He didn't say nothin' about it that night. What happened?"

"Is there someplace we can sit down and talk about this?"

"I guess we could go out back. I call it my patio. Actually, it's three or four chairs in the grass and a barbecue."

Gibbons stretched out his pronunciation of patio and barbecue.

I noticed that he had a considerable limp as he led us around the house to the back. We each took a seat, choosing three of the four metal chairs that looked like they were nearing antique status. Gibbons grimaced and used his arms to take most of his weight as he sat down.

"So, Mr. Gibbons, tell me about what all happened that night. Did you participate when everyone toured the school before dinner?"

"No, you mighta noticed I got me a limp. It hurts most of the time, but it really hurts if'n I try to go up or down steps. As you can see, I ain't got no steps here. But that night, I got there a few minutes before 7:00, before we ate."

"Was Jimmy Conkwright there when you got there?"

"No, but Jimmy got there not long after that. he was there when it come time to go through the food line."

"So, tell me about what went on that night?"

"Well, there ain't much to tell. It was our twenty-year reunion. There ain't many of us, and most of us still live 'round here, but Jimmy had moved away. It was good to see him again. He was kind of feeling his oats that night. I had to calm him down a mite."

"How was he feeling his oats?"

"Well, you know how some people act when they see some old friends. 'e was a little on the rowdy side."

"What kind of things did he do?"

"Oh, nothing too much. He was just talkin' a lot, and he asked some o' the guys' wives to dance. Flirted with 'em a little, too. Some of the guys took it the wrong way."

"Almost come to blows?"

"Well, I don't know about that. I stepped in and pulled Jimmy away before that happened."

"Did he hit on any more of the women before the night ended?"

"A little bit. Ruffled some more feathers. Then, when Betty Gail Spencer came in without Duck, he took up with her."

"Was he drinking?"

"Not at first. Then, someone riled him up and he stomped out. Betty Gail took off after him. They was gone a while. When they got back they'd been drinking a little."

"Did this lead to anything?"

"Oh, that Rose Ellen Calvert had her panties tied in a knot. Everybody always said she was such a prude because none a the guys were innerested in her. The first time Jimmy left, she followed him. I think she was 'afraid he might do something to the school. She tried to do it again when Jimmy and Betty Gail left together, but somebody stopped her."

"Do you know who it was?"

"Naw. I just remember that somebody said something to her, kept her from leaving. She ended up leaving anyway, said she had to go to the restroom, but that was about five minutes later. I had to go myself, and when I come out I seen Rose Ellen coming outa the kitchen. When she seen me, she hightailed back to the cafeteria."

"Did anyone leave the cafeteria to go look for Jimmy and Betty Gail?"

"Yeah, but not right away. At least I don't think it was right away. Anyway, Duck showed up a few minutes later. I think George Justice musta called him. At least he got on his phone and called someone when they left together. Anyway, he showed up, and he, George, and Billy Korlein were gonna look for Jimmy and Betty Gail. I was afraid that the three of 'em would beat Jimmy up if they found him, so I butted in and went looking with 'em."

"So the four of you looked for them together?"

"Well, we did at first, but when we didn't find 'em right away, Duck was just gittin' madder and madder, so somebody suggested we'd do better if we spread out. I told 'em to holler if they found 'em, but nobody ever hollered."

"Do you have any idea if anybody saw either of them?"

"Don't know. I went outside, thought maybe the two of 'em mighta gone back to Jimmy's car. I hunted 'round out there for a while, but I didn't see nothing except'n one of the other guys. Time I got back, the other three was back with everyone else and Duck was raving and decided to leave."

"Did you see Jimmy's car?"

"Yep, but they wasn't in it."

"Were you and Jimmy good friends?"

"Still are. Oh, we had some words on occasion. Usually when we were out drinking somewheres. We were still in high school, but Jimmy always knowed where to find something to drink. I don't drink no more. That night that Jimmy and that girl was out ridin' 'round and she got killed, that cured me. I never took another drink after that. That was just before the end of the school year. Jimmy's daddy got things hushed for a while, but everybody turned against Jimmy after that, so his daddy had him leave town. I didn't see much of Jimmy after that."

"Did you know Miriam Van Meter?"

"That was the girl who was with Jimmy, weren't it?"

I nodded and he continued.

"I knowed she was a freshman. She wanted to be liked, wanted to be noticed. She chased all the boys, but most of 'em got tired of her real quick like."

"Was she new to the school? Did any of you go to school with her before?"

"Don't think so. She just seemed to show up one day somewheres 'round the beginning of our senior year. She was a freshman."

"What can you tell me about Betty Gail Spencer?"

"Well, she was Betty Gail Reynolds then. She didn't become Spencer 'til she married Duck. She was all right, I guess. I never asked her out or nothing."

"Jim Bob, have you heard the rumors?"

"You mean about Jimmy and Betty Gail running away together? Some people was talkin' that nonsense. I don't think it's true."

"Why's that?"

"Well, I have to admit that I ain't seen Betty Gail much lately, but used to be she only did stuff like that to make Duck jealous, make him want to buy her stuff. Duck called her his princess. I do know that one day I ran into Duck in the auto parts place, and he was upset with her. He said she'd changed, started doing things she'd never done, staying out late at night and drinking."

"Do you think Duck would hit her?"

"Duck? No way. He loved her too much. He mighta hollered at her if she made him mad, but that's all. Why you askin' all this stuff, anyways? Did they really run away together?"

"No, they were murdered together."

"You don't say. Any idea who done it?"

"Not yet. You have any idea?"

Gibbons gave me a funny look. I don't know if that meant he knew or didn't know who did it.

"One final question, Mr. Gibbons. Do you know anyone named Jennifer Garner?"

"Is she one of your suspects?"

"I don't know. Her name came up in regard to this investigation, and I wanted to check and see if you've heard of her."

"Sorry."

I decided to leave him to his thoughts. I told him I'd let him know if I had any more questions. He didn't seem pleased with that.

"Listen, fellas, if'n it's all right with you, I'll let you see yourselves out. I think you know the way."

13

I was hungry, but I wanted to get to all my suspects before any of them had a chance to compare stories. We were given two days to work on the case before news of the murders would be made public. Of course, that didn't stop anyone I'd talked to from letting the cat out of the bag. That was fine. I just wanted to talk to each of my suspects before he or she knew anything about the murders.

Before I visited the Korleins, I dropped by my house and picked up a couple of apples, a container of almond butter made from raw almonds, and two spoons. That had to do us until after we'd questioned four more suspects, two married couples.

Magnolia Lane wasn't too far from my house, in a middle-class neighborhood, so it was only a little after 6:30 when we pulled up in front of the Korlein's house. It looked like they were home. There were a car and a truck in the driveway. The two of us got out, looked around. It was still a little on the warm side, so we didn't see any of their neighbors. I suspected most of them were taking advantage of their air conditioning. However, my ears told me that one poor, misguided soul a few doors away had chosen that moment to mow his grass.

I walked up to the front door, rang the bell, and waited. Ten seconds or so later, a man came to the door. He had dark brown hair, had on a red sports shirt and khakis. He was about my height, and carried a few extra pounds, but less than most men his age. He opened the door slightly.

"I'm sorry, but we're busy right now."

"So are we. I'm Lt. Dekker. This is Sgt. Murdock. We're with the Hilldale Police Department. Are you Billy Korlein?"

"I am, but why do you want to talk to me?"

"Actually, we'd like to talk to both you and your wife."

"Well, we're just finishing up supper. Do you mind waiting in the living room a couple of minutes while we finish eating?"

In past days, I would've wanted to join them, but I told him that Lou and I could wait in the living room if they'd hurry. I refrained from asking him if we could bring in our apples, almond butter, and spoons.

A couple of minutes later, Korlein returned, had a woman with him. Lou and I stood up to greet April Korlein. I could see where she might have been a cheerleader in high school. Her dark hair matched her husband's and her shape told me she worked out or had good metabolism. She looked good enough that she could still turn men's heads.

"Hi, I'm April Korlein," she said, as she came forward and stuck out her hand. "I guess this is as good of a time as any to talk. Our kids are visiting their cousins for a few days."

I introduced myself and Lou to her. She motioned for us to be reseated.

"What's this about, Lieutenant? We can't imagine why the police would want to talk to us," Korlein asked.

"I just wanted to talk to you about the night of the high school reunion."

"Don't tell me that Jimmy Conkwright has filed some kind of suit against me."

"No, Mr. Korlein, nothing like that. I just want you to tell me what happened that night. Did you and Mrs. Korlein take part in the tour of the school?"

"Yeah, that was a lot of fun. Me and George Justice swapped stories of things we did back then."

"Give me a for instance."

"Well, when we got upstairs, anytime we saw something, it reminded us of things we did when we were in school. We both started laughing when we passed the restroom. See, the boy's restroom was just above the entrance to the school, and since teachers were already in their classrooms getting ready for whatever we were to do that day, none of them were standing at the school entrance. From time to time, some of us guys would open the boy's bathroom window, and toss a water balloon on an unsuspecting girl. We had our favorites we watched for. Like girls who were already developed, or ones who were stuck up. We smacked Rose Ellen Calvert right in the kisser one day. Naturally, she reported us, but they didn't ever find out who did it. And then, on occasion, we'd see some girl walking down the hall and shove her into the boy's bathroom. Some of them loved it, but others hid their eyes. One time, we almost got caught. We didn't know that Mr. Tompkins, the math teacher, was in there at the time. And that night, I'm talking about the night of the reunion; we went in and sat down in a few classrooms. That gave us a chance to talk about some of the things we put in teachers' desk drawers or girl's hair. And one day, Jessica Tyler opened her notebook and found it was full of shaving cream. Nobody admitted doing that, either, although Miss Thorndike questioned us about it for over ten minutes. And another time, someone put some water on Angie Crowder's seat, and she didn't see it before she sat down. Someone did pass her a note telling her that next time she should stop off in the girls' bathroom before coming to class. Several of us noticed that her backside was still wet when class was over. She had a couple of her friends walk behind her on her way to her next class."

I smiled at some of the things he talked about, although I never attempted any of those things. We were more civilized at Hilldale High.

"So, you swapped stories and relived some old memories. What then?"

"Well, that put most of us in a good mood, and we were well on our way to having a good reunion. Everybody seemed happy to see everybody else. Oh, some of us run into some of the others at the Piggly Wiggly from time to time, but that's different. Anyway, as I said, we were on our way to having a good time, talking about high school, music, the way we all looked back then. That was until Jimmy showed up, then Betty Gail Spencer showed up without her husband and started carrying on with Jimmy."

"I understand that Jimmy Conkwright hit on your wife."

"So, you've already talked to some others. The truth is that Jimmy hit on practically everyone that ever wore a skirt. Well, everyone except Rose Ellen Calvert. I doubt if anybody's ever hit on her. She really doesn't look that bad. It's just that she expects everyone to be so perfect. I admit that Jimmy was way out of line, both in high school and that night. But Rose Ellen always had this thing about her that repelled both guys and girls."

"Do you agree with that, Mrs. Korlein?"

"Well, Billy's thinking is a little stronger than mine, but I never really felt comfortable around her. She always expected everything to be a certain way. I don't mean that she's a bad person. She just seemed like someone who never had any fun and didn't seem to want anyone else to have fun, either. Of course, I don't call any of those things Jimmy did fun."

"So, Mr. Korlein, Conkwright came in and made a pass at your wife, or something like that?"

"Yeah. See Sandy Justice and April were cheerleaders. The Justices were there that night too, so when Jimmy came in he came over and said something like he wanted them to do a cheer just for him. I never liked Jimmy in high school, so I got riled up pretty easy, but I never hit him, and nobody else did, either. And later, after Jimmy started drinking, he came over and tried to pull April and Sandy to the dance floor. It was then that a few of us threw Jimmy out. Betty Gail left right after that. Jimmy had paired up with Betty Gail after she showed up without Duck. Jimmy shared some of whatever he was drinking with her. They'd gone out once before. Evidently, he had a bottle on him or in his car."

"When you say threw him out, do you mean you saw that he left the cafeteria, or left the school building?"

Korlein laughed.

"I mean threw him out. We hustled him out the door. I took one arm and George took the other one and we threw him out the front door."

"And he hit the sidewalk and landed on his face."

"That's right! He was already drunk, so he had trouble getting up. It was about that time that Duck's wife pushed me aside and went to his rescue. We just left the two of them to themselves and went back to the cafeteria."

"You had to pass the janitor's office on the way to and from the front door. Did the janitor see you throw Conkwright out?"

"Naw, he had his door closed most of the way. I think he was listening to make sure we weren't going to do anything else. He'd already threatened to call the police if things got out of hand."

"And what was Jim Bob Gibbons' take on all this?"

"Evidently, you've done your homework. I see we're not the first people you've questioned about this. Can I ask you why you're here asking all these questions? Something bad must have happened."

"All in good time, Mr. Korlein. Just tell me about Jim Bob Gibbons."

"Well, back in high school Jim Bob was one of the few male friends that Jimmy had. I think Jim Bob liked all the things that Jimmy's money could buy. Anyway, they hung out some together. That is if Jimmy wasn't pawing some girl. Anyway, I didn't care to be around either one of them, although it seems like Jim Bob might have changed some. It sounds funny that the two of us live in the same town and never see each other, but it'd been a while since I'd run into him until I saw him at the reunion. Anyway, Jim Bob tried to settle Jimmy down. Each time it worked for a few minutes, but then Jimmy'd get going again."

"And what did Gibbons think of your rough way of removing Conkwright from the premises?"

"Oh, he said something like, 'You didn't need to be so rough.'"

"Tell me about when Duck Spencer showed up."

"Lieutenant, if you already know all this stuff, why are you bothering to question us? What did happen that we don't know about?"

"In a minute. Just tell me about when Spencer showed up."

"Well, when Jimmy and Betty Gail left, I looked over at George Justice, and he took out his phone and dialed someone. I wasn't sure if it was the police or what, but a while later Duck showed up, wanting to know where Betty Gail was."

"And did anyone know?"

"I'm sure Jimmy did, but Jimmy wasn't there to answer him, so we took off looking for them. I didn't want Duck to do anything he'd be sorry for."

"You say 'We took off.' Who's 'we'?"

Oh, me, and George, and Duck, and Jim Bob."

"All of you stick together?"

"We did at first, but it seemed like Jim Bob was itching to go look for them by himself, so he did. The rest of us stuck together, didn't find them, though. Later, I saw Jim Bob coming out of the kitchen. He just looked at me, smiled, and gave me a palm's up sign, as if he hadn't had any luck."

"Are you sure Jim Bob was the one you saw coming out of the kitchen?"

"Yeah, it was Jim Bob. The rest of us had just gotten back. Duck and George went back to the cafeteria. I had to use the restroom. I saw Jim Bob as I was coming out."

"Do you remember Miriam Van Meter?"

When Korlein didn't say anything right away, his wife broke in.

"Wasn't she the girl that Jimmy killed?"

"She was the one who died in an automobile accident when Jimmy was driving drunk one night."

"She was kind of different. It was like she wanted to start out on top. I guess that's why she hooked up with Jimmy. It's funny. She just showed up one day, out of nowhere. No one knew who she was. I never had any classes with her, but since we were a small school I kind of knew who she was. I could tell she wanted to be liked, but just like Rose Ellen, she never went about it the right way."

"Mr. Korlein, you've been after me to tell you why we're here. I'll tell you now. We found Betty Gail Spencer and Jimmy Conkwright dead. We're pretty sure they were murdered."

"I'd heard the rumors that they might have run away together, but nobody ever guessed that they might have been murdered. I guess this puts a whole different spin on things. Do you have any idea when they were murdered?"

"Possibly that night. We're not sure."

"Well, neither of us saw anything out of the ordinary. Well, nothing we haven't already told you. Nobody followed them when they left the school. At least I'm pretty sure no one did because I think all of us were in the cafeteria most of the time. I'm pretty sure no one went out and got in their car and took off then."

"And did you see either of them again that night after Duck Spencer got to the school?"

"I didn't. I don't know about anyone else. I know that nobody said anything about seeing them, at least not to us."

April Korlein broke in.

"I hope we've been able to help you some."

"We're just putting together what everyone says and see if we can learn anything from those who were there."

"Well, I can't see anyone at the reunion doing anything. We might have wanted to throw Jimmy in the river and sober him up, or hope he'd float away. But I'm sure none of us saw anything. Anything else we can do for you, Lieutenant?"

"No, I guess that's it. For now, anyway."

I swear I saw Mr. Korlein flinch when I added those last three words.

"Oh, one final thing, do either of you know someone named Jennifer Garner?"

Korlein grinned.

"You mean the actress?"

"I don't know. I just wanted to know if you know anyone by that name."

"Well, if you mean the actress, I'd sure like to know her."

April Korlein's elbow connected with her husband's ribs about the time Lou and I got up to leave.

"So, you think she looks pretty good, huh?"

"Don't you, Lieutenant? You're a man. What man wouldn't want to spend time with her?"

April Korlein's elbow was a little harder the second time.

"Now, honey, you know I'm just kidding. Remember how I'm always telling you about how all the guys are jealous of me because I've got you."

Steve Demaree

14

Neither of us said a word until we were safely ensconced in Lightning.

Lou turned to me as soon as he was sure no one could overhear us.

"So, what do you think, Cy?"

"I think April Korlein looks pretty good. And you?"

"Me, too, but I also think she looks pretty married."

"Maybe not for much longer after those remarks her husband made. Anyway, Lou, I forgot to mention this earlier, but I think Rose Ellen Calvert has the hots for you. Did you see the way she looked at you? Of course, she needs a makeover, but not an extreme one."

"You interested in double dating, Cy. Me and Rose Ellen, you and your next-door neighbor?"

I knew it was time to change the subject.

"Does this make you think about our high school days, Lou?"

"A little. I can remember when you stuck Ruby Hatcher's pigtails in your inkwell."

"There wasn't any Ruby Hatcher at our school, and there weren't any inkwells, either."

"Well, Cy, I can remember back when I was prom king."

"You didn't even go to the prom, Lou. Neither did I."

"I know you didn't. So, how do you know I wasn't prom king?"

"Maybe because the students at our school were smart enough not to do something like that. By the way, speaking of the prom, I remember going to school the Monday after the prom. Rachel Robinson came up to me and said, "Cy, I was hoping you'd be at the prom. It was the only reason I went. So, you know what I did?"

"Yeah, you asked her out, dated her a few times after that, didn't you?"

"Yeah, we dated a few times until she went off to college. She was kind of cute with that red hair and freckles. Of course, it wasn't long after that that I met my Eunice."

I started getting sentimental, so Lou brought my mind back to the murders.

"You think some actress might be mixed up in this?"

"I don't know. But from the look on Korlein's face, I sure hope so. I'll make sure I Google her as soon as I get home tonight."

Evidently, Lou's clue of the day had something to do with an actress. I wondered how an actress might figure into our case. It wouldn't be the first time his clue was a famous person. I'd try to find out how famous this Jennifer Garner was before I let anybody downtown know her name meant nothing to me. At least most of our suspects didn't know her. Well, the ones who lived way out in the country. Plus, Rose Ellen Calvert, who I assumed was more into books than movies or TV.

I knew Lightning wouldn't give away any of our secrets, so we talked as we headed to the Justices' house. Five minutes later, we pulled up in front of our last house of the night.

A pretty blonde-headed woman answered the door, admitted to being Sandy Justice. I told her who we were and that we needed to talk to her and her husband. She told me her husband was on the phone. She seemed a little miffed when I asked her who he was talking to. I was a little miffed when she told me Billy Korlein. She invited us in and I saw George Justice sitting in a chair, talking on the phone. I told him I needed him to get off immediately. Justice was short and thin and had hair the color that some people would refer to as red, others as blond.

When Justice ended his call, he turned to us and said, "I would ask who's ordering me to get off my own phone in my own house, but I already know who you are. I also know why you're here."

So much for pretending he didn't know who we were, but also so much for my surprise attack.

Mrs. Justice looked as if she didn't have a clue what was going on, so her husband filled her in.

"That was Billy Korlein. Jimmy Conkwright and Betty Gail Spencer were killed the night of the reunion. These two gentlemen are investigating the murders. Am I right...? I'm sorry. I didn't get your names."

"I'm Lt. Dekker and this is Sgt. Murdock. So, what else did Mr. Korlein tell you?"

"Just that you were over to his place asking him and April questions about what happened that night. We don't know any more than they do."

"Sometimes one person may notice something that another person doesn't. That's the reason it's a good idea to talk to anyone who was a witness."

"You mean someone there that night might have witnessed the murders?"

"They could have, but I'm talking about anything that went on that night. Why don't I start with you, Mrs. Justice? Tell me all that you can remember about that night."

"That was a few weeks ago, now. I'm not sure I can remember everything, but I'll try."

Her husband interrupted, but I asked him to be quiet until it was his turn. His wife seemed to be waiting for something. I told her to go ahead, tell me what she could remember, and I'd ask any questions that might fill in the holes.

"Well, as you probably know, it was our twenty-year high school reunion. Ours wasn't a big school, so there weren't a lot of people there that night, but most of us made it. It was fun at first, and then Jimmy came in. It had been a while since I'd seen him or even thought about him, but I recognized him. I'd hoped that he'd changed, but he didn't seem to be any different, except that he looked older, like the rest of us. I remember my mouth flew open when I saw him. George looked at me, then turned and looked in the direction I was looking. He was next to me, so I laid my hand on his arm and said, 'Now, George, calm down. Let's see how Jimmy acts.' George said something like, 'Murderers like him don't change.'"

Mr. Justice opened his mouth to defend himself. I silenced him before he could start, and directed his wife to continue.

"Well, it wasn't any time until Jimmy came over to me and April. We were cheerleaders in high school, and Jimmy said something about us doing a cheer just for him. I was thinking, I bet my husband has something just for you. George stood up and was about to get in Jimmy's face when Jim Bob Gibbons stepped in and pulled Jimmy away. I can't remember much else, except that Jimmy lost interest in me when Betty Gail Spencer showed up without Duck and didn't ward off Jimmy's advances. Anyway, at some point, Jimmy left with Betty Gail right behind him and they came back a few minutes later. It was obvious both of them had been drinking. I remember somewhere in there Jimmy tried to pull me to the dance floor, and the rest of the guys threw him out of the cafeteria. A couple of times my husband and some of the others went looking for

111

Jimmy and Betty Gail. One of those times was after Duck showed up. George called him and told him what was going on. When Duck got there, the guys went looking for Betty Gail."

"Do you remember which guys?"

"Not really. I know that George and Billy were two of them because April and I started talking about what might happen if they found them. We were worried, thought about calling the cops, but we decided to wait until our husbands came back."

"And how long before they came back?"

"I'm not sure exactly. It probably seemed longer than it was. I know before they came back to stay, a couple of times one of them poked his head in to see if Jimmy had come back."

"Weren't they concerned that Jimmy might come back when they weren't there and try something with you?"

"No, because before they left, all the guys got together and some of them volunteered to stay in case Jimmy came back."

"Mrs. Justice, do you know whether or not anyone else left the cafeteria while your husband was gone?"

"Several people did, but just to go to the restroom. They were all back really quick."

"What about Rose Ellen Calvert? Did she leave?"

"I know she left once, right after Jimmy left. I'm not sure if it was the first or second time he left. I think she left one other time. I know one time she told us she had to go to the restroom, but I can't remember when that happened. It could have been early or late."

"Did all the guys come back at once?"

"No, but there wasn't much difference between when they all got back. At least I don't think so."

"And what did your husband have to say when he got back?"

George Justice tried to interrupt again, but again I silenced him. His wife didn't seem to notice and continued with her answer.

"Just that they didn't have any luck finding Betty Gail, and they didn't run into Jimmy either."

"Did you believe him?"

"Of course! Anyway, the school is small enough that we would have heard them as loud as they would have been."

"What if they saw Jimmy, sneaked up behind him, and bopped him on the head?"

"I imagine Betty Gail would have screamed."

"Not if they bopped her at the same time."

"Lieutenant, I know you don't know us very well, but the men I know would never bop a woman on the head."

"Not even Duck Spencer, if he was mad at his wife?"

"I don't know Duck as well as I do some of the other guys, but we've been around him some. He and George are good friends, so George would know better than I would, but I don't see him doing anything like that to his wife."

"What about if Jimmy Conkwright or Betty Gail Spencer made someone good and mad?"

"Well, they say that all of us are capable of murder if provoked. I guess anything is possible. I just don't believe any of us murdered anyone."

"Well, someone there did."

When I made that statement, neither of the Justices had a thing to say.

"Let me ask you something else, Mrs. Justice. What can you tell me about Miriam Van Meter?"

"The mystery girl. Now, there's a name I haven't heard in forever. She just wandered in from out of nowhere our senior year. Well, we were seniors. She was a freshman. Usually, seniors and freshmen never have any classes together, but I needed one more class to graduate, and since my other classes were hard, I opted for a nice, easy class to fill out my last requirement. Miriam was in that class. We were given an assignment where we were to pair up with another student and give a report in front of the class. Miriam seemed to be the class outcast, because of the way she was, and the rest of them were all friends, so, as it turned out, Miriam and I were the last two without a partner. I suggested that I come over to her house or she come over to mine to work on the project. She finally agreed to come to mine. Well, she came over one afternoon, right after school, and we did the work we needed to do, and then she left. Not long after she left, I remembered that I needed to ask Miriam something before the next morning. Miriam had told me that she was Mrs. Edwards' niece, and was living with her. Well, I didn't really know Mrs. Edwards, but I knew where she lived. My mom drove me over there and planned to wait on me because what I needed would only take a minute. Well, I knocked on the door and Mrs. Edwards came to the door. She told me Miriam didn't live there. When I told her, Miriam had told me that was where she lived, she said something funny. She said, 'Oh, Miriam, I thought you said Mary Ann.' I didn't want to cause a scene, but the next day I made it a point to seek out Mrs. Edwards' daughter, who was a junior at our school. She told me that evidently some friend's daughter was out of district and wanted to attend our school, so her mother agreed to pretend that the girl lived there. I tried to find out who it was, but Carrie Edwards had no idea."

Like Jimmy Conkwright, no one seemed to like Miriam Van Meter, and everyone seemed to agree about her, but this was the first time anyone had volunteered that all was not right with her. She might need some looking into.

I turned to Mr. Justice, who seemed to have turned reticent.

"So, Mr. Justice, what have you got to add to what your wife told us?"

"The way she told it, it looks like all of us guys were murderers. It wasn't that way at all. Jimmy got out of line, and we did the best we could to see that he didn't cause any more trouble. None of us saw Jimmy or Duck's wife other than when we were in the cafeteria. So, that let's all of us off."

"How does that let you off?"

"We were together the whole time. Unless you're insinuating that we all chopped him to death. Her, too."

"I'm not insinuating anything. But we have had three people tell us that the four of you separated after you left the cafeteria."

"They must have meant after Jimmy left the first time."

"No, they were talking about the second time."

"Well, then whoever they are they're lying."

"Even your own wife said you didn't all come back in together."

"Well, we might not have done that. It's possible one of us might have stayed out in the hall. Oh, yeah! I remember. I think Billy and Duck might have stepped outside for a smoke."

"Was this before or after the two people were murdered?"

"How do I know? I didn't kill them."

"Maybe someone who makes an excuse to smoke a cigarette waited until you'd left and then ran into Conkwright and Mrs. Spencer and whacked them to death."

"Didn't nobody do no whacking. At least none of my friends."

"This time I believe you because neither of the victims was whacked to death, but someone did murder them, and it was someone at the school who did it. Only four of you left the cafeteria."

"That's not true. Almost everyone left at some point. Maybe someone who left to go to the restroom did it. Or

115

what about the janitor and his friend? They could have done it anytime."

"Do you figure they did it together?"

"Could be. How would I know? Or what's to keep someone from outside the school, someone who didn't attend the reunion, from sneaking in and murdering them."

"You mean someone who just happened to be in the neighborhood and looked up and said, 'There are two people who need to be murdered. Why don't I go do it?'"

"No, but someone could have driven by when Jimmy and Duck's wife were outside at his car, recognized Jimmy from way back, saw that he was drunk, and decided to get even for some old grudge."

"You see someone driving down the road?"

"You act like it couldn't happen."

"Well, it does seem a little farfetched. They would have to have great vision in the dark to recognize Jimmy Conkwright."

"Not if he was near his car. He always drove some kind of red Corvette. I don't know anyone else around here who's ever had one. It could've caused someone to slow down, spot Jimmy, and then kill him. Of course, they would have to kill Duck's wife too, so she wouldn't tell on them. And by the way, it wasn't all that dark when we threw them out."

"So how do you know they were ever at Jimmy's car?"

"I don't. But they went somewhere. And I don't think Jimmy had any liquor on him when he came in the first time. I think he had it all planned. He would either lure some old high school flame away, or he'd bring it in later."

"But Conkwright and Mrs. Spencer came back in after they were at the car, if the car was where they went to get something to drink."

"And they could've gone back out to the car."

"And maybe they stayed in the school."

"You don't know that."

"No, but I know their bodies weren't found near the car."

I'd been careful not to tell anyone where we found the bodies, in case someone might let something slip. So far, no one had. Then, I remembered I did let it slip once.

"Mr. Justice, tell me about your phone call to Duck Spencer."

"Not much to tell. Duck and I are pretty good friends. I knew he wouldn't like his wife running around with Jimmy Conkwright, so I called him to let him know what was going on."

"And when was this?"

"I can't remember if I called him after they left together the first time or the second time. I just remember I called him, let him know what was going on. He told me to try to get his wife away from Jimmy. I told him I didn't think I could. Then he told me he'd be there as soon as he could. It took him longer than he thought it would. Turns out that storm we had earlier knocked down a tree across his road, and he had to run down the road to get the old janitor to bring him in his boat. He called me back after he ran into the tree, told me to hold the fort, and he'd get there as soon as he could. That was when he told me he was going to check with old man Spickard, see if he could bring him in his boat."

I'd talked to several people. None of them mentioned anything about anyone's phone ringing. Either no one heard it, no one remembered it, or no one thought it was important.

"And did you leave the cafeteria again when Spencer called you back?"

"I wasn't in the cafeteria when he called. I was out trying to find Duck's wife. Actually, I was on my way back to the cafeteria. I'd decided to wait until Duck got there."

"So, you'd gone out by yourself to look for them?"

"No. No. No. Billy Korlein and I were together. Jim Bob Gibbons had been with us, but he went off on his own."

"And this was after Jimmy and Betty Gail were drinking and had left."

"I'm not sure. I think it was before. It might have been when they were out at Jimmy's car drinking. That might have been the reason we didn't find them the first time."

"And what might be the reason you didn't find them the second time?"

"Maybe they were already dead. You seem to know more about this than I do. Where did you find them, anyway? Maybe I can tell you if I saw anyone anywhere near the place."

"I think I'll save that little bit of information for later."

"Suit yourself. I'm just trying to help. Anyway, I know it had to be outside someplace."

"And how do you know that?"

"Well, I don't for sure. But when the four of us first went to look for them, after they came back in drunk and we threw Jimmy out, we walked down the hall together, then one of us came up with the idea of looking on both floors at once. So, me and Duck took the downstairs floor and Jim Bob and Billy took the upstairs. They climbed the steps and looked down the hall. They didn't see anybody. We hollered that we didn't see anybody, either."

"Did you check all the rooms?"

"They did upstairs. One of them walked down the right side, the other one the left, and they tried every door. All of them were locked. Downstairs there are not as many locked doors. Only the principal's office and the counselor's office. Both of those doors were locked."

"Did you look in the gym and the kitchen?"

"We did. I took the gym, Duck the kitchen. It took me longer 'cause the gym is a larger place. I had to go up on the stage and check behind the curtain. First of all, I had to find the light switch. After I found it, I realized there wasn't anyone in there, anywhere. When I walked out, Duck was coming out of the kitchen. He told me they weren't in there, either. That means they had to be outside someplace. We looked out there, too, but of course, it's a lot bigger area out there. I suspect you found them down by the river somewhere. Is that where you found them, Lieutenant?"

"I can't say."

"I knew that's where they were. Had to be. There wasn't anywhere else. And if that's the case, it means it could have been anybody who did it. Probably somebody drunk out on the river."

We sat there silently for a few minutes, and then Justice spoke.

"Lieutenant, I've been sitting here listening to everything you've said, but there's something that puzzles me. Can I ask you a question?"

"You may, but I'm not sure I'm allowed to answer it."

"How does Jennifer Garner fit into all this?"

Before I could open my mouth, his wife said, "Jennifer Garner? The Jennifer Garner?"

"Yeah, Billy said the lieutenant asked him about Jennifer Garner. But then, what man isn't interested in Jennifer Garner? There'd have to be something wrong with him if he wasn't."

+++

Again Lou waited until we were safely ensconced in Lightning before he opened his mouth.

"Cy, can I go home with you?"

"Why would you want to do that?"

"Well, I don't have a computer, and it looks like going to your house is the only way I'm going to find out who Jennifer Garner is."

"Lou, you could care less who she is. You just want to know what the babe looks like."

"Well, I do have room for a poster on my bedroom wall."

"You mean you don't have a picture of Heather there?"

"Nope. Betty Lou, either."

"Cy, do you have a picture of your next-door neighbor on your wall?"

"I used to until I woke up in the middle of the night, saw the picture, and it almost frightened me to death. At least, while the picture was there, I didn't have any problem with rats. Now, bats, that's another story."

We shared a laugh and then Lightning lurched forward.

+++

It was late when Lou and I left our last suspects of the day. My stomach had been growling for quite some time. We'd eaten our snack and cleaned up on the way to the Justices, and it was past my supper time. In years past, I would have taken out a Hershey Almond candy bar, my staple food, and munched on it, one almond and surrounding candy at a time. But I was trying to turn over a new leaf. I thought I was off the hook with Doc when I went back and met his weight goal, but he wasn't sure I had conformed, and actually, I wasn't sure, either. When Doc told me I had to continue to lose at least two pounds a month to stay on the force, I knew I had to keep up with my newfound regimen. Sometimes, that would be tough.

Both Lou and I were tired, so we refrained from talking about the case or Jennifer Garner and made plans for the next day.

"Lou, I'll probably be a little late in the morning."

"Oh? Exercising a little more or sleeping a little later?"

"Neither. I need to call Sam and see what he can find out about these people. Then, I want to Google Jennifer Garner to see if I can find out what today's clue means."

"Did you say Google or ogle?"

"Maybe both. It depends on what she looks like. Anyway, I want to see if I can find something on the computer that will tell me what our clue means. And of course, I plan to exercise, fix breakfast, and read my daily devotionals and my Bible before I come, so I expect I'll be a few minutes later than usual. I'll call you before I leave the house. So far, all I have planned for tomorrow is for us to go where Betty Gail Spencer worked and see what they can tell us about her and her relationship with her husband. Also, I want to check to see if Mrs. Edwards is still around. If so, I want to see her and try to get her to tell us what she can about that girl that died in the wreck twenty years ago. So far, it looks like someone's motive either has something to do with that wreck or something that happened at the reunion. I'm leaning toward the latter since I don't think this thing was premeditated, but then I want to see if anyone knew that Jimmy Conkwright was coming to the reunion."

"I would think that Rose Ellen Calvert knew since she took care of the reservations."

"I think we'll end up seeing most or all of our suspects again, as we learn more, but probably not until after we hear from Sam."

I dropped Lou at his place and then rushed home to fix myself some supper. I wasn't in any mood to cook, so I opened the refrigerator and took out some shrimp and cocktail sauce to make myself a shrimp cocktail. The shrimp weren't large, and according to the container, I could eat ten of them. I could've eaten twenty of them, but I wasn't going to revert back to the old Cy. Not yet, anyway. I had a tray full of carrot sticks, celery stalks, sliced green and red peppers, and some cherry tomatoes. I filled my plate with them and added four olives to my display. As soon as I poured a glass of water, I was ready to eat. I knew I was too tired to Wii, but that was okay. I would make up for it the next day.

Curiosity had the best of me, however, so I went to the computer and Googled Jennifer Garner. I could see how Korlein and Justice were enamored with her. I didn't know a woman could look so good. The next morning I planned to find out more about her. But then, the next morning was still several hours away. It was time to go to bed. And dream about Jennifer Garner and any other beautiful women who might be future clues. On the way to get ready for bed, with my thoughts still fixed on Jennifer Garner, I realized that sometime, somewhere, she too went to high school. I wondered if she was a cheerleader, the prom queen, and whatever else she wanted to be, and how many of the guys hit on her. I thought back to my days at Hilldale High. We had some nice-looking girls there too, but I don't think any of them became famous.

15

I woke up the next morning feeling better than I did the night before. I sat up, remembered what I had planned for the day. I didn't know how long it would take to talk to the people where Betty Gail Spencer worked, plus see Mrs. Edwards. I picked up the phone book. Mrs. Edwards was still listed, and at the same address. I figured she'd be up in age by now and would be home during the day. I would soon find out.

In the past, I stumbled to the shower to wake up. That was before I started exercising. I had no idea if the Wii Fit would make me sweat in January, but it sure did in July. Also, I'd heard that a body should eat something before exercising, so I took a few minutes to read my daily devotionals, and then headed to the kitchen.

I'd settled in on oatmeal, bacon, and scrambled eggs most days. On occasion, I fixed an omelet, but omelets take longer than scrambling eggs, and I wanted to leave as much time as possible for working on the case. Once I ate, I dashed to the computer. Jennifer Garner was waiting for me. The night before I'd clicked on long enough to see what Garner looked like. I now knew that my blind date was worth every click I could muster.

I sat down in front of the computer, eager to give Garner my full attention. Besides, I needed to allow my food ample time to settle before I Wiied. I learned a little about her and looked at all the things the actress had appeared in. Four of them stood out; *Alias, The Invention of Lying, Catch Me If You Can,* and *The Pretender.* I didn't know whether this was important or not, but she was married to some guy named Ben Affleck. I wasn't sure if he too is an actor, or if his family is the one that owns the insurance company that uses the duck in its advertising. See, I don't watch TV, and I haven't been to the movies in years. I don't watch sports either, so I'm clueless when it comes to entertainment.

I sat there mulling over my possibilities. Was God trying to tell us something which had something to do with one of those four movies or TV shows in which Garner appeared? Alias was easy enough to understand. That meant that one of our suspects was not who he or she said they were. If that was the case, that made it easy. All of them knew each other except for the current custodian. It would have to be him. I planned to have Sam check on him. Oops, I'd gotten so involved in looking at Garner that I almost forgot to call Sam. I'd make sure I did that before I left.

It was time to move on. Obviously, someone had lied to me. Maybe a whole lot of someones. This meant that several of them were in cahoots or they were protecting themselves or others for some reason other than murder. If the first turned out to be the case, my guess would be some or all of the guys who were at the reunion. At least three of them seemed to be close-knit.

"Catch Me If You Can," told me that someone had been playing games with me. While I'd had that happen before, I hadn't run into anything having to do with this case that indicated that. "The Pretender" meant that someone was pretending to be someone whom they were not, or pretending that something happened that didn't happen. This sounded more in line with the "Alias" suggestion. I decided not to take any more time thinking about them at the time, so I wrote them down, so I could see what Lou thought of our possibilities. I'd spent enough time with Jennifer Garner. It was time to make myself look more appealing in case I ever ran into her.

After the first few days, I had no trouble doing the aerobic exercises on the Wii. Well, I had no trouble doing the Step exercise, even the Advanced Step. But hula hooping and running were a different story. If I attempted to do either of them, I would huff and puff for a minute or so after I quit. And that was if I merely attempted to do them one time. There was no way I was in shape to repeat either of them. The strength exercises were even worse. I still didn't attempt any exercise where I had to get down on the floor. Instead, to get myself in shape, I practiced falling toward and pushing myself away from a wall. I hoped that would help make my arms strong enough to support my body. I was told I needed to rotate between strength and aerobic exercises, but where was I to get the strength to do the strength exercises?

+++

After I'd run so much hot water over my aching muscles that the water was no longer hot, and I had stumbled from the shower and managed to dress, I went to the phone to call Sam Schumann. Each time Lou and I worked on another murder investigation I called Sam to do any legwork that I didn't have time to do myself. Sam was the best at what he did, and while I wouldn't want him to know it, he'd been quite helpful to Lou and me over the years.

"This is Sam I Am dining on green eggs and ham. I'm Sam the Man, the cop who assists all other cops from A to C, and from E to Z."

"Very funny, Sam. Well, I'm one of the cops from A to C, as in Cy."

"I thought you were one of the cops from D to D, as in Dekker, as in the one letter of the alphabet I don't have time to help."

"Sam, if you don't cooperate over the phone, I'll just come over there."

"Won't do you any good. I've already eaten. Some of us have been up for hours."

"Some of the rest of us have, too."

"Is there a barking dog in your neighborhood, or did your conscience got the best of you? Huh, Cy?"

"Listen, Sam, it's time for you to go back to work. I've got some people I want you to check on."

"When I heard that a couple of bodies were found the other day, I put paper beside the phone. I knew you'd be calling, so, shoot, just as long as you have only a couple of suspects."

"Well, some of my suspects are couples, but I'll start with a couple of unmarried ones. See what you can find out about Walter Gillis. He's the custodian at the county high school. He hasn't been here long, and I don't think he knew either of the victims, but check him out, anyway. See where he came here from, and why he came here. See if he knew either of the victims or if he knew anyone in Hilldale before he moved here. Also, see what you can find out about the retired custodian, Earl Spickard. He's been here for a long time. He doesn't seem to have been able to have done in the victims, either, but check him out nonetheless."

"I'll do that. Bye, Cy."

"I'll 'bye, Cy,' you! Keep writing! Next, check out Rose Ellen Calvert. She works at the library. She was in charge of the reunion. If possible, I want to know if she knew that

Jimmy Conkwright was coming to the reunion. See what you can find out about her. She went to school with the victims."

I continued reciting names until I'd given Sam the names of all the people I had questioned so far.

"Now, what were those names you gave me after the custodian? My pen ran out of ink and I couldn't write the rest of the names down."

"Very funny, Sam. One other thing. Supposedly, Conkwright still had a lot of his dad's money. See if you can find out how much he had, and who inherits. I guess that's it for now. And no hurry on this. Noon will be fine."

"Cy, I promise you I'll have everything by noon. I can't make any promises as to which day. One question. Do you want me to feed you this a little at a time, or all at once?"

"How long do you think it will take you to come up with all of it?"

"Oh, probably two or three days."

"You can just wait. We still have people to question, and then Lou and I will mull over what we know so far."

"Mull over. Is that another way of saying you'll hang out at your house, order good fattening food, and eat it in front of Lou who doesn't eat that stuff anymore?"

"Well, I do mull better at home, Sam. Oh, one other thing. I'm curious about something. Do you know who Jennifer Garner is?"

"Do I know who she is? I have all the DVDs from that TV show. I'm still upset they canceled it."

"What about movies? Have you seen any of her movies?"

"Every one of them."

"What if it's a bad movie?"

"If she's in it, it's not a bad movie. Listen, Cy, does she have something to do with this case? If so, I'm your leg man."

"She's only involved indirectly."

127

"Cy, you know she's married to Ben Affleck, don't you?"

"I'd heard that. What do you think of him?"

"Oh, some of his movies are good, but she's much easier on the eyes. Back to his wife, when she gets involved directly, let me know. Also, another Jennifer that I'd be happy to help out with is Jennifer Aniston. She floats my boat, too."

I wish he had used a different description. My thoughts immediately went back to my rowboat experience, but I did think another excursion would be better if I had a woman with me. Unless that woman was my next-door neighbor, but then I never think of her as a woman.

Sam and I continued our folderol until I realized that I had places to go, people to locate. We hung up, and I rushed to use the information I'd gotten from Sam. I Googled Jennifer Anniston. I misspelled her last name, but Google knew who I wanted. I had one too many n's. A few seconds later I realized that I haven't been watching enough movies and TV shows. I wondered what other beautiful creatures I've missed out on and if all of them were named Jennifer. When I have more time, I plan to call Sam back and ask him. Well, after I've gotten tired of my two Jennifers.

16

"9-30-55."

Those were Lou's first words as he got in Lightning and buckled his seat belt.

"I think your watch is a little slow. I've got 9:42."

"I wasn't giving you the time, Cy."

"Then, what are you doing, Lou? Giving me your locker combination after all these years? Or did you rob a bank a while back and you're letting me know where the money is in case you keel over before I do."

"Those numbers are today's clue."

"And we still haven't decided what yesterday's clue means. God seems to be getting a little ahead of me."

"Cy, I hate to break this to you, but God's always well ahead of you. Besides, you're the one who says these messages come from God. You may be right. Like I said I don't hear any voice, just a thought. But just in case you're right, do you want me to tell God He's moving too fast?"

"I wouldn't do that. He might do something we don't like. I guess we just need to ask Him for more wisdom."

"Or more patience."

"Before we get into today's clue, let's talk about yesterday's. I Googled Jennifer Garner. Hatchet-faced, oh you wouldn't believe how bad she looks."

129

"You're right, I won't. Mrs. Eversole was taking out the trash when I got in last night. I asked her if she knew who Jennifer Garner is. Even she told me how good Garner looks. Do you know she used to be the star of some TV show? Mrs. Eversole is still mad at the network for taking it off."

"Your neighbor was on some TV show?"

"Not my neighbor. Jennifer Garner."

"I know she was on some TV show. I don't know if it matters whether she was the star or not. Anyway, that TV show, in case you don't know, was called *Alias*. She also appeared in some things called *The Invention of Lying, Catch Me If You Can,* and *The Pretender*."

"And you think that one of these things she appeared in or on will help us solve the case?"

"Well, maybe. At least after seeing Garner, I know she's not some suspect in the Witness Relocation Program."

"She does look good, doesn't she, Cy? And if she wants to relocate, she might try my neighborhood."

"How would you know how she looks?"

"Well, you wouldn't let me come over to your house while you Googled her, and when Mrs. Eversole invited me in and asked me if I'd like to see one of her shows, well, I couldn't disappoint Mrs. Eversole. She's such a lonely woman."

"So, where were you and Jennifer in your dream last night?"

"On some deserted beach. And you?"

"Well, part of the time lying around the pool at some resort, holding hands, but every now and then Garner faded out and I was stuck in a rowboat with my next-door neighbor."

I knew that would make Lou laugh.

"Cy, you need to treat your neighbor better. Maybe if you do, she'll invite you over to watch TV, as Mrs. Eversole did me."

"Oh, she's invited me over often enough, but I don't think she wants to watch TV. By the way, since you and Mrs. Eversole are on such good terms, why don't you ask her what she thinks of Jennifer Aniston?"

"What did you do, Cy? Google every woman in the world?"

"No, just the Jennifers, and I didn't Google Jennifer Aniston until after Sam recommended her to me."

"Sam? Have you been discussing this with him?"

"I just wanted to see if you and I and those who live out in the wilderness are the only people who've never heard of Jennifer Garner."

"And what did Sam have to say?"

"Well, he has some of those TV episodes on DVD, too, and he's seen some of her movies. Actually, I think he said all of them."

"She makes movies, too? Mrs. Eversole didn't tell me that."

"Well, maybe she's saving that for your second date."

"Cy, Mrs. Eversole is eighty-two."

"In that case, I wouldn't waste a lot of time before you ask her out again."

All of our back and forth about Jennifer Garner meant that we arrived at the shoe factory where Betty Gail Spencer worked before we'd had a chance to get serious about what the previous day's clue meant. Oh, well! We did have the rest of the day to mull it over.

+++

I let Lightning rest in "Visitor Parking" while Lou and I went inside the small factory where Betty Gail Spencer worked. I showed my credentials to someone at the front desk, who headed off to find someone in authority. I went through the process again, told the manager why we were there, and he led us to the area where Betty Gail Spencer worked. He then excused himself and allowed us to go about our business. We talked with Mrs. Spencer's immediate boss, who called over a couple of people who worked in the same area she did.

"Miss Collins, how well did you know Betty Gail Spencer?"

"Well, we worked together for over four years. I guess I knew her fairly well. We never did anything together away from work, but we talked almost every day."

"What kind of person was she?"

"Well, she changed not too long ago. Used to be, she was kind of quiet, mainly talked about her husband and her home life. Then she got to where she started to complain about him."

"In what way?"

"Oh, she'd say things like, 'Duck doesn't ever want to go anywhere. He's an old stick in the mud. All he does is work and go fishing."

"Did she ever say anything about how her husband treated her?"

"Oh, she said she had him wrapped around her little finger. If she'd so much as pout, he'd go out and buy her whatever she wanted, if it didn't cost too much."

"Do you have any idea if he ever hit her?"

"If he did, she never said anything about it. And I never saw any bruises on her face or arms."

"Did she change in any other way?"

"I'll say she did. She started going out bar-hopping after work, without her husband. She'd laugh about picking up men. I told her she'd better watch herself. One night, she went to a bar with one of the guys who works here. Floyd, the one over there. Every Friday just before we got off, Floyd would come by and say, 'Hey, ladies, I'm going bar hopping tonight. Anybody want to go with me?' He did it mainly as a joke, and we'd all laugh and tell him we already had a date. Then, this one night, Betty Gail up and says, 'Yeah, I'll go with you,' and Floyd said, 'Ain't you married?' and she said, 'Yeah, you got a problem with that?' and Floyd, 'I guess not.' That next Monday morning Floyd came in and said, 'I'll never do that again.'"

Lou and I didn't seem to be learning much about Duck Spencer, but what Miss Collins said seemed to agree with everyone else. We excused ourselves and headed over to talk to Floyd. We learned his last name was Hampton, and when he found out who we were and why we were there he moved away from his work and the people around him so we could talk more privately.

"Mr. Hampton, I understand you went out with Betty Gail Spencer one night."

"Oh, yeah, but I'm not sure I'd call it going out together. It was a standard joke that I'd walk by and tell the ladies I was going bar hopping every Friday, just before we got off. Most of the time, I did nothing of the sort, but there were times I'd go somewhere for a drink before going home. Well, this one night Betty Gail offered to go with me. I said, 'Aren't you married?' because I knew she was. She said something about that didn't matter. Did I want to go, or not? Well, I decided to cover my backside, and told her, okay, but we needed to drive separately. I didn't want her husband to catch us out somewhere and beat my face in. I'd never met him, so I didn't know if he was twice my size, or not."

"Had you heard that he was a man who settled things with fisticuffs?"

"I didn't know anything about him. I didn't even know her that well. She worked over on the other side. We just smiled and said, 'hi' each day, when we passed each other. Well, anyway, I met her at a nice place, and we had a drink. We hadn't been there long, when she said, 'I don't like this place. It's too stuffy. Don't you know any place else?' Well, I'd heard of this one bar, sort of a western kind of place, and I asked her if she wanted to go there. She said 'yes' and she followed me to it. Well, that was a mistake. She started drinking, and she couldn't hold her liquor. I never have over two drinks anywhere I go, but she didn't stop with two. She got drunk, and when I quit paying any attention to her, she started hitting on some other guys, even got up on the mechanical bull to get their attention. Well, she fell off that thing, threw up all over herself. I felt responsible since I was the one who suggested we go there, and I went over and told her it was time to go. She said it wasn't. Anyway, the bartender and I convinced her to call her a taxi."

"How did she act that next Monday?"

"I saw her, asked her if she got her car okay, and she laughed, and said, 'Yeah, Duck and I went to pick it up on Saturday. I asked her if her husband was mad, and she said, 'He blew a gasket,' Then, I asked if that meant he hit her or tore things up, and she said, "Naw, Duck isn't like that. He just hollers a lot.' Well, he must have really started hollering a lot because before long she started going to bars two and three times a week. A couple of times she came in here all hungover, and once she almost lost her job over it. That's about all I know about her."

I thanked Floyd Hampton for his help, and Lou and I turned to leave. I didn't think we'd learn anything else if we stayed there.

17

"Well, Lou, what do you think?"

"It sounds like she was quite a character."

"Yeah, everyone says the same things about her. Same about her husband, too. Everyone seems sure that he wouldn't do anything to hurt her."

I wondered if that was true, or if the reunion was the straw that broke the camel's back. Maybe time would tell.

"Well, Lou why don't we get back to Jennifer Garner?"

"I wish we could."

"What do you think of those things I told you she was in. Do you think one of them is supposed to help us solve this thing?"

"I'm not sure. I remember one of them says something about lying and another about deception. Personally, I think that several of our suspects are guilty of that, but I've seen that freezer door, and it only took one person to close it and padlock it."

"Unless whoever it was had to corral them and throw them in. Then it might take two people."

"I don't think that's the case."

"Why's that, Lou?"

"Because both victims prints were on the freezer door as if they unlocked it."

"But it takes only one person to unlock a padlock."

"You're right about that."

"What do you think about the word 'Alias'?"

"I think it means someone has another identity. And if that's the case, it has to be that new janitor. Everyone else knew each other. None of them could have aliases."

"From what we've heard, the one most likely to have a second identity was Betty Gail Spencer."

"What about those still living?"

"Do you think one of them has a second identity?"

"And the two victims found out about it? I doubt it. I'm more inclined to think that if someone has a second identity, it has something to do with that new janitor."

"But, supposedly, he didn't know any of these people. He's the only one who didn't, which makes him the only one who definitely didn't have a motive."

"Well, that does it. The current janitor is our man. Should I swear out a warrant now?"

"Cy, I don't think it's nice to swear."

"Then I'll at least wait until I hear back from Sam and find out if this guy is who he says he is, or not. Let's move on to today's clue. What do you think about it? Is it the combination to a safe or a lock, or a date?"

"I'm not sure if it's either, although a combination lock makes more sense. Could it be that someone's been blackmailed, or someone has something valuable put away somewhere?"

"I'm more inclined to think that it has something to do with a date, except for one thing."

"What's that?"

"If it is a date, the year is 1955. Neither of our victims was alive back then, and none of our suspects were either, except for the retired janitor, and he was just a kid. too young to have done anything wrong."

I looked up to see that Lightning had stopped in a residential neighborhood. There were two little boys staring at us from across the street. I got my bearings and realized that we had arrived at Mrs. Edwards' house. Who knows how long we'd been there, and how long those two boys had been staring at us. I smiled at them. They frowned back at us. I got out of the car, and the two boys took off running.

Lou and I approached Mrs. Edwards' house. There was no doorbell, so I knocked on the door. A younger woman came to the door. She couldn't have been Mrs. Edwards and might have been too young to be her daughter.

"May I speak to Mrs. Edwards, please?"

"I'm sorry, but Mrs. Edwards passed away this spring. My husband and I just moved in last month."

"Do you know anyone on the street who might have known her?"

"Well, there's Mildred next door. Everyone smiles when they see us, and says 'hi,' but she's the only one I've spoken with. She knew Mrs. Edwards, but I'm not sure how well. She's at the grocery now, though. Left about thirty minutes ago. Stopped and asked me if I needed anything."

I thanked the young woman and turned away. As we walked down the steps, I perused the street, looking for cars. There were only a couple, and each of them was a few doors away, in two different directions.

"Left or right, Lou?"

"Oh, I prefer to be right rather than left."

"I mean which house do you want to try first?"

He shrugged his shoulders, so I picked the one that was on the same side of the street we were on. No need walking any extra steps that the Wii wouldn't give me credit for.

We arrived at our second house, and I knocked on the door. An elderly woman answered the door, a woman old enough to have known Mrs. Edwards for a long time.

"I'm sorry, but I don't live here, and my daughter's not at home right now."

She smiled quickly and shut the door.

No sooner had we turned away from the house than the two boys who had run away reappeared from around the corner of her house.

"Does too."

"Does too what?" I asked.

"Does too live there. My momma says she says that anytime somebody suspicious, like a salesman or a preacher, shows up at her door. Men selling TV dishes and stuff like that are thicker'n thieves around here. And momma says that from time to time some people come by in pairs trying to convert us to their religion. Momma calls them alternative religions. She don't take much stock in them."

I wondered if I looked more like a salesman or a preacher. I also wondered how thick the thieves were in that neighborhood.

"What's your name?"

"Momma says that we're not supposed to give our names out to strangers."

"And your momma's right."

I took my badge out to pacify the young boy who was the spokesman for the duo.

"See, I'm a cop."

"Momma says fake badges are easy to come by, too."

"Well, tell me this, Son. Did you know Mrs. Edwards?"

"I don't guess there's no harm in answering that. Is she the old lady who keeled over not too long ago, the one who lived in the first house you went to?"

"That's the one."

"Yeah, I knew her. She was a nice old lady. Always called my momma any time she baked cookies. Told her to send me down. She let me bring P.J."

The other boy smiled when he said this. I assumed that meant the other boy was P.J.

"Did anyone live with Mrs. Edwards?"

The boy laughed.

"Naw, she wasn't that kind of lady. She'd make sure he married her first."

"No, I mean like her daughter."

"Naw, she lived alone. She baked a lot. I miss her."

I didn't figure that I would learn any more from these two young tikes, so I told them goodbye and Lou and I set off to the other house with a car in the driveway. The two boys followed us up the street, crossed the street when we did, and stood behind us in the yard when I knocked on the door.

Another young woman opened the door. Before I could open my mouth, the spokesman for the younger set opened his.

"Momma, these two men have been pumping me about poor old Mrs. Edwards. I didn't tell them nothing exceptin' that she made cookies for me."

Before anyone could utter another word, I introduced myself and Lou. The young woman did likewise.

"Mrs. Perkins, we're looking for someone who might have known Mrs. Edwards twenty years ago, like a neighbor or her daughter."

"I don't think anyone else on the street has lived here that long and her daughter died of cancer a couple of years ago."

"Any friends you might have heard her talk about who've lived in Hilldale for twenty years or more."

"Sorry, I can't help you there. She was really neighborly with a couple of people on the street, but I never noticed any cars stopping at her place."

I thanked her for her time and turned to leave. The household spokesman followed us.

"Hey, Mister, I knowed you was all right."

"Knew you were all right," his mother corrected.

"Yeah, but I knowed it first, Momma."

139

The boy's mother looked at me, smiled, and shook her head.

When we got back in the car and shut the door, Lou turned to me and said,

"Well, Cy, that looks like a dead end."

"I'm not so sure. How would you like to go back and ask that boy what he and P.J. were doing on the night of the reunion?"

+++

"Cy, what are our plans for this afternoon?"

"Nothing set in concrete. I can't really think of anyone else to talk to until we learn a little more. It'll be sometime tomorrow or the next day before Sam gets back with me on what he's learned. Sometime before that, I want the two of us to get together at my house and mull over what we know so far. Why did you ask, anyway?"

Lou turned to me with a sheepish grin on his face.

"Well, Cy, I figured I'd be better able to do my job if I had a computer. I thought I might go shopping this afternoon. The problem is, I don't know anyone to hook it up for me. Should I pay the place where I buy it to do that?"

"You could check with my yard boy Mark. He knows all about computers. He hooked up mine, my Wii, too. It's summer. You can probably catch him at home."

+++

We drove to my place. I went in and called Mark. He told me he'd be happy to fix Lou up, even had me put Lou on the phone so he could recommend where Lou should get his computer and what kind to get. Then he told us to call when Lou got home.

I invited Lou to stay for lunch, Then, I ended up going shopping with him, even though I wanted to rest, read, and

Google. That saved Lou from driving and allowed me to learn a little more about computers. I ended up buying a thumb drive, just in case I wanted to store something somewhere other than the hard drive. So far, I've saved very little to the hard drive. I've spent most of my computer time on the Internet. One day I overheard someone say something about a Facebook and a Farmville. I might check those out someday, but for the time being, I was giving myself to Google.

We had no problem finding the computer Mark recommended to Lou, and he turned down all the other things the salesman said he needed. Lightning offered her back seat for Lou's purchases, and we headed back to his place. I helped him carry his things in and had an opportunity to meet Mrs. Eversole. Lou asked her what she thought of Jennifer Aniston and she invited Lou over that night to watch *Friends* together. I assumed that was either a movie or a TV show that Aniston was in. When Lou found out it was a TV show, he agreed to come over, but he could watch only one episode because he wanted to play with his new computer. Mrs. Eversole said that was fine with her.

I left Lou with his computer and his date and headed for home. I too planned to spend some time with Jennifer Aniston, and Jennifer Garner. I could handle ogling and Googling two babes. I wanted to read too, but I didn't want to get too far ahead of Lou, and I didn't figure that Lou would be doing too much reading that night. When a boy gets a new toy, the boy has to take the time to play with that toy. I shook my head at what was happening. A year before, I would never have figured that Lou and I would own computers and Wiis. What next? Surely we weren't going to succumb to the cell phone craze.

18

I awoke the next morning, lay there until the cobwebs had flown from my brain and I remembered what was on our agenda. Lou was coming over for breakfast. We were going to mull over the case, see if we could make any sense out of what we'd learned so far. Lou wasn't coming until I called him, so I had plenty of time to do whatever I wanted prior to that. I began by spending a few minutes in prayer and devotional reading. Since Lou and I would be eating together, I peeled a banana, ate it as I drank a glass of water, and prepared to Wii. I'd Wii, then shower, then call Lou.

I continued to set new record highs in Advanced Step, while I struggled along with the same low scores in many of the other exercises. So that I wouldn't get too full of myself, I clicked on Yoga and tried the Tree exercise. I'd remembered to put a chair within lunging distance, so I didn't hit the floor when my leg gave out before my cartoon drill sergeant called time. I was feeling particularly good, so I tried a couple of new Balance Games. I continued to be unbalanced.

I showered, dressed, and then gave Lou a call. He picked up on the first ring as if he had nothing to do except wait for my call. I hung up, unlocked the front door, and opened it a little so Lou would know to come on in. Then, I went to retrieve the notes I'd made on the case, which I'd placed on the dresser in my bedroom.

I picked them up and had just about gotten to the bedroom door when I started to suspect that all wasn't right. Two more steps showed me that something was very wrong. I looked down to discover a ball of white fluff trotting down the hall in my direction. I'd lived next door to that ball of fluff long enough that I knew it was incapable of opening any of my doors by itself.

"Miss Humphert, you had better not be in my house. I'm coming out shooting. And if that mutt of yours so much as touches my pant leg, it will be the first to go."

"So, you're taking off your pants, Cyrus."

"No, I'm taking off your head."

I made it to the living room and saw that I would have to fumigate. I might even have to burn the couch. But first, I would throw out what was slithering on it.

"Oh, Cyrus, it was so nice of you to leave your door open for me. Twinkle Toes noticed first."

"Miss Humphert, if you don't get up right this minute, I'm going to call the police."

"Oh, Cyrus, don't you remember, you are the police, and believe me, you won't need any help. You're man enough for me. You can even handcuff me if you wish."

I leaned over and shouted at her.

"Up! This minute!"

I did this at the exact time Lou opened the front door.

"If I'm interrupting anything, I can come back later."

"Oh, Cyrus, I didn't know it was going to be a foursome. I'll call my sister Hortense right now."

"No, you'll leave right now."

She didn't make a move, so I called downtown and had them send someone out.

"Oh, Cyrus, will there be more people coming? I didn't know this was going to be a party. I thought it would be just you, me, and Twinkle Toes."

"This is your last chance to leave."

Heloise Humphert turned to Lou and said, "I think he's talking to you."

What seemed like well over an hour was only five minutes. A black-and-white pulled up and an officer I didn't know except by face came to the door. Lou motioned him in, and I let him know that my next-door neighbor had entered my house without my permission. My neighbor peppered him with some of her gobbledegook from the fantasy world in that mind of hers, but the young officer held up well.

It didn't take my neighbor long to find out we were serious. She pleaded with me, but I needed to teach her a lesson. When she fought off the officer and resisted arrest, he had no choice but to take her to the floor and cuff her hands behind her back. When the officer led her to the car, she kept crying and hollering, "My baby! My poor baby! I want my baby!"

That poor baby, the one who tried to bite the officer who was handcuffing its owner and anyone else who tried to restrain it, yipped and yapped and jumped around the room. When Lou saw where things were headed, he took the dog back to where it belonged and then came back to my house

+++

Lou and I stood on the front porch until the black-and-white disappeared out of sight. I called downtown, talked to my good friend Lt. George Michaelson, and asked him to make sure she received the third degree, which included questioning Miss Humphert with a bright light shining in her face, and her spending time in the same holding cell as the drunks who had come in the night before and had not yet been released. Then, I told him to hold her until she stated that she would never set foot in my house again.

+++

I sat down, physically and emotionally spent. It was a couple of minutes before I realized that I'd sat down on the same couch that woman had slouched on. I expected to break out in a rash any second. Lou, on the other hand, was in a different state of mind. He couldn't stop laughing, now that he was sure that I was out of danger.

"Just keep it up. Your day is coming."

"No, Cy, I don't want her. She's all yours. Can't you see how much she loves you?"

"That woman needs to donate her brain to science."

I sat there, exhausted.

"Cy, I can see what this has done to you. Do you want me to fix breakfast?"

I hoped I could eat. I knew I couldn't fix anything. I needed to get this incident out of my mind so Lou and I could concentrate on the case. I sat frozen to that couch until Lou hollered and told me breakfast was ready. I summoned whatever strength I had and stumbled to the kitchen to find a plate containing an omelet with peppers and onions, and two slices of bacon. My hand shook as I poured myself a glass of water and sat down to eat.

Since we were alone, there was no problem discussing the case, but I needed a few more minutes, so we discussed more mundane things while we ate. At least Lou had quit spewing out his jokes about me and Heloise Humphert.

In order to function better, I changed the subject from myself to Lou.

"So, Lou, how did your date with Mrs. Eversole go?"

"Just one episode, Cy. And Cy, I could go for Jennifer Aniston, too. She's hot."

"Watch yourself, Lou. I don't want you to get burned."

"Oh, by the way, I had to go back to my place and Wii."

"Jennifer Aniston did that to you?"

"No, Mrs. Eversole did."

"Lou, from what I've heard of Jennifer Aniston, she doesn't look anything like Mrs. Eversole."

"No, I mean Mrs. Eversole baked some homemade cookies, and I couldn't refuse her. She's so nice. But just to make sure I'm not packing the pounds on again, I went back to my place and Wiied for fifteen minutes."

"What kind of cookies were they?"

"Macadamia nut."

"Oh, Lou, you should've Wiied for twenty minutes."

"Nope, I weighed this morning and I've lost another two tenths of a pound."

"Yeah, but I lost four-tenths."

"But you're a lot bigger than I am."

"You'd better watch out. I'm gaining on you."

"Don't you mean you're losing on me?"

19

Lou and I talked a few minutes about the Wii and the two Jennifers. After we allowed the food and the mood to settle, we turned our talk to the case at hand.

"So, Lou, what do you think?"

"Well, I checked out Jennifer Garner pretty good last night, and the more I think about it, the more I think our clue has to do with her show *Alias*. It's what she's best known for."

"Yeah, but God knows everything she's ever done."

"But He knows we don't."

"But He also knows that now we're armed with Google."

It seemed like both of us were taking both sides of the argument, even though we weren't arguing.

"Okay, Lou, let's say you're right. What do you think 'Alias' means?"

"The only thing I can come up with is what we talked about before. Someone having to do with this case has an alias. The only way that can have anything to do with anyone other than the custodian is that one of our suspects is leading a double life."

"Let's travel down that road for a minute. Which one would you say is most likely?"

"Well, I would hope it's the librarian. The life we know about must be very boring."

"Well, maybe not to her, and that's what matters."

"Do you think maybe that one of the others might be involved in something illegal, and maybe that Spencer woman caught him or her?"

"Maybe she found out something about someone when she was bar hopping and started blackmailing that someone."

"That doesn't seem likely, either. Let's move on to something else. My guess is if the janitor is the one who's actually someone else, Sam will be able to find out for us. Is it possible that there's someone who's a suspect that we haven't thought of?"

"I thought about that last night, too, and I couldn't come up with anyone. How about you?"

"No, it's not me. I really am Lou Murdock. And I'm not leading a second life, except in the world of Google."

"Let's try something else. Let's say that it's not *Alias*, but the one that has to do with lying."

"I don't think that's it, because I think that most of our suspects have lied to us. They can't even agree as to who was with whom when they went out looking for Spencer's wife."

"Why would someone lie if he or she wasn't guilty?"

"Maybe to protect a friend."

"Could be."

"Maybe we should take each person one at a time, in the order we talked to them."

"Okay, first was Walter Gillis, the new janitor. He seemed to be telling the truth. And as far as we know, he didn't know either of the victims. Of course, I reserve judgment until we hear from Sam."

"What about Rose Ellen Calvert?"

"Well, I can't see why she'd do it, other than the reason that she definitely is the kind of person who didn't like anything about Conkwright, and she wouldn't approve of a woman going out on her husband, or a woman bar hopping."

"Judge and jury kind of motive."

"Right."

"Well, at least that's something. And some of the guys did say she left the cafeteria. We'll have to follow up on that."

"What about Duck Spencer?"

"Was he mad enough at his wife to kill her? It's obvious that he hated Conkwright, but then everyone hated Conkwright."

"What about the old janitor?"

"Earl Spickard. Well, he definitely knew both of the victims. The problem with him is that he's the one guy who seems to have an alibi the whole time he was at the school."

"Maybe we should check with some of the others, see if they can tell us anything about Spickard's movements."

"That leaves us the two married couples."

"And that's the way I think of them, the two married couples. I don't see either of the wives doing anything like this, even though it only involved shutting a door and locking it, but still, they had to think that those two would die in time if left in the freezer."

"Well, there is the possibility that one or both of them did it, told their husbands what they did, and asked their husbands to let those two out after they'd had time to cool off and sober up, and then the husbands didn't let them out."

"Or maybe the husbands locked them in, planning on letting them out after Spencer arrived, but then Spencer talked them into letting them stay in there, or else he promised to let them out, but he didn't."

"You know, I've got a feeling this one might be tougher to prove than any case we've ever tackled."

"You could be right."

We sat there, not sure what to do next. If only Sam would solve the case for us. We were quiet for a few minutes until Lou broke the silence.

"Oh, Cy, I almost forgot. I haven't told you today's clue. Try Googling."

"'Try Googling' is today's clue."

"That's right."

"Did He by any chance tell you what to Google?"

"No, that's it. Maybe we should try Googling all of our suspects, see if we find out anything more about any of them."

I approved of Lou's idea, and Lou drew a second chair up to the computer. I started with the janitor. Nothing. Maybe he isn't who he says he is. I moved on from there to Rose Ellen Calvert, the librarian.

"Aha! We have something."

A few minutes later, it turned into a double aha, as we delved into the private life of the librarian. It turned out that the woman spent time on Facebook, and the photo she used there wasn't a picture of her, but of someone younger and better looking. I clicked and went to Facebook. The woman had friends. Lots of friends. Most of them male. All of them from somewhere else. And some of what she'd written to them was a little flirtatious. It gave me a whole new opinion of Rose Ellen Calvert, but it didn't increase her likelihood of being a murderer, just a liar.

A few minutes later, we'd Googled all the people we'd talked to. None of the men showed up on Google. All of the women did. Most of them on Facebook, but none of the others were flirting with men on there. Actually, we did find some of those men's names on there, but in every case, it was someone by that name who lived somewhere else. None of them were our suspects.

We still had nothing. We decided to see if we could find anything on the victims. There was nothing on Betty Gail Spencer, but a lot on Jimmy Conkwright. We studied what we found for over an hour, but found nothing that could tell us a thing about who might have murdered him.

"Cy, I've got an idea. We Googled Jennifer Garner, but we never checked on 9-30-55. Why don't you key that in and see if anything comes up? Maybe it's like Jennifer Garner. Maybe it has nothing to do with any of our suspects, but it could take us a step closer to solving the case."

I couldn't believe that I'd forgotten to Google the second clue. Maybe that's what God was telling us to do.

I keyed in the numbers, looked at what came up, and smacked myself in the head for taking so long to get there. September 30, 1955, was the day that film icon James Dean died. While Dean has no more to do with our case than Jennifer Garner, we were meant to read the clue. Dean, like Miriam Van Meter, died in a car wreck. In both cases, the car was a sports car, although the make and models were different.

I turned to Lou.

"Well, what do you think?"

"Maybe it means we're supposed to look for someone who might hold a grudge because Conkwright's drunken carelessness killed Miriam Van Meter."

"You mean that Conkwright might have been killed because of something he did a long time ago, not that night?"

"It's possible. At least it gives us something else to look at."

I grabbed the phone book and looked for any Van Meters who might be listed. There were only two. I dialed the first of the two numbers. It rang a few times and then went to voice mail. I tried the second number. Another voice mail. Well, it was the middle of the day, almost lunchtime.

"What do you think, Lou? Think a lunch break might increase our brain cells?"

"I doubt that, but we probably should eat soon. You realize we forgot our mid-morning snack again?"

I must be turning over a new leaf. I'd completely forgotten about eating. My mind was totally on the case.

I went to the kitchen, opened the cupboard and lifted out two tins of sardines.

"Sardines okay with you, Lou?"

"I haven't had any in a while, but I love them."

I tossed some spinach into a saucepan with water and let it heat while I opened the refrigerator door and plucked two shiny red tomatoes (actually orange ones) to have with the sardines and spinach.

We ate lunch and sat back and let it digest. Each time one of us came up with another idea, we rushed to the computer to Google it. None of them led to anything. Maybe Google only knew about the clues God gave us.

When nothing turned up anything and frustration began to set in, Lou and I took a break to Wii. I was amazed at how much better Lou was at everything. I only beat him at Advanced Step. He scored much higher than I did on the Balance Games. He bested me a little on Yoga. We refrained from attempting anything on Strength Training.

We were having so much fun we didn't realize how much time we'd spent there. It was 3:47 when I looked at my watch. I remembered that we forgot our mid-morning snack and made sure that we ate our daily regimen that afternoon. I gave Lou a spoon and a plastic container of almond butter made at the grocery. We washed that down with water, and then I dashed to the refrigerator and palmed two apples. Well, I grasped one in each hand. I tossed one to Lou. We both still had our cloth napkins from lunch, and they came in handy since we were eating juicy, red delicious apples.

We cleaned up from our snack and were trying to think of what to do next when the phone rang. It was Sam.

20

"Cy, it's Sam. I hope I didn't wake you."

"Very funny, Sam! Lou and I have been working on the case all day. We were wondering when you'd get started so we could have something else to do."

"So, not much has changed, Cy. I still have to solve all your cases for you."

"I hope that means you've solved this one."

"Well, let's just say I've come up with some possible motives."

"Let's hear them."

"Well, first let's start with your janitor friend, Walter Gillis, who was the reason it took me so long to get back to you. After I was able to track him back to northeastern Ohio it didn't take long, but it took me a while to find out where he lived before he came here. Cy, I'm sorry to disappoint you on this one, but he is who he says he is. He doesn't have any criminal record. As a matter of fact, I talked to his former boss and one of his co-workers. He was a janitor at a school up there too, and they said he was a fine worker. I even double-checked with the Board of Education up there, and I talked to the school principal. No one had anything but good things to say about him. His co-worker did give me an inkling as to why he ended up here. Gillis told him that every few years he was going a little farther south until he got to where it's warm all year long. He said that Gillis said when he left Ohio that he was going to drive until he used up one tank full of gas, and wherever that happened to be was where he planned to put down roots. Well, whatever roots you can put down in a few years. Everyone up there described Gillis as nice, quiet, and a hard worker. I checked other places, both here and there, and I can't come up with anything that says Gillis knew anyone here before he arrived here four-and-a-half years ago. The principal at the school here is the one who turned me on to checking in Ohio. He couldn't remember the exact place where Gillis was from, but he said he could find out if I couldn't. He told me that he called up there and talked to someone at the school where Gillis used to work and they told him that Gillis would be a good hire."

"I thought you said you were going to give me some motives."

"I am, but I thought I'd start with the guy you know the least about. What if I move on to who inherits?"

"Only if it's one of my suspects. I don't want any more suspects."

"How about two of your suspects?"

"You're kidding, aren't you?"

"Do you want me to be kidding?"

"No."

"Well, then the timing is right because the will was read this morning. Conkwright was well-heeled. Are you ready for this? It might surprise you."

"Just get on with it, Sam. We don't need a drum roll."

"First of all, let me ask you a question. Does Jim Bob Gibbons limp?"

"He sure does. You know something about that?"

"Nothing concrete, but it's enough for me. Back when this bunch was in high school, Gibbons went to the hospital drunk one night. He said he had accidentally shot himself in a hunting accident. Now, I can see where someone might believe that, well at least the part where he said he shot himself accidentally, except for a couple of things. One, someone at the hospital spotted Gibbons being dropped off that night by someone in a red Corvette. Of course, we all know who that was. Also, the next day Gibbons made a deposit of $2,500 in his bank account. Each month, on the same day each month, there was another $2,500 deposited in the bank. For the first few years, he deposited $2,500 in cash, but just before Big Russ Conkwright died, that money started moving from one account to another, and that first account was a trust fund that Big Russ set aside to take care of Gibbons. I checked, and that money is still coming in today and will continue to come in until Gibbons dies. At that point, the remainder of the money will go to charity.

"Now, let's move on to the will, which was made out by Jimmy, not his father. There are two beneficiaries. Jim Bob Gibbons will receive one million dollars. Now, get this next part. The rest of the money, which is over eight million dollars, all goes to Rose Ellen Calvert. Jimmy, being an evil person to the end, stated that he wanted to give her the money, because he had no family to leave it to, and a lot of money was the only way Rose Ellen Calvert could ever lasso a man, and he knew how badly she wanted one."

I whistled at that remark.

"So, it looks like I've got a couple of suspects."

"I've got another one for you if you want."

"Shoot."

"Again, back to high school. Duck Spencer was expelled from school because of Jimmy Conkwright."

"I know that."

"But, did you know that he was first suspended because of fighting with Conkwright and that Conkwright wasn't suspended. Then, when Spencer came back to school,

155

Conkwright lured him into another fight, and this time Spencer was expelled for good. Even though several students went and told the principal that it was Conkwright's fault, Big Russ's money prevailed, and Duck Spencer was barred from ever being a student at County again."

"How did he take it?"

"Not too well from what I heard."

"Did he try to go to school anywhere else?"

"Hilldale didn't want him either. He was going to have to go outside the county, so he decided to get a job instead. He could only find menial jobs, and he detested any job he had until he started working at an auto body shop. Turns out that he liked that so much that later he started his own business."

"Anything on anybody else?"

"Nothing that you don't have. I assume you know that everybody hated Conkwright. Other than that, I couldn't find anything specific about anyone else."

"Well, thanks for this much. This might be enough. If I need you for anything else, I'll let you know."

I hung up and turned to Lou and filled him in on everything Sam had told me.

We mulled over what we'd learned. The janitor was who he said he was. So was everyone else. Everyone but the janitor, and the possibility of Jim Bob Gibbons, hated Conkwright, so that must mean the janitor was our killer. I smiled. We'd check out those three who stood out all of a sudden. If we couldn't pin anything on any of them, we'd consider it a *Murder On The Orient Express* type of murder.

+++

I wasn't sure if we were going to interrogate everyone again, but I definitely had questions for Rose Ellen Calvert,

Jim Bob Gibbons, and Duck Spencer. I looked at my watch. It was almost 5:00. We had enough time to question two of the three before calling it a day. I figured Duck Spencer could be found in his shop during the day. I could find Miss Calvert during the day too, but I preferred to question her at her home, rather than the library. We were off to see the two people mentioned in the will and see what new story they had for us.

+++

Lightning was ready for us when we walked out of my house. I looked next door. It was nice to know I could leave my house without being pawed. I wondered when George would release my neighbor. I hoped for some date in the far distant future, like the turn of the next century.

After weighing our options, Lou and I decided to begin with Rose Ellen Calvert. I could tell when she came to the door that she was excited to see us.

"I don't know anything else about that night, Lieutenant."

"But I do. Why don't we come in and talk about what I know?"

Rose Ellen Calvert seemed a little shaken.

"I'm sort of busy right now."

"We are too. That's the reason we'd rather talk here than downtown."

"You act as if I'm a suspect, Lieutenant."

"Everyone's a suspect, Miss Calvert. If you're not guilty, you might want to cooperate, so we can get this wrapped up as quickly as possible."

Reluctantly, she opened the door and let us in. My guess was that she wasn't going to ask us to stay for dinner.

"So, Miss Calvert, are you sure there's nothing else about that night that you want to tell us?"

"Absolutely."

"How about when you followed the victims?"

"I only followed them far enough to see that they were leaving the building."

"And then you went to the kitchen."

"I did not."

"We have witnesses."

"Oh, all right. I didn't want to share this, because it has nothing to do with the murders. Jimmy and Betty Gail turned left as they left the school and headed toward the parking lot. I was curious as to whether or not they planned to leave, and I knew that I could look out the kitchen door and see what they were doing. Well, at first he was pawing her something awful, and then he reached into the glove compartment and pulled out a bottle of something. I don't know what, because I don't drink, but I know enough to know that it was booze of some sort. Jimmy took a big drink and then offered a drink to Betty Gail. She grabbed it with both hands and drank until Jimmy took it away from her and took another drink. Well, I contemplated calling the police, but instead, I merely hoped that they wouldn't come back into the school or take off driving. I could tell that they weren't going to quit drinking until the bottle was empty. So, I closed the door and returned to the cafeteria."

"Did you lock the door when you closed it?"

"No, I figured the janitor would check the doors before he left, and I left it open in case I wanted to go back and see if they passed out in the parking lot."

"Did you mention to anyone else that the two of them were drinking?"

"No, I was afraid of what some of the men might do."

"So, tell me, Miss Calvert, what was your relationship with Jimmy Conkwright?"

"I had no relationship with Jimmy Conkwright. I despised him when we were in school together, and I still do."

"Did he ever hit on you in high school?"

"A couple of times. I think as a joke. He would come up to me and say something out of the way and then laugh when I said something about his manners."

"So, were you surprised that you were the largest beneficiary in his will?"

"So, you know about that, too."

"We know about a lot of things, Miss Calvert. That's why it would be better for everyone if they told us the truth."

"Okay, I was surprised. But then when the lawyer read why he left all that money to me, I thought it sounded just like Jimmy Conkwright."

"When did you first find out that you were mentioned in his will?"

"When the lawyer called me last night and invited me to the reading. I thought it was someone pulling a not-very-funny practical joke. I even called the lawyer's office back to make sure they were the ones who called."

"And you didn't know anything about it before the reunion? The will was written before then, you know."

"Obviously, and no, I didn't know."

"And when did you find out how much you received?"

"Not until the reading of the will. I knew that Big Russ had a lot of money, but I never suspected he had that much and I figured that Jimmy would have squandered all of it by now. It's a good thing I was sitting down when the lawyer told me, although at the time it seemed like something out of a nasty dream."

"An eight million dollar nasty dream?"

"Well, considering where the money came from."

"So, you turned down the money?"

"No, I've decided to accept it to teach Jimmy a lesson. Besides, Big Earl made that money, and he made it honestly."

The days of Jimmy learning a lesson were over, so I figured that Rose Ellen Calvert accepted his money because the idea of having money sounded good to her.

"Back to the night of the reunion. How many times did you return to the kitchen that night?"

"Maybe once."

"And was anyone in the kitchen at the time?"

"No."

"Was the door still unlocked?"

"I can't remember if I checked."

I didn't want to make the kitchen so obvious, so I asked another question, so she wouldn't think too much about the kitchen.

"What about the second floor of the school? Did you go back up there after dinner?"

"No, there was no need to."

"Isn't there a window up there that overlooks the parking lot?"

"Come to think of it, there is, but it takes longer to get to it."

"Did you go outside anytime after dinner?"

"Not until I left."

"And when was the last time you saw Jimmy Conkwright and Betty Gail Spencer?"

"When the guys threw them out for coming back in the school drunk."

I'd learned what I wanted to know from Rose Ellen Calvert, so I thanked her, and Lou and I turned to leave, but before I'd taken a step, she interrupted our departure.

"Lieutenant, can I ask you a question?"

"Go ahead, Miss Calvert. I'll answer it if I can."

"Well, this is the second time you've been here, and he hasn't opened his mouth yet. Can he talk?"

I turned to Lou and used hand signals. When I quit, he signaled me back.

"What did he say?"

"He said he can talk, but he's not to open his mouth until I mess up. So far, I've done everything right."

"Oh, I see."

"Anything else, Miss Calvert?"

"No, I guess not."

+++

Lou and I managed to keep a straight face until we'd pulled away from Miss Calvert's house. Then, we both burst into laughter.

"Cy, in case you want to know, the reason I talk more when we're not interrogating our suspects is that you mess up a lot when you're not working so hard."

"Watch it, Lou, or I'll mess up your face."

"I'm sorry, oh Exalted One."

21

I left Rose Ellen Calvert knowing that if I ever have an overdue library book, I'm in big trouble. I wasn't her warm fuzzy of the day, but then I hope no one ever refers to me as a warm fuzzy. Since Jim Bob Gibbons' house in the country was a few miles from Calvert's, I turned to Lou to see what he had to say.

"Well, Lou, how does she grab you?"

"Well, so far she hasn't, Cy. I've just been sitting here wondering if it would be worth $8,000,000 to let her."

"Money talks, huh, Lou?"

"Well, I could buy a lot of books if I had $8,000,000."

"But then you'd be stuck with her."

"Who said anything about being stuck with her? If she grabbed me, I could sue her for the $8,000,000."

I laughed.

"Okay, Tonto, what do you think about what she had to say? Do you believe her?"

"I'm not sure I believe any of them."

"I'm not sure I do, either. It's just a matter of weeding through all this information and figuring out which one did it."

"Or which two or three."

I was beginning to think we could solve the case more quickly if we stayed home and rotated between Googling and Wiiing. Maybe that's what we'll do on our next case. Sort of a modern-day Nero Wolfe with Sam as our Archie Goodwin.

+++

We arrived at Gibbons' place and saw his truck in the driveway. I contemplated whether to knock at the front door or try the back "patio" first. Gibbons decided that for me when we slammed Lightning's doors and he hollered, "I'm 'round back." We rounded the corner of the house and spotted Gibbons sprawled out, holding a bottle of water. While the patio was in the shade and it was late in the day, it was still late July, so Lou and I didn't turn Gibbons down when he asked us if we wanted a bottle of water. We nodded and he reached into the cooler beside him and tossed us a couple.

"Let me guess, Lieutenant. You heard about the will and thought it might make a good motive. Well, let me tell you right off. I didn't know nothing about that will 'til the lawyer called me last night. I still didn't know how much he'd left me until we got there this morning and the lawyer read the will."

"What about Miss Calvert? Do you think she was surprised?"

"I don't know, but I sure was. I never expected Jimmy to leave that broad anything, but then when the lawyer read the reason, it was hard to keep from laughing out loud. That was just like Jimmy."

"I was planning on asking you about that, but I want to know something else, too. I can't help but notice that you limp when you walk. How did that happen?"

"Hunting accident, when I was in school."

"What kind of hunting accident?"

163

"The usual kind, with a gun."

"Do you usually go hunting at night, Mr. Gibbons?"

"It took a while to get to the hospital."

"According to the hospital records, it happened not long before you got to the hospital, which would make it at night."

"Well, I meant hunting in the sense it happened with a rifle."

"And did you do it yourself?"

"More or less."

"And you'd been drinking at the time?"

"That's right! Guns and alcohol don't mix."

"Just like driving and alcohol don't mix."

"That's right."

"And did you drive yourself to the hospital?"

"It hurt too much, and I was bleeding. A friend drove me."

"And the friend was?"

"Some guy I went to high school with."

"Mr. Gibbons, why don't we quit beating around the bush? Jimmy Conkwright was seen dropping you off at the hospital."

"Well, if you already knowed, why'd you ask?"

"I wanted to see if you'd pass the test of telling the truth. You didn't."

"I didn't lie. I said it was a friend."

"But did you say that it was your friend who shot you?"

"He didn't."

"Even back then, doctors were pretty smart. The report says that from the angle the bullet went in that there was no way it could have been self-inflicted."

"I was just trying to protect a friend. I didn't want to get him in trouble. He'd been drinking, too, and he didn't do it on purpose."

"But he could have gotten in trouble if it came out that he did it. I guess that's what the $2,500 was for."

"I won that money betting on the horses."

"Wow, underage drinking, underage betting. What else did you do?"

"That was pretty much it."

"You know, Mr. Gibbons, you're probably the first person who has won exactly $2,500 a month every month for twenty years."

"Well, that's money I got for working."

"Working at what, Mr. Gibbons?"

"This and that."

"And you were doing that work for Jimmy's father?"

"That's right."

"Mr. Gibbons, I bet there are times when your knee really hurts."

"Most of the time."

"Have you ever resented Jimmy Conkwright because he shot you? You know, $2,500 a month isn't that much when you're in pain all the time."

"And sometimes I have 'expenses out of that money, 'cause I need some pain medication or something."

"So, tell me, Mr. Gibbons, was Jimmy really a friend, or did you just hang out with him for the money?"

"He was okay most of the time."

"But some of the time he wasn't. Is that why you killed him?"

"I didn't kill him!"

That wasn't the answer I had hoped for. I was hoping he'd say something like, "I didn't lock him in no freezer." My trick didn't work.

"No, I suppose you didn't, unless you knew about the money you'd get if you did kill him and get away with it. A man can do a lot more with $1,000,000 than he can with $2,500 a month."

"I'm about to find out. I'm tryin' to decide whether or not to quit my job. A million might last me the rest of my life if I don't do nothing stupid."

"Like murder someone."

He was starting to protest, but I waved my hand.

"Okay, so you didn't kill Jimmy. Who do you think did? It had to be someone who was at the school that night."

"I've been thinking about that. All of 'em hated Jimmy. Still, I can't see any of 'em being a murderer."

"Let's talk a little bit about that night. Some people say they saw you coming out of the kitchen. Did you see anyone in the kitchen or anywhere else other than the hall and the cafeteria after Conkwright and Mrs. Spencer were shoved out the front door?"

"First of all, let me tell you I didn't go in no kitchen, except far enough to look in and see if Jimmy was in there. He wasn't, so I left right away. And yeah, I did see a couple of other people in the kitchen, Rose Ellen Calvert and Duck."

"Together?"

"Naw! You kidding?"

"And did you see both of them in there after the victims left drunk?"

He smiled.

"What's so funny?"

"I just have trouble thinking of either of those two as victims."

"I thought one of them was your friend."

"He was, but he ain't never been no victim."

"He was that night. Anyway, answer the question."

"I forget what it was."

"When did you see Rose Ellen Calvert and Duck Spencer in the kitchen, before or after the two...dead people disappeared?"

"I think she was in there both times. Duck didn't get there until after they disappeared."

"And did they see that you saw them?"

"That stuck up woman did."

"And how did she react?"

166

"Embarrassed."

"You have anything else for us, Mr. Gibbons?"

"I can't think of nothing."

"Well, let me know if you do. We'll be in touch."

Gibbons's knee must have acted up as I added that last sentence because he looked in pain. Was there a reason that my words should have bothered him?

+++

It looked like another late dinner. I turned to Lou to see if he wanted to cook or go to Burkman's for a steak. We opted for Burkman's. It was hard getting used to not eating out all the time. It was also hard getting used to asking for a "to go" box, too. I thought of what we had planned for the next day. We'd go talk to Duck Spencer, stop in on Conkwright's attorney, and then late that afternoon we'd see if we could locate some Van Meters, just in case that girl's death twenty years ago had anything to do with the case. When I relayed this information to Lou, he agreed to keep his leftovers at my house. We'd either eat them for lunch or dinner.

+++

Lou and I ate what most people call a sensible meal; steak, baked potato, and a salad. The salad was the toughest part for me. Well, other than the fact that both Lou and I turned down an offer of dessert. If only we could lose weight on a sugar diet. I could've gone for something like that years ago. Maybe I did. Maybe that's the reason that my circumference was second to that of the Earth. But back to the salad. Salad is bad enough on its own, but I have trouble covering it with a minute amount of some see-through dressing. I had no problem with steak or the potato. Before I began eating, I cut both the steak and the

167

potato in two and asked for a to-go box. I think our server had waited on us before because she laughed. She thought I was making a joke until I assured her I was serious. I'm sure she had encountered other people who'd done something similar, but in January, when some people had not yet broken their New Year's resolutions, not in July, after most of them had long since forgotten they ever made any.

Lou and I refrained from talking about the case until we were safely ensconced in Lightning. We kept no secrets from Lightning, just from the rest of the world.

"So, Lou, did that steak enlighten you as to who might be our murderer?"

"A little bit. I've narrowed it down to those who were at the school that night, and I've eliminated two of those people."

"Oh, which two?"

"Jimmy Conkwright and Betty Gail Spencer."

I pulled over, rolled down the window, and dangled Lou's leftovers out the window. He merely smiled. I'd forgotten that losing food no longer had an effect on Lou. So, I changed tactics.

"Lou, I've known for a long time that I'm the brains of this outfit."

"Is that why it takes us so long to solve a case?"

"No, it takes us so long because even the innocent lie to us."

"I think you've hit on something, Cy. Do you think we just need to round up all of them?"

"Maybe eventually. For the time being, we'll just keep plodding along. Can I assume that all your folderol means you have nothing important to say?"

"I think my folderol is among the best in the county."

+++

I started to head to Lou's place, then he reminded me that his car was at my house. I'd completely forgotten about the nightmare my next-door neighbor had caused. I looked at my watch. It was 9:00. I wasn't used to working so late. At least I didn't have to go home and cook. Just toss a couple of boxes in the refrigerator.

I drove down the street, looked and saw lights on in the house next door. Could it be that the woman from another planet had returned? I didn't plan to go next door and knock in order to find out. I left Lightning in her customary sleeping place, got out, and sniffed the air to see if there was any sign of my next-door neighbor. There wasn't enough of a breeze to answer my question. I bid Lou good night. He headed down the driveway toward the street to his car, while I walked up to my back door and inserted my key.

22

We'd been working on the case for almost a week, and I wondered if we were getting anywhere. At least that was my thought when I woke up Friday morning and took stock of what we had planned for the day. We had planned to work three angles. I hoped that one of them would pay off. We'd start with another visit with Duck Spencer, see if he'd confess that he closed and locked that door while in a rage. If that didn't work, we'd move on to the attorney who handled Jimmy Conkwright's will. While I didn't expect him to tell me that either of the parties confessed to murder during the reading of the will, maybe he would be able to tell me something about the state of mind of either of the windfall's recipients. Last, we'd visit with the two families named Van Meter to find out if they were related to the mysterious girl who died in that car wreck twenty years ago.

I got up, went through my morning routine, which was everything from eating to showering to working out, then called Lou and told him I was on my way.

I walked out the front door and froze. It was the first time I'd seen Heloise Humphert since she was incarcerated. She looked at me and stuck out her tongue. I swear, it looked like the furball did the same. Evidently, she'd learned her lesson, because she made no move to jump my bones. She remained in her yard, and her small companion did too.

+++

I pulled up in front of Lou's place and he rushed out to join Lightning and me. He slid onto the seat, buckled up, and as I was about to take off, he said, "Don't start yet."

"Don't start yet is today's clue."

"No, I'll share that with you in a moment. Cy, we need to talk first."

I'd heard those same words spoken on occasion, usually by a man or a woman who was about to break up with someone. Lou and I weren't that type of a couple, and I didn't think that Lou wanted to quit working with me. But I could contain myself no longer.

"Lou, have I done something wrong?"

"Many times, but that doesn't have anything to do with what we need to talk about. Thelma Lou called last night."

"Oh, Lou, I'm so sorry. And I thought that maybe someday the two of you would end up getting married."

"We're not breaking up."

"Oh, I always thought of you as someone who would wait until he got married to have kids. That's okay, Lou. I don't agree with it, but I'll still support you."

"Cy, will you shut up for a minute so I can tell you what I have to tell you."

"You don't mean Thelma Lou has..."

"Cy, button your lip!"

"Go ahead. I'm all ears."

"No, you're mostly mouth. Well, you are now that you're losing weight. Anyway, Thelma Lou's cousin is coming to visit this weekend. She's thinking about moving here and wanted to get a feel for the place."

"But she doesn't need my okay."

171

"But she does if Thelma Lou gets her way. She wants us to have a double date this weekend."

"How old is she? We really don't know much of anyone except for the guys on the force. Most of them are married, and we're doing our best to pair up Officer Davis and Heather. Who's left?"

"Who do I usually double date with?"

"Me, but that's with Betty McElroy."

"That's another thing we need to talk about. Betty called Thelma Lou and told her that she's moving to Indiana to be close to her grandchildren. She wanted to tell you as soon as possible, but she knew we were busy with this case. Besides, you and Betty weren't more than friends."

"But how do you know I'll even like this cousin?"

"Well, I think your best chance will be if you meet her. Thelma Lou wants to schedule something for tomorrow, and then Sunday after church. It's not like you're getting married. If there aren't any sparks, then you don't have to see her again."

Lou laughed.

"What's funny, Lou? Does she look that bad?"

"It's not that. It's that her last name is Sparks. I'm kidding. It's Sparks, and maybe there will be sparks between you."

"What's her first name?"

Lou laughed again.

"That's why I think it'll work. It's Heloise."

I shot him a nasty look.

"I was just kidding, Cy. It's Jennifer, as in Garner and Aniston."

"Yeah, but those two are babes. What if this one's ugly?"

"Cy, have you ever met a Jennifer who was ugly?"

I thought for a moment and then admitted I hadn't.

172

"Okay, I'll go along with tomorrow, since you're my friend and I can tell this means a lot to you and Thelma Lou, but if I can't stand this Jennifer, I can see myself coming down with something on Sunday."

Lou wanted to protest, tell me something like "it's only one weekend", but he remained quiet and agreed.

"By the way, Lou, what do they have planned?"

"I don't know, Cy. Thelma Lou said they'll fill us in when we get there on Saturday. We're supposed to get there around 11:00 a.m. And it is both a day and night date."

This time I gave him a look, but I kept my mouth closed.

+++

After Lou had finished telling me about Thelma Lou's cousin and I agreed to go out with her, he gave me the okay to take off, and we started off, headed out into the country to see Duck Spencer.

"By the way, Lou, what's today's message?"

"It's no French kissing on the first date."

"I'm serious here."

"Wyatt Earp."

"So, it's a lawman that did it. But none of our suspects are lawmen. I guess that narrows it down to you or George. Where were you on the night of the reunion?"

"Out looking for a new best friend. And you?"

"Out on Thornapple River Road with Heather, showing her how to do a stakeout. Now, back to the clue. Do you have any idea what it means?"

He gave me the look he usually gave me when I asked that question, then responded.

"Maybe we're about to take a trip out west."

"Maybe we'll go back to my place for lunch and Google Wyatt Earp. You know, Lou, sometimes I wonder how we

173

were able to solve all those murders before we found Google."

+++

We turned into Duck Spencer's driveway and changed another person's disposition. He looked up as we got out and left Lightning at the front of the house. It looked like his next blow with the hammer was a tad bit harder than the previous one.

"Back again, huh Lieutenant. What this time?"

"Oh, we thought it was a great day for a drive in the country and decided to see how you're doing."

"I'm doing fine. Goodbye, Lieutenant."

"Mr. Spencer, if everyone would cooperate a little better we'd be through with this case a lot sooner. So, unless you have something to hide, why don't we be a little more cordial, so we can be on our way?"

"Fine."

"Mr. Spencer, we just found out that you were expelled from County High after fighting with Jimmy Conkwright."

"I told you that when you was here before."

"But what we learned is that it happened twice and the second time you weren't allowed back at school. You didn't quit, Mr. Spencer. You weren't allowed to return to school."

"So?"

"From what I understand, you weren't too happy with that. When Hilldale High wouldn't accept you and your parents refused to let you go to an out-of-the-county school, you had to go to work, and from what I hear, you weren't too pleased with the jobs you were able to get."

"That's true. But it might have been the best thing that ever happened to me. I ended up finding a job at a body shop, loving the work, and now I've got me my own body shop. I might not have been this happy if I finished school."

"But you had to hate Jimmy Conkwright."

"You bet I hated him. That's the only good thing about all this. He's dead. He's not gonna cause no more trouble for nobody else."

"So, did it feel good to kill him?"

"I don't know. You'll have to ask the killer that."

"Are you saying you didn't see him or your wife that night?"

"That's right! And that might be the second-best thing that happened to me, 'cause I ain't a very good liar."

"Oh, I beg to differ, Mr. Spencer. I think all of you are very good liars. I just wonder if any of you are good at telling the truth."

I could see Spencer's anger, but he made no move toward us.

"Why don't you get outa here and find out who murdered my wife and that no good so-and-so?"

"Do you have any idea who that is?"

"Not a one."

I couldn't think of anything else to question Spencer about at that time. So, I bid him goodbye, told him we might be back. He didn't appear to be too pleased.

+++

"Well, Lou?"

"I don't have any idea if he did it or not, but if so, I think we know what his motive was."

With a guy like Jimmy Conkwright, it was easy to see what someone's motive was. It was merely a matter of figuring out which one of those people who wanted him dead did something about it. We mulled it over silently as we headed back to town.

+++

175

"I'm Cy Dekker. This is Lou Murdock. We're here to see Lee Goodwin."

"Are you expected?"

"No, but we're here on police business."

I took out my credentials as I spoke.

"Just a moment, please."

The receptionist got up from her desk and walked to a nearby door and knocked. A couple of minutes later, she returned, followed by another woman, a well-built, well-dressed woman. One look at her made me wonder if she got her position because she could type, or for other reasons.

The second woman led us into an office.

"Have a seat, gentlemen."

Lou and I took a seat in front of the desk. The young woman sat down behind it. I continued to look at the bombshell in front of me while we waited for Mr. Goodwin to come in.

"Well, gentlemen. What can I do for you?"

"If it's all the same with you, we'd rather wait for Mr. Goodwin."

She laughed.

"I don't think my father will be coming."

My puzzled look allowed her to embellish.

"I'm Lee Goodwin. Don't worry. I get this all the time. Some people don't expect to find a woman lawyer."

"I just assumed that with the name Lee, that Goodwin was a man. You know, like Lee Majors."

"Sometimes it's a woman, like Lee Remick."

I realized when I was out of my league and decided to get on with business.

"Ms. Goodwin, we're here about Jimmy Conkwright's will."

"Someone from the department has already called about it. We gave him all the information."

"Oh, we know that, like who gets what. What I want to know is how the two that inherited reacted when you told them."

"I'm not a mind reader, Lieutenant."

"But could you tell if either of them seemed to know if they inherited before they arrived?"

"Not really. Lieutenant, I won't testify to this in a court of law, but I'll give you my gut feeling. If either Miss Calvert or Mr. Gibbons knew they were inheriting a lot of money before they showed up, I'd have to call them good actors. I did kind of get the idea from watching them that it was sort of like watching their mother-in-law drive over a cliff in their new car, only in reverse. I don't think either of them felt saddened by Conkwright's demise."

We talked a little more, but I felt like we'd gotten as much as we were going to get. I thanked her for her time, apologized again for thinking she was a man, and Lou and I got up to leave.

+++

As soon as we returned to Lightning and buckled up, Lou turned to me and grinned.

"What?"

"Sometimes, Cy, I'm glad I'm not the one who does all the talking."

"Lou, could you do me a favor? Could you check with Thelma Lou and see if Lee Goodwin is also her cousin?"

Lou grinned again.

23

It was a little before noon when Lightning eased into the driveway. It was time for lunch and to Google Wyatt Earp. In the past, lunch at my place meant Strombolis, and French fries with lots of gravy, delivered by Antonio's. I tried to dismiss that thought. Otherwise, there was no way I'd enjoy what I was going to fix us for lunch. Sometimes losing weight is not all it's cut out to be.

+++

Lou and I enjoyed lunch. The conversation made it more palatable. Our conversation consisted of talking about Wii Fit and how much weight we'd lost. Lou had lost close to fifty pounds. I was gaining on him but from a distance. When I weighed that morning, my Wii Fit told me I'd lost fifteen pounds so far. A long way from fifty, but a beginning. Of course, all of that meant that I had to work a little harder getting dressed each morning. I had to yank on my belt until I got to the next notch. I wondered if the Wii would let me count that as strength training.

+++

I turned on the computer and clicked on the favorite of My Favorites, Google. I typed in the words "Wyatt Earp" and Lou and I perused the material. After fifteen minutes of looking, we sat back and silently mulled over what we'd read. When I gave the sign, it was time to compare mental notes.

"What do you think, Lou?"

"The only thing I saw that stood out was that after Wyatt Earp left Dodge City, Kansas he moved on to Tombstone, Arizona. I was wondering if we should be looking at someone's tombstone."

"I was thinking the same thing, Lou, and my someone is that Van Meter girl. I hope one of those people we talk to later today is related to her. Maybe they can tell us where she's from and what brought her to Hilldale. From everything anyone's telling us, she seemed to appear out of nowhere, and didn't even live where she said she lived."

+++

I looked at my watch. It was only 2:46. I remembered we couldn't locate either Van Meter when we tried to call them during the day, so we'd wait until after they got off work to call on them. We had some time to spare, and I came up with a brilliant idea.

"Hey, Lou, we've got some extra time. How about if I Google Jennifer Sparks and see what I can find out about her?"

"You just want to know what she looks like, Cy. You'll find out soon enough."

"That's what I'm afraid of. I want to be prepared for this. What if she's as ugly as a one-hundred-year-old outhouse? It won't look good if I get there and react to it, because she's so butt ugly. Besides, if she looks okay, it might be better if I can find out what she's interested in. I could find out, then bone up on her interests, and make a good impression."

"Just keep calm, Cy. Tomorrow will be soon enough."

"It might be too soon."

"You don't think that Thelma Lou would fix you up with an ugly woman, do you?"

"Not unless she's trying to help her cousin's self-esteem, and she thinks I'm butt ugly, too."

"Cy, I've never thought of you as ugly. Just as someone most women wouldn't be interested in, and that has nothing to do with your looks."

I wasn't about to ask him what it had to do with. Instead, I thought of ways to get even with Lou in case Cousin Jennifer looked better with a bag over her head.

+++

We wiled away the afternoon, then decided to chance it and see if either of the Van Meter families was at home. Lightning seemed eager to leave the house. Was this a good sign, or had my neighbor and her wee one been sticking their tongues out at her, too?

We arrived at the first of the two Van Meter residences but saw no cars in the driveway, and no garage. It looked like we were too early, but since we were there, we got out, sidled up to the front door, and knocked. A welcome blast of cool air hit me in the face as an elderly woman opened the front door.

I held out my credentials before she could close the door.

"So, you're police officers. I don't have too many policemen calling on me. What can I do for you?"

"Are you Mrs. Van Meter?"

"I am. Am I under arrest?" she asked, and then laughed.

"I'm sorry, but we don't have enough evidence to arrest you yet, but I do have a question for you. Were you related to Miriam Van Meter?"

"You said 'were' did Cousin Miriam die?" She grabbed the door facing and her jovial manner left her face.

"The Miriam I'm talking about died a long time ago. Twenty years to be exact. Maybe she was named for your cousin. She was only in high school at the time."

Mrs. Van Meter breathed a sigh of relief.

"I don't know any other Miriam Van Meters. My cousin lives just outside Pittsburgh. I assume that's not the same one."

"No, this one lived here, died in a car wreck twenty years ago."

"I've only been here for fifteen years. My husband was transferred here and then died shortly thereafter. I decided not to move back home, although I did give it a lot of thought. I've enjoyed it here."

"Do you know a Robert Van Meter over on Gimlet Place?"

"That's my son. What do you want him for?"

"Nothing, now that we know he wasn't related to Miriam, either. We had hoped that we could find some of Miriam's family."

"You waited a long time to look for them, didn't you, considering she died twenty years ago?"

"She wasn't a motive for murder twenty years ago."

"Oh, so that's it. I thought you said she died in a car wreck."

"That's right! Drunk driver."

"Seems like someone's waited a long time to get revenge."

"Probably too long. More than likely her death is a dead end. But we have to check out all of our leads."

"I'm sorry I wasn't able to help you gentlemen."

I thanked Mrs. Van Meter, and Lou and I turned away. On the surface, the two murders didn't look premeditated, but then there is always the possibility that someone had carried a grudge a long time. At any rate, the line of people who wished Jimmy Conkwright dead was a long one, the line of mourners non-existent.

+++

I couldn't think of anything else to do. I wasn't through looking at Miriam Van Meter, but any place I needed to check would be closed until Monday. That was okay. Maybe my blind date would keep my mind off the case until then. On Monday morning, I would call Sam, and maybe Lou and I would look for that tombstone. I'd have Sam check out of town possibilities first, then check in Hilldale, in case we were no closer to finding out all about Miriam Van Meter.

+++

The Van Meter excursion didn't take long, so I followed the only lead I had left, another visit with Rose Ellen Calvert.

"Lieutenant, if you show up any more I might start charging you rent."

"Sorry, I just have to clear up something. This won't take long. Miss Calvert, you said you went to the kitchen only one time. We have a witness that says they saw you coming out of the kitchen after Conkwright and Mrs. Spencer were thrown out for being drunk."

"I thought I said I couldn't remember whether or not I went back to the kitchen. Now that you mention it, I remember going back to the kitchen a second time."

"And what was the inspiration for this second trip?"

"I overheard someone say something about Jimmy and Betty Gail heading toward the parking lot. This was after the guys threw Jimmy out for being drunk. I waited about fifteen minutes, and then I made an excuse of going to the restroom and rushed down to the kitchen to look out the door. I was curious as to whether they'd gotten in their cars and left."

"And what did you see when you opened the door?"

"They were still there, only this time they looked up and saw me watching them. Jimmy Conkwright, who was in a drunken stupor by this time, stumbled toward the school, toward the kitchen door where I was standing. I was scared of what he might do. He was always making smart remarks about me when we were in school. I wondered what he'd do to me if he got me alone, with him being drunk and all. When I saw him heading toward me, I took off running. I didn't even take the time to close the door. On the way out of the kitchen, I saw Jim Bob. I bet he's the one who told you he saw me coming out of the kitchen. I'm sure I was a frightful mess at the time. Anyway, I said, 'excuse me,' brushed past him, and hurried back to the cafeteria."

"And did Jim Bob Gibbons go into the kitchen to see what frightened you?"

"I have no idea. I didn't look back. I was too scared."

"Anything else, Miss Calvert?"

"Only that I was surprised when Jimmy didn't come charging back into the cafeteria. I guess he was afraid of what the guys would do to him."

Lou and I had to put our game faces on when we talked to Rose Ellen Calvert because we both remembered Silent Lou the last time we visited. On this, our third visit with her, I noticed that from time to time, even though I was the one questioning her, she turned to look at Lou. Maybe she wanted to be looking at him if I happened to mess up.

Finally, she could control herself no more and spoke to Lou.

"Sir, do you have any questions for me?"

"Ooga wong bowie Zulu dong."

She was surprised at the words that sprang from Lou's mouth. She wasn't the only one. I refrained from looking at Lou because I knew if I did I wouldn't be able to keep a straight face. After a few moments, she turned to me.

"What did he say?"

"I assume this means that you don't speak Swahili."

"Swahili? But he's a white man."

"That's the reason he's here."

"I don't understand."

"Miss Calvert, this is Little Chief Kabongo. He was supposed to become the Chief of the tribe after the tiger came into the camp, entered their tepee, and ate his father, the Big Chief. But the Witch Doctor of the village wouldn't allow him to become Chief. See, he was the white sheep of his family, and tribal law says that no white man can become Chief, but must be boiled in a pot instead. After dark, on the day before his pot-boiling experience, his mother put him in a canoe and pushed him downstream, trusting the gods to save him. He fell asleep, and the next thing he remembered was arriving in Jamestown, Virginia. When he arrived there, they asked him his name, and he said, 'Little Chief Kabongo.' He spent the next three months in a sanitarium until the doctors realized that he wasn't crazy. When he was released and adopted by a white family, all he remembered was that one day he was supposed to be Chief. That's why today, he's a cop, and someday he hopes to become Chief of Police."

"You are kidding, aren't you, Lieutenant."

"Miss Calvert, we wouldn't kid about such grave matters. We are merely thankful that Little Chief didn't see his father being eaten by that tiger."

"Are you sure he doesn't remember?"

"Very sure, Miss Calvert. He smiled the first time I showed him a box of Frosted Flakes. He would have run or lashed out at that box if he had remembered that terrible night."

"I guess he would at that. But do you think he will ever become Chief of Police without knowing the language?"

"Only God knows what the future holds. But enough about Little Chief. If that is all, Miss Calvert, we have other people to question."

"I understand, Lieutenant. I'm sorry to have kept you."

+++

Again, we were able to drive away before bursting into laughter.

"Cy, I like it when you call me Chief."

"I didn't call you Chief. I called you Little Chief."

"But in this country, I can become Big Chief."

"Lou Murdock, Big Chief of Boloney."

"Jealous. By the way, do you think she was dumb enough to believe you?"

"I hope not. If she was, we might want to scratch her off our list."

"Why, Cy? Dumb people commit murders, too."

I tried to focus on the case instead of our ruse. Finally, someone had narrowed down the time of the murders, provided Rose Ellen Calvert was telling the truth.

+++

Lou and I purposefully saved our leftovers from Burkman's until dinner, just in case we had something worth talking about. I felt that was finally the case, and since neither of us minded the other talking with his mouth full, we talked all the way through dinner. However, we didn't wait until dinner to get started. As soon as Lightning lurched off down the street, I opened my mouth.

"What do you think, Lou?"

"It looks like one of the nouveau riche is about to be disinherited. At least, it seems like Rose Ellen Calvert or Jim Bob Gibbons had the best opportunity."

"Could it be that it was clever of Miss Calvert to turn around Gibbons' seeing her in the kitchen to where it might incriminate him? Did she wait until the couple gained entrance to the kitchen and shove them into the freezer before she left? Or linger nearby and take advantage of Conkwright entering the freezer on his own?"

"We know that Conkwright and Mrs. Spencer entered the freezer of their own volition. At least we think they did. That would sound more like a little time elapsed, and Gibbons, who was standing at the kitchen door wondering what scared Miss Calvert, took advantage of the opportunity when Conkwright entered the kitchen and walked into the freezer. Of course, maybe neither one of them did it. Maybe a third person came along after both of our suspects had left the area."

"Of course, either of the first two could have shut them in the freezer without any intention of killing them. Maybe they told someone else, and told them to go back and let them out after so long a time."

"You mean after they had a chance to cool off?"

"Oh, Lou, you certainly have a way with words."

"Remember, I've been doing crossword puzzles for years."

Lou and I continued to talk about the case, hoping we could make an arrest before 11:00 the next morning, but to no avail. We would pick up the case again on Monday, where we left off that Friday night.

+++

An elephant and Cy Dekker never forget, so as soon as I returned from taking Lou home, I headed to the computer to Google Jennifer Sparks.

Anxiously, I typed in the name Jennifer Sparks. There was a reference to a Facebook page, so I clicked on it. There was a picture. The first thing I noticed was her harelip. The second was her misshapen head. It looked like the doctor had used forceps to remove her from her mother, while in a fit of anger. I had seen the movie *The Elephant Man*. I'd seen the classic movie *Freaks*. I'd seen my next-door neighbor. But never had I seen anyone who was as hideous looking as Jennifer Sparks. I looked at her list of Friends. A picture identified Thelma Lou as her cousin, so it had to be the same Jennifer Sparks who would soon make my weekend miserable. If someone had scanned the Internet for the ugliest person alive, they would have ended up with Jennifer Sparks. There was no way I could go through with this date. Maybe if I called Lou and had him Google her, he would understand. Then I remembered. Lou had told me that under no condition was I to Google the woman. Somehow, I had to get even with Lou. I wondered if there was any way I could fix Lou up with my next-door neighbor.

I thought of ways to get sick. One came to mind immediately, but that one wouldn't work. That one would happen tomorrow if I couldn't get out of the date. I thought of Googling "Desperate Women," see if I could find one that didn't look too bad. If so, maybe we could find a Justice of the Peace before nightfall, then have the marriage annulled on Monday. Then I remembered that Lou said this woman might be moving to Hilldale. Would it be better to stay married to my Desperate Woman just in case?

I wondered what I had done to make God do this thing to me. And what if I couldn't get out of the date? Lou said Thelma Lou and Jennifer were planning the date. What were my chances that we'd go somewhere so dark that I couldn't see the woman across from me, and that no one else could see who was with me? I wondered if I should call Thelma Lou and let her know how much I love spelunking.

That caused my thoughts to turn to Thelma Lou. I'd always thought that Thelma Lou liked me. What had I done to gain her wrath?

My phone rang. It was Lou.

"Listen, Lou, I think I'm coming down with something. I don't think I'll be able to make the date tomorrow. Maybe you can find someone else."

"Cy, you went to the computer and Googled her, didn't you?"

"How did you know?"

"I just did the same thing myself. I thought I'd better call you and remind you that you promised me you'd do this."

"But, Lou, she must be at least seventy."

"Seventy-two, I believe her page said."

"What did I ever do to you to deserve this?"

"That was a gruesome picture, wasn't it, Cy?"

"It's not funny, Lou."

"Look at it this way, Cy. She can't look any worse in person. Besides, it's only one weekend."

I hung up. If I went to bed early and had nightmares, at least that would be an improvement over the last few minutes. Only one weekend. There are a lot of seconds in one weekend. Maybe something would prevent the world's only ugly Jennifer from getting to Hilldale. If I prayed earnestly, would God cause it to snow in July? Somehow, I didn't think so. What options did I have left? I thought of hypnotism. I wondered if there were any lingering effects. I thought of my next-door neighbor. I knew there would be lingering effects there. I wondered if there was a waiting list to join a monastery. What if someone from the department saw the two of us together? I did promise that

I'd go out with her, but I didn't promise where. I wondered if I called Lou and offered to meet the three of them somewhere in Pittsburgh if he would go for it. As far as I knew, I didn't know anyone in Pittsburgh.

24

I awoke the next morning, realized that it was Saturday, and then remembered our plans. There was no way to get out of it. All I could say is that whoever I would interrogate on Monday had better watch out. I might get a confession out of someone who isn't guilty.

I slunk out of bed. I thought briefly about not showering or using deodorant but quickly dismissed that notion. I had to live with me, too. I would look my best. I burned my bacon at breakfast, and my oatmeal stuck to the pan. I took my frustrations out on the Wii Fit board and did better on the exercises I had somewhat mastered and turned in my usual bad scores on the others. Except for the one time I tripped over the board stepping up onto it and almost saying a bad word, I survived with flying colors. I took a shower, shaved, and fixed my hair the best I could, which means I swiped at it a couple of times with a brush.

I needed to calm down, so I saved my prayer time and devotional reading for last. I asked God to get me out of the mess. I felt like He was telling me that everything would be just fine. I assumed that to mean that Thelma Lou's cousin had decided to go home early and have reconstructive surgery. Shortly after I finished that prayer the phone rang. I've never known God to call on the phone, either in my life or in scripture, so I answered it, figured it was Lou. It was. He told me he was on his way to pick me up. He didn't say anything about Thelma Lou's cousin's surgery. As I hung up, I realized that God's definition of "all right" was much different than the one I had in mind.

Lou pulled up in front of the house. I spotted a shopping bag lying on my kitchen counter. I thought about picking it up, taking it with me and asking my date to put it over her head before I came in. If she got mad and wouldn't go out with me, so much the better. But then I realized if I took the bag there was a good chance I would lose two friends, so I refrained from grabbing the bag.

It was too late to put up the quarantined sign, so I opened the door and stepped out into Saturday morning. I took my time getting to Lou's classy 1957 Chevy, just in case my next-door neighbor rushed over, mauled me, and gave me some kind of contagious disease. The one time I wanted to see her she failed me.

I opened the car door, got in, buckled up, and looked over at Lou. He was smiling. I returned his smile with a frown. That turned his smile into a big grin.

"I can tell you're excited, Cy."

"You're gonna owe me big time."

"Maybe she looks better in person."

I couldn't see how. I'd double-checked her friends' list on her Facebook page. It said she was Thelma Lou's cousin. I had the right Jennifer Sparks. Actually, it was the wrong Jennifer Sparks, but it looked like she was mine, at least for a weekend. I could see why Lou warned me to stay away from Googling her. I could also see why Thelma Lou had to get blind dates for her. I tried to think of someone who might enjoy a blind date with the woman. Only Stevie Wonder and Ray Charles came to mind. That is if they didn't touch her face, which looked craggier than Mt. Rushmore, and if her voice sounded much better than her face looked.

In milliseconds, we pulled up in front of Thelma Lou's house. I recognized it because Lou and I had double-dated many times.

Reluctantly, I got out. Wobbly-legged, I followed Lou up to the front door. His knock garnered an immediate reply of, "It's open." Lou motioned for me to go first. I gave him a dirty look, and said, "After you, Friend."

I followed in Lou's footsteps, which means I did my best to hide behind him. I saw no one but Thelma Lou. Maybe they were saving the surprise until I arrived. Maybe her cousin left to have surgery after all. My jubilation was short-lived.

"Oh, Jennifer's in the other room putting her face on."

I refrained from commenting, but that didn't stop me from thinking. *I hope she uses a pound of make-up.*

Nervously, I shuffled from one foot to the other. What seemed like an hour couldn't have been more than thirty seconds. I failed to notice Lou and Thelma Lou grinning at each other. Then, the earth moved. This gorgeous creature entered the room. Her honey-colored hair, full of body, hung down and caressed her shoulders. Her tan was just right, not too dark, and not too pale. Her body contained all the necessary parts, and in the right proportions. She had on shorts and was barefoot. Even her feet were beautiful.

She walked toward me, with her hand stuck out.

"Hi, I'm Jennifer Sparks. You must be Cy."

The laughter from my so-called friends alerted me to the fact that my mouth was wide open. I didn't improve matters when I said, "Yes," in a voice much higher than one that had ever come out of my mouth, even during puberty. They laughed again, and I soon realized why. I'd failed to let go of that gorgeous creature's hand, but then, when I realized that I hadn't, I wasn't sure I wanted to. I let her hand go, and all I could do was utter, "Bu...bu...bu...but."

The gorgeous creature spoke to me, again.

"It wasn't my idea."

Since she was looking at me, I figured she was addressing me, so I responded, this time in a voice closer to the one I usually use.

"What wasn't your idea?"

"To put all that false information on my Facebook page. Thelma Lou said that Lou came up with the idea, just in case you peeked. At least the fact you peeked told me you were looking forward to our date."

As soon as I could take my eyes off her, which was no more than a day or two later, I looked at my friend who was grinning. I would tell him later that he was dead meat.

"Why don't we all sit down?" Thelma Lou asked, and I thought it was a good idea. My legs were started to feel rubbery again.

Lou and Thelma Lou made some pretense for leaving the room, which gave Jennifer and me a few minutes to get to know each other in private. In a matter of moments, my desire for the itinerary for the blind date changed. I wanted to parade her back and forth in front of the police station, in case any of my co-workers were there. Actually, I wanted to parade her by every person I knew, particularly the males, and then take her to my place.

As it turned out, she already knew a lot about me. I soon learned that she was forty-two and had been a widow for two years. She shared about the loneliness of suddenly being a widow and how her family reached out to her to help her through a difficult time. We briefly compared our loneliness, as I knew what it was like to lose a spouse to death, and then she told me that the one thing this had enabled her to do was to spend time with family members she would not have spent time with otherwise. She told me that Thelma Lou had suggested that she relocate to Hilldale and had invited her to visit to check out the town. In just a few minutes' time, I had a change of heart. I totally agreed that she should move to Hilldale, although I didn't want to appear too eager, so I didn't suggest it. After all, we were only to the handshake stage.

What seemed like seconds later, but was actually fifteen minutes, a couple of heads peeked around the corner, and they emerged with bodies in tow.

"So, did Jennifer tell you our plans for the day?"

"No, we hadn't gotten that far yet."

"Well, Cy, the weather is so pretty, and Jennifer loves sports so much, we decided to go out for lunch, then on to play miniature golf."

"Do you play miniature golf, Cy?" the gorgeous creature asked.

If I was going to have to play, I knew better than to lie.

"It's been a while since I've played."

It had been a while. I think someone made me do it once when I was a teenager.

"Well, I'm sure it will all come back to you," GC said.

Then, Former Friend butted in.

"If it's slow in coming back to you, Cy, I'm sure that Jennifer would be more than happy to help you with your game, wouldn't you, Jennifer?"

"Oh, I love giving pointers."

At that point, I knew that even if I had been a miniature golf champion, I was going to need pointers. Hands-on help would be even better.

Thelma Lou spoke next.

"I know you boys have been watching what you eat and losing weight, so I took that into consideration when I chose a place for us to eat lunch."

If it had been me, I would have taken lighting into consideration. I wanted a dark place, but for a much different reason than the one I had before we arrived.

Lou and I did our best to act like gentlemen, which means we opened the car door for both of the girls. As I walked around the car to the other side of the back seat in order to get in and sit next to Jennifer, Lou whispered to me, "You owe me."

I most definitely owed him, in more ways than one.

I can't tell you what we had for lunch; but somehow, I kept from getting whatever it was all over me. From time to time, someone from the other side of the table spoke to me, which were the only times I became aware that someone was on the other side of the table.

While miniature golf isn't a vigorous exercise, we lingered at the table for a while, after we finished eating, to give our food time to settle. I was sure those on the other side of the table were talking about the two of us on our side of the table, but I didn't give that any thought.

A few minutes later, we arrived at the miniature golf course, and then at the first hole.

Jennifer turned to me and said, "Cy, this hole looks easy. It's a good one to start with, but then usually the easier holes are first."

I smiled and nodded. Being the gentlemen that Lou and I are, and the fact that neither of us knew a thing about miniature golf, we let the girls go first. Jennifer promptly stepped up, lined up her putt, and knocked it in the hole. Thelma Lou went next and missed holing her putt by a couple of inches. I motioned for Lou to go next. He putted and I was thankful that I wouldn't be the only doofus there. His ball rolled up, hit the concrete barrier behind the hole, and rolled back to where Lou was standing. He smiled, embarrassed. He tried again, with slightly better results.

Finally, it was my turn. I hoped I needed some personal instruction. I wanted to make sure that was the case. My ball didn't become airborne until it hopped over the barrier and out into the grass. Jennifer retrieved my ball and handed it back to me.

"Not quite so hard this time."

The second time my ball moved no more than three feet. I gave her the palms up sign. I was thankful that all it took was two bad shots to get personal instruction.

"Here, let me show you, Cy."

To put your hands over the top of someone else's on the putter, you have to get close. Real close. When she got close enough to help me, it caused me to mishit, only this time not on purpose.

"Sorry," I muttered.

"That's okay, Cy. Take your time."

I tried hard to think of putting that golf ball, but that was hard to do. It had been too many years since I had had a woman that close to me, and since I had felt that good. I suddenly realized that there's more to life than solving murders and reading about other people who do the same. I did my best to regain my composure, but it took a few strokes before I settled down. Finally, I hit a reasonably good shot and everyone clapped for me. I wanted more instruction, but I had to put away my thoughts and concentrate on that stupid game.

Over the course of eighteen holes, I improved. I hit the ball over the barrier only one more time, although I had a lot of uphill putts come back to me because I had either hit the ball too hard or not hard enough. I did come in fourth, but not a distant fourth. Sometimes it's nice to have Lou around.

"So, what's next?" I asked, more eager to continue the date than I had been early that morning.

Thelma Lou answered my question.

"Well, I thought we'd go back to my place and hang out. Jennifer and I will fix dinner for you boys, and then I thought we'd play some games on the Wii. Lou's been telling me about how good you're getting on the Fit."

"Only on the Advanced Step. The rest of them are still a lot tougher than what I can handle."

196

"Well, I've got Wii Sports and Wii Sports Resort, too. Let's see how you are at some of those games."

Ordinarily, I wouldn't be in favor of "Let's see Cy mess up at something else," but if it was Wii games with Jennifer or go home without Jennifer, I was in favor of those Wii games. Besides, I expected to thoroughly enjoy watching her Wii.

Lou and I were instructed to sit and talk while the girls fixed dinner. After dinner, and a sufficient amount of time to let our food settle, Thelma Lou pulled out the Wii Fit board.

"Let's start with Wii Fit. Then we'll play some sports games. Cy, why don't you show us your Advanced Step moves?"

Reluctantly, I complied, followed by my three companions. I was surprised that I turned in the best score of the foursome, and Jennifer eagerly congratulated me on my great moves. I was glad she didn't have to win at everything.

While it was good to see that I could do well at something compared to others' efforts, the highlight of my Wii Fit exercises was when I was coerced into doing the Tree exercise with Jennifer as my crutch, and when I got to watch Jennifer do the Hula Hoop exercise. Afterward, I congratulated her on her moves. What made the Tree exercise much better than before, was that I tried to maintain the pose and almost fell off the board. I fell into Jennifer and wasn't eager to regain my balance. But all good things must come to an end, and around 10:30 Lou suggested that we had better go because we had to get up for church the next day. While Jennifer was going to Thelma Lou's church, rather than mine, I found out that the girls had planned a picnic for the four of us for the next afternoon. I gave Jennifer a goodbye hug and Lou and I left.

+++

I looked over at the grinning man in the driver's seat.

"Listen, Cy, if you're too tired to come back tomorrow, the girls will understand. I'll let them know."

"That might be best, Lou. Why don't you stay home and I can pick Jennifer up and take her to my house for a while."

Lou laughed.

"See, Cy, I told you that she'd probably look better in person."

I shook my fist at Lou.

"Remember, Cy, you owe me."

Again I thought to myself, *in more ways than one.*

25

Lou dropped me off. I skipped a few times before I walked into the house. It was a good thing I didn't fall down when I kicked up my heels. The woman of my dreams wasn't there to pick me up, and I was still a long way from being able to get up off the ground by myself.

It was a good thing it was late. It would have been useless for me to try to read. I stripped down to my boxers and undershirt and went to bed. An hour later, I was still thinking about "Her". These were feelings I hadn't had in a while. It had been over twenty years since my Eunice died.

+++

After tossing and turning, and smiling each time I woke up during the night, daylight arrived. I lay there thinking of Jennifer, wondering if she was thinking of me. Suddenly, I became aware of the time. I had already planned to forgo my daily Wii workout, as most of the time I skipped Wiiing on Sunday. I fixed breakfast, hopped in the shower, and paid extra attention to my grooming. As I was getting dressed, the phone rang. Could it be "Her"?

"Oh, it's only you."

"It's good hearing your voice too, Cy. I just called to remind you that I'm picking you up today since we're going on a picnic with the girls after church."

"I almost forgot."

"About the picnic?"

"That I wasn't driving. I'll be ready when you get here."

+++

We arrived at church, entered the building, and were immediately reminded of where we were. The smell of pecan buns and cinnamon rolls wafted through the church. It had been only a couple of weeks since I'd given up eating them. Lou, on the other hand, gave them up months ago, so more than likely he paid no attention to the smell.

We went downstairs for the fellowship time anyway. My will power was good. I wasn't tempted. Well, not much. After chatting with a few friends, Lou and I hurried to the sanctuary to get our customary back row seats. I didn't want visitors to take what was rightfully ours. Besides, we could hear quite nicely from the back. As it turned out, we could be seen on the back row, too. I didn't know this until we were greeted by our pastor on the way out after the service.

"Cy, as always, good to see you. You must have liked today's sermon in particular."

"I like all of your sermons."

"But today I could see the smile on your face, the joy in your heart."

I elbowed Lou so that he wouldn't comment on the joy in my heart, and he took the hint. Of course, he had a few words about my joy after we'd left the congregation behind. Lou and I are not prone to dressing up or dressing down, so we didn't have to bring a change of clothes for the picnic. The girls, on the other hand, did change from their church clothes. We arrived at Thelma Lou's house just after the girls had changed into casual attire.

We walked in to encounter a luxurious creature hidden behind a paper mask of grotesque proportions. Evidently, someone had had enough time to print a picture from her Facebook page. I walked over and took the hand that held up the paper mask, lowered the hand and the mask.

"I like this face better."

"I have a confession to make."

"Oh, what's that? You mean that this mask is what you really look like?"

"No, I mean I had trouble sleeping last night. I kept thinking of you."

A lump formed in my throat. I finally managed to whisper, "Me, too."

"You mean you thought of yourself last night, too?"

I love a beautiful woman with a sense of humor.

We stood there, staring into each other's eyes, until Thelma Lou said, "Jennifer if you're busy I can pack the food by myself."

I was starting to let her go, when she replied, "Sure, if you don't mind."

Those words were music to my ears. Almost as heavenly was when Lou said to Thelma Lou, "Let me help you."

Jennifer reached out and did her best to put her arms around this big, burly guy. I don't know how long we stood there and embraced, but at some point, before we were joined by Lou and Thelma Lou, we stepped back, while still holding hands. Again I gazed into her eyes, and I was the first to speak.

"How soon can you move here?"

"How does yesterday sound?"

A clearing of the throat, voices, and approaching footsteps alerted us that it was time to separate completely.

"Well, are you two ready to go?"

"If you two are," Jennifer replied.

+++

Thelma Lou directed Lou toward Lakeside Park, a city-owned park on the outskirts of town. We arrived a few minutes later, realized that we didn't have the place all to ourselves, and looked for a place to park the car and our carcasses. The first was easy. The second took a couple of minutes, but finally, we spotted an empty picnic table. We took our time eating, even fed each other. Well, Lou and I didn't feed each other, but Jennifer and I did. However, we refrained from eating from both ends of anything until we met in the middle. After all, I had no idea if the Chief or some of my friends from the department were there. I could imagine what they'd have to say, simply seeing me somewhere with a woman. We were close enough that none of them would have believed she was my cousin from Alabama.

After we finished eating, we must have sat and talked for thirty minutes or so, as a foursome.

"What do you think of going out on the lake in a couple of those paddle boats?" Jennifer asked.

"Jennifer, how about you and I taking a walk down the woodland trail instead?"

"Sounds good to me. But Thelma Lou and Lou, you feel free to give one of those paddle boats a try. Let us know what you think of it."

I was glad that she was not someone who had to plan everything. And that she wanted to be alone with me as much as I wanted to be alone with her.

We took off down the woodland trail and were thankful that we seemed to have the trail all to ourselves. She reached over and took my hand, and we swung them back and forth, as we walked slowly down the trail. I assume that we walked slowly because neither of us was ready for the moment to end. Plus, we looked more at each other than we did the pathway, so we had to go slowly so as not to fall down.

Hidden from the rest of the world, we talked about ourselves. She asked me questions about myself that she didn't already know the answers to, and I learned what I could about her.

We walked for a while, and then we stopped. I looked around, saw no one. Then I looked at her, so close to me. I'm five feet ten inches tall, so I guessed her to be around five-eight. I looked at her, mere inches from me. I don't know who made the first move, but our lips met, and our kiss lingered.

When we parted, she looked at me and saw that I had tears in my eyes.

"What's wrong, Cy? I'm sorry if I did something wrong."

Tears began to form in her eyes, too.

"It's just that you're the first woman I've kissed since my mother died. And the last woman I kissed on the lips was my Eunice, and she's been gone over twenty years."

"I'm sorry. I guess I should have waited."

"But I'm not sorry. I'd just forgotten what it's like to have feelings for a woman."

This time I'm sure she was the one who kissed first, and the second kiss lingered longer than the first. We parted only when we heard the snickers. I looked up to see a boy and a girl. They looked around twelve years of age.

"Sorry to interrupt you, but there's not enough room for us to get by. If you could let us by before you carry on."

We stepped aside to let them pass but heard their remarks as they walked on by.

"They are supposed to be our role models."

"Yeah, they tell us no PDA, but I see they don't practice what they preach."

We gave them time to move away from us, and then we too walked on, but happy we'd taken the trail.

+++

We'd agreed to meet at Lou's car, and we returned just as two leg-weary people stepped from a paddle boat back on to the hard ground. Their first few steps were wobbly. I was glad we'd chosen the trail instead.

It was time to leave. Neither Jennifer nor I wanted the day to end, but Jennifer had already told me that she needed to leave town before 4:00 in order to get home before dark. Luckily, it was summer and darkness didn't arrive until somewhere around 9:00.

Lou drove back to Thelma Lou's. Jennifer and I were silent, both of us wrapped up in our thoughts. A few minutes later, we stood in Thelma Lou's living room saying our goodbyes.

"I've made up my mind. I'm definitely going to move here, but it might be a few months before I can sell my house and find one here. But, I can probably arrange another weekend trip before long."

I nodded, and reached out and hugged her. She broke apart from me long enough to put her arms around my neck and pull my lips to hers. It didn't matter what Lou or Thelma Lou saw. That kiss had to last us for a while.

She had already packed. I helped her carry her things out, kissed her one more time, and the three of us stood there and watched her drive off.

Thelma Lou walked over and gave me a hug.

"Thanks for making my cousin feel welcome," and then she laughed. We all did.

"Thanks for having a cousin," I replied.

+++

I expected Lou to let fly as soon as we left, but he left me to my thoughts. He drove me home. I got out and said, "Thanks."

He replied, "Remember Cy, we have to go back to work tomorrow."

"I know, but that's tomorrow. Tomorrow is another day."

He laughed and backed out of my driveway.

I gave myself an hour to think of Jennifer, and then my thoughts returned to the murder case.

+++

I had trouble leaving my thoughts of Jennifer behind and moving on to the case at hand. For the first five minutes, I did nothing but rescue Jennifer from the freezer at the school. Finally, I was able to move on.

I pictured each of the suspects, none of whom looked any guiltier than any of the others. When I thought of what I had planned for the next day, to see what I could find out about Miriam Van Meter, the girl who died in the wreck twenty years ago, I wondered if her death had anything to do with the murders. From everything I could ascertain, the murders were not premeditated. No one, including Rose Ellen Calvert who organized the reunion, seemed to have any knowledge that Jimmy Conkwright was coming to the reunion. I couldn't even find out how Conkwright knew that the reunion was taking place, but he did. Obviously, someone saw an opportunity to rid the world of a bad person and took advantage of that opportunity. But who?

+++

I continued to ponder the case until the phone rang. I looked at my watch. It was almost 9:00. I couldn't imagine anyone calling me at that time on a Sunday night except Lou. Maybe he'd been thinking about the case too, and had come up with a lead.

"Dekker here."

"Sparks here," came the reply.

"There were definitely sparks between us."

"I just wanted to let you know I made it home okay. The drive home didn't seem as long. I thought of you all the way back."

"Why don't you just turn around and come back, and think of me all the way here?"

"I can't do that yet, but I will as soon as I can. Besides, aren't you working on a case?"

"I was just going over it when the phone rang."

"Well, I'd better let you go, then. I miss you already."

"And I missed you already before you disappeared out of sight."

I hung up and gave up. There was no way I could focus on the case again until the next morning. I went to the computer, Googled Jennifer. It was just as I hoped. The ugly picture had been replaced by a gorgeous one. It was all I could do to keep from kissing the computer screen.

26

I awoke Monday morning and made myself focus on the case. Once I got back into the routine of fixing breakfast, Wiiing, and heading out to bring the case to a conclusion I would be all right. I sprang from the bed a little quicker than I was able to do a few weeks before and set about doing just that, whatever I could do to bring the case to a conclusion. I could think about Jennifer while I Wiied, but after that, it was back to business. I set a new high score in Advanced Step and even attempted the Tree exercise. I still wasn't able to support myself with one foot tucked underneath me, so I had to put my foot down since Jennifer wasn't there to catch me.

+++

"Good morning, Sam."

"You seem especially chipper this morning, Cy. Are you calling me to tell me you've solved your case?"

"Not yet, Sam, but I am calling you to give you a little work to do."

"So, you've come up with sixteen more suspects you want me to check on."

"No, just one name, and she's not a suspect. She died twenty years ago."

"If she died twenty years ago, why do you want me to check on her? I doubt if she's gone anywhere."

"I'm not sure about that, but if she did, she went twenty years ago. Her name is Miriam Van Meter. She was the girl who was killed in the car wreck one night when Jimmy Conkwright was drunk."

"I vaguely remember something about that. It caused quite a stir around here for a while. So, what do you want from me?"

"I want you to see if you can figure out where she came from. All anyone I've talked to seems to know is that one day she arrived at County High. No one seems to have seen her before that. Check with the school. Find out where she came from. Then check there to see if she still has family there. Find out as much as you can about her. In the meantime, Lou and I are going to check on where she went. Maybe take a look at her tombstone, see if it tells us anything. We're on our way to the cemetery."

"Well, I'm glad you're getting out of the house for a change. Is that all you have for me?"

"It is for now, and I have been out working on the case every day."

"If you say so. Well, I should be able to get back to you with the information you want some time today or tomorrow."

+++

I pulled up in front of Lou's apartment building. He was sitting on the front porch. He got up quickly and seemed to bounce as he made his way to Lightning.

"After the dash," he said, as he tucked himself into his seatbelt.

"Huh?" was all I could mutter.

"I said, 'after the dash.' Cy, you need to get those love stars out of your eyes and focus on the case again."

"I am focusing on the case."

"Then why don't you recognize the clue of the day?"

I stared at him dejectedly.

"What's the matter, Cy?"

"You said, 'After the dash?'"

"That's right."

"It's just that it doesn't sound like something that Google will be able to help us with."

"Remember, Cy, we were always able to figure things out before we ever heard of Google."

"Yeah, but it always took us longer. Do you have any idea what it means?"

"Absolutely."

"You do?" I couldn't believe Lou's answer because he always gave me a strange look or a rebuke when I asked him that before.

"Sure. It means that you are to run a fifty-yard dash, and I will be there at the end. At that time, your adrenalin will be so strong that you will know what this clue means."

"You know, Lou, I do think I'll be ready to do the ten minute run on the Wii before long."

"You mean within the decade?"

"Yeah, and maybe within a month."

"You know, Cy, love does some strange things to people. Now, where are we going?"

I informed Lou that it was time to see if Miriam Van Meter's death had anything to do with the murders, so we needed to see what we could find out about her.

+++

We arrived at the cemetery, found Lightning a comfortable place to rest, then got out and made our way to the office.

209

"Hi, I'm Lt. Dekker with the Hilldale Police Department. This is Sgt. Murdock. We're here to inquire about someone who was buried here twenty years ago."

"Do you have the exact date this burial took place?"

"No, but it was sometime in May, and we do have her name. It's Miriam Van Meter."

The woman turned to the computer and hit some keys, then hit some more. She sat there puzzled for a moment, and then turned back to me.

"Is this the correct spelling?"

"That's right. At least I think it's right. Just tell me where to find her grave. And if you have any information on her next of kin, that would be appreciated, too."

"I'm sorry, Lieutenant, but she doesn't seem to be buried here. What made you think that she was?"

"She lived here, and she died here."

"Was she born here?"

"I don't think so. Where she was born is what I'm trying to find out."

"Well, if her family came from somewhere else, there's a good possibility that they might have buried her back where they came from. Was she an older woman?"

"Quite the opposite. She was a teenager."

"Well, sometimes when a tragedy strikes a family, like when a young person dies, that family tries to rid themselves of anything or any place that might conjure up memories of the awful occasion. It could be they moved back where they came from and they had her buried there. I'm sorry I can't help you."

+++

If the cemetery couldn't help us, maybe the mortuary could. Hilldale had two of them, McPeak's and Herrington & Sons. We would check both places. We began with McPeak's since it was closer.

Lou opened the front door and someone came rushing out of the office to meet us.

"I'm sorry, for the delay, but some of our people are still out at the cemetery. We had a funeral this morning."

I said I understood and told the man who welcomed me why we were there.

"What was the name again?"

"Miriam Van Meter."

As was the case at the cemetery, the man sat down in front of a computer and pushed some keys.

"I'm sorry. I don't seem to have anything. Are you sure we served the family, or could it have been Herrington?"

"I'm really not sure. It was a long time ago."

"Oh, I didn't realize that. How long ago?"

When I said twenty years, the man turned and smiled at me.

"That might explain it. See, twenty years ago we weren't computerized. All of those files are stored in the basement. As time permits, we're trying to convert everything to the computer, but we've been so busy lately we haven't had time to get all of them done. We'd be glad to check on that for you, Lieutenant, but we have another funeral today. It would probably be tomorrow sometime before we can find what you want."

I was disappointed, but I understood. I agree to check back the next day.

Lou and I left and made the short drive to Herrington & Sons. We left five minutes later, with the same response.

I was at a loss as to what to do next. All I could think of was for Lou and me to head to my house and mull over what we knew. There had to be something out there that could help us. Otherwise, our only hope was if Sam had more luck than we had had.

+++

"Any ideas, Lou?"

"None, Cy."

"I guess all we can do is lay it all out on the table, clues, suspects, motives, and see if anything jumps out at us."

Both of us grabbed a legal pad and headed to my dining room table. We put down who we had talked to, who might have had a reason to murder either or both of the victims, and the clues we had been given. In Column A we had Walter Gillis, Rose Ellen Calvert, Earl Spickard, Jim Bob Gibbons, Billy Korlein, April Korlein, George Justice, Sandy Justice, and Duck Spencer. We refrained from putting down Mrs. Eversole, Lou's neighbor, because she had a good alibi for the night of the murders. She was watching Jennifer Somebody on TV in her apartment. I was sorry I thought of Mrs. Eversole because the thought of Jennifer anybody made me think of Jennifer Special. I needed to focus on the case.

Column B was much shorter than Column A because we didn't know as many possible motives. Rose Ellen Calvert and Jim Bob Gibbons were richer with Jimmy Conkwright out the way than with him living. Also, not only did Conkwright cause Duck Spencer to be expelled from school, but it was Spencer's wife that Conkwright was carrying on with the night of the reunion. Was it possible that the fact that Conkwright had hit on Korlein's or Justice's wife at the reunion was enough of a reason to end Conkwright's life? I didn't think so.

It took a few minutes for me to remember the clues I would list in Column C; "North To Alaska," "Jennifer Garner," "9/30/55," "Wyatt Earp," and "After The Dash." The first one had to do with finding the bodies in the freezer at the school. I had no idea what the last one meant. The second one meant somebody was not who he or she said he was, and the other two had to do with Miriam Van Meter. At least that's what Lou and I thought.

We were getting nowhere, and we weren't even getting there fast, or were we? At any rate, I looked at my watch and we agreed to take a break for lunch. After all, there wasn't much we could do. We hoped that we'd get a break when Sam called.

Sam called just as we were finishing lunch. I swallowed my last bite and picked up the phone.

"This had better be Sam."

"And this had better be Cy. Otherwise, I'm calling downtown and report a burglary in progress. It must be nice to get to stay home all day and do nothing."

"You ought to know. So, did you learn something about Miriam Van Meter?"

"It all depends upon what you mean by *learn something*. Did I find out anything that might help you? I don't know. What I do know is that I called the school, found out she transferred to County High from a small town in Tennessee. At least that's what County High said. When I called that small town in Tennessee, I found out there's no school there by the name County gave me. When I checked with the schools there, I found out that the county high school had never had a student by that name. So, I checked with the county clerk. They have no record of any family named Van Meter living in the town, at least not in the last fifty years."

"Thanks, Sam," I said dejectedly, and then hung up.

I shared Sam's findings with Lou.

"Do you think all this about a girl being killed in a car wreck was someone's idea to throw us off?"

"No, because I vaguely remember this happening and so do some other people. Could it be that the girl didn't want us to know what town she came from?"

"Obviously."

"Is it possible that she could have grown up right here in Hilldale?"

"I don't see how. If so, wouldn't you think someone would've known her? If she didn't go to school, neighbors would've reported her. If she did go to school here, there would be a record. Let's check the middle schools here, see if they have a record of Miriam Van Meter. There are only three of them, two that move on up to Hilldale High, and one that sends their students on to County. It shouldn't be that tough to find out."

It shouldn't be that tough, yet everything about this case was that tough. Everyone seemed to be lying to me. A mysterious girl was thrust upon us. Maybe she did die in a car wreck with Jimmy Conkwright behind the wheel. That doesn't mean that her death had anything to do with Conkwright's and Betty Gail Spencer's death. I tried to think of who first told us about that wreck. Could it be that someone who had no connection to Miriam Van Meter dropped her name in order to send us on a wild goose chase? I was beginning to think that. Whatever their reason, whoever opened that can of worms had gotten me to where I wanted to find out who this girl was and where she came from. What if we checked back with the two mortuaries and neither of them knew a thing about Miriam Van Meter? I needed to know where to turn. Could it be that the next clue would give us what we needed to solve the murders?

I could see that Lou was as frustrated as I was. At times like that, it was always a good idea to step away, regain our bearings.

"Lou, I think we need a break. I know it's still early, but what do you think about shutting things down for the day. I can take you home and both of us can kick back and start reading a new book."

"Sound good to me. What book do you have in mind?"

"I don't know. Let's look and see which ones we have left."

Lou and I looked over our possibilities. We opened dust jackets and read.

"What do you think of this one?"

"I was leaning in that direction, Cy."

I reached down and plucked *Loves Music, Loves To Dance* by Mary Higgins Clark from my stash. I laid it on the table next to my recliner, put my shoes on, grabbed my keys, and headed out the door to take Lou home. There was no way that Lou or I could finish the book that night, but there was something that appealed to me about a murderer finding his victims by running personal ads in a newspaper. And unlike our case, I knew exactly how long that case would last.

27

I woke up the next morning and couldn't believe it was Tuesday already. Where had Monday gone? And then I remembered, Monday had been a dead end. I wanted to get a head start on Tuesday, so I Wiied the first thing, then gave Lou a call. I wanted to know the clue of the day.

"Don't tell me you're ready already, Cy."

"No, Lou, I just wanted to see if God had given you our message for today."

"It won't do you any good."

"It won't do me any good. Is God trying to tell us to forget about this case?"

"No, I mean it won't do me any good to tell you. Today's clue is "The same as before.""

"The same what?"

"I assume it means that He's already given us everything we need to know to solve this case. Maybe we need to focus on the clues we've already been given."

"We did yesterday and what did that give us."

"Cy, sometimes we can look at something many times before we figure out what it means. Just look over the clues again, and I'll do the same until you get here."

"You mean you're already ready for me? I haven't eaten breakfast, read my devotionals or showered yet."

"I've done all of those things except eat. I'm about to fix my breakfast, but I can fix food, eat it, and think of clues at the same time."

I decided to spend my time with God first. I needed to concentrate on Him during that time, but after that, I too could cook, eat, and shower while I mulled over our clues.

+++

I picked up Lou and we headed back to the cemetery. Maybe their computers don't have records as far back as when the Van Meter girl died. Maybe those early records were buried in a grave somewhere. I was willing to dig to find what we needed, but not that kind of digging.

On the way to the cemetery, I continued to mull over the clues.

"Lou, have you ever heard anyone say that the difference between one person and another is what they do with their dash, which means the time they are alive. Well, maybe our clue "after the dash" means that we should concentrate on Miriam Van Meter's death, or what happened after her death."

"It kind of looks like we're doing that, Cy."

"Yeah, but there's something else. You know how she appeared out of nowhere. Maybe she's the one who has the alias. Maybe Van Meter isn't really her name. I think when we check back today we need to check on any teenage girl who was buried here during the month of May twenty years ago."

"I thought we were already going to do that, too."

"Oh."

We arrived at the cemetery and encountered the same woman in the office.

"Checking on someone else, Lieutenant?"

"No, the same person. But there's a possibility she might have been buried under a different name. Can you check and see if any teenage girl was buried here during the month of May twenty years ago."

"I can, but it might take thirty minutes or so. Do you want to wait or come back later?"

"We might as well wait. No need in wasting gas."

Lou and I sat down. I tried to be as patient as I could. Patience has never been my strong suit. Still, I refrained from jumping up every five minutes to see if she found anything. However, I did frown a time or two when the phone rang and she had to stop searching for what I wanted and answer the blasted phone. Finally, around thirty minutes later, she got up from the computer and peered over the counter at us.

"I'm sorry, Lieutenant, but as I said before, her family could have taken her back where they came from. A lot of families do. Is there any way you might be mistaken as to the date of the death? Could it have been another month or another year?"

"I don't think so, but I'll double-check. I might be able to come up with an exact date."

+++

"Evidently she was buried somewhere else, Cy."

"Either that or somebody has their dates wrong. After we check back with the two funeral homes we can run by the newspaper office and check old newspapers, see if they have a record of the wreck."

"Library, Cy. Remember, when we looked for that before, we found copies of old newspapers at the library, not the newspaper office."

"Oh, yeah, now I remember."

+++

Lightning entered the mortuary parking lot and headed for the same spot she rested in the day before. Lou and I got out to see if someone at the funeral home had found the information we needed.

"Oh, hi, Lieutenant, I guess you didn't get my message. I just called and left one for you. We don't have a record of a Miriam Van Meter."

"I think they might have brought her in under another name. At any rate, whatever the name, she's not buried here in Hilldale. Could you check back through your records for May twenty years ago and give me the information for anyone who might have been sent to you, and you shipped her body out of town. It could be somewhere else in the state, or to another state. And to make it easier for you, we're looking for a teenage female."

"I'm glad you came in before we put the records back. Still, we can't get to it right now, but we'll get to it as soon as we can. However, it might not be until tomorrow."

We left McPeak's and dashed over to Herrington & Sons. We received a similar answer there, although they expected to have something for me by the end of the day.

+++

Going through a month's worth of newspapers might take us a while, although I expected to find what I wanted on the front page. While it was just a little after 11:00, Lou and I took a break for lunch and let our lunch settle while we tried to come up with another plan of attack before we left for the library, in case this one failed.

+++

We opened the front door of the library and the first person we saw was Rose Ellen Calvert. Although I knew she worked there, it didn't register that the place we had to go to was the place where she worked, because she wasn't the reason we were there. However, I could tell by the look she gave me and the fact that she hurried over to us, that she didn't know our reason for being there.

"Please, Lieutenant, not here."

"Where then, Miss Calvert?"

"Well, if you must, please wait until I get off and come by my place."

"You keep old newspapers at your house?"

"Pardon?"

"We're here to look through old newspapers, Miss Calvert. Is there some reason we need to talk to you some more?"

"Of course not, Lieutenant. It's just that you keep bothering me. I thought you came up with some other reason to badger me."

"I'm not badgering you, Miss Calvert. I'm merely following the information I receive and talking to whoever I need to talk to."

"Old newspapers, you say. What year did you need?"

"I need to see the papers for the month of May twenty years ago."

"But...that was my senior year, just before we graduated. And that was the month Jimmy Conkwright killed that girl."

"Exactly. Now, where did you say I could find those files?"

She had no desire to spend any more time with us, but she was trapped.

Follow me," she said and took off to the other side of the library. She walked through an archway and led us to a series of filing cabinets.

"It should be in here somewhere. Oh, yes, here it is."

I was expecting her to tell me that someone else was looking at the month we wanted, but she located what we needed, led us to an unoccupied machine, threaded the machine, and showed us how to find what we needed.

While everything else was taking a lot longer than we'd hoped, ten minutes later we had located the article telling about the young woman's death. I read the article and then continued perusing the month's newspapers. I found one subsequent article. The first one merely reported that the wreck had happened and that there was one fatality. The second article said the victim's body had been released to a local mortuary, but any details of the victim or the driver would not be released until notification to the next of kin.

It had to be the same girl. The article mentioned the victim was a teenage girl, and that the car was a red Corvette. I wrote down the date in case I needed it.

+++

"Why was everything so secretive, Cy?"

"I suspect because the driver was Jimmy Conkwright. My guess is that the newspaper didn't breathe without checking with Big Russ to see if it was okay. I just wish the article had told us a little more. We already knew or thought we knew, when it happened. This just confirmed that she did die in a wreck, and that wreck happened in May twenty years ago."

"So, what do we do next?"

"The only chance we have of finding out any more about her will be if one of the funeral homes turns up anything. The article did say that her body was released to one of the local funeral homes. Is it possible there was another funeral home at one time?"

"Not twenty years ago. Remember, we both lived here then. Although, there is one possibility, Cy."

"What's that, Lou?"

"Funeral homes are still pretty much segregated here."

"As many people as we've talked to, I don't think all of them would have told us about her and none of them mentioned that the girl was black. Besides, there aren't a lot of black families in Hilldale. At least there weren't back then. Let's wait and see what we find out this afternoon and in the morning, and if we don't turn up anything we'll check with Bledsoe."

+++

I dropped Lou off and headed for home. Around 4:30 I received a call from downtown. Herrington & Sons had called. There were no teenage girls brought in at any time during the month of May. My hope rested with McPeak, which meant I would learn nothing until the next morning. It was looking more and more like I would solve Mary Higgins Clark's classified ad murder before I'd solve my own. Maybe I should quit working and start writing murder mysteries. It wouldn't be nearly as stressful on me.

+++

I needed to get my mind off the case. I called Jennifer to see if time was still flying by because she spent all of it thinking about me. We talked for thirty minutes, and then I hung up and continued to think about her. My thoughts were only of her until I heard my stomach begin to grumble. It was time for me to go fix my meager portion. At least all wasn't lost. But I had found out that another two pounds had been lost.

28

I woke up, stirred, and lay there until I could remember what day of the week it was and what I had scheduled for that day. It was Wednesday. It had been over a week since we found the bodies. Halfway through the second week. After that long, I'm always ready to put an end to things. I took stock of what I'd learned so far. It seemed like I didn't know much more than when I started. I didn't want to have to go through the third week of an unsolved case. I sat up in bed and tried to think. What were our plans for the day? Actually, they weren't much. I'd told Lou that we'd be lazy. I'd wait around the house for a while to see if anyone called from McPeak's. If they didn't come through for me I thought about putting everyone in stocks until someone confessed. I wondered where I could find stocks, and how much they would cost. Colonial Williamsburg immediately came to mind. Maybe I could find them in Boston, too. But I couldn't think of anywhere else. See, Wal-Mart and Lowe's don't have everything.

It wasn't doing me any good to lie there, so I extracted myself from the bed. I had to admit doing so had become easier after I started exercising every day. I could begin to tell a little bit of difference after two weeks. So far, I hadn't seen anyone from the department, so I had no idea if anyone could tell I'd lost weight.

I picked up my Bible and my devotional books and headed for my recliner. I didn't spend as much time with God as Lou did each morning, because he took part in an in-depth Bible study, but I was faithful enough that I took time for God every morning, no matter how busy we were. I read, reflected, and prayed. I asked God for the wisdom, the strength, the courage, and the desire to do what He wanted me to do each day. I couldn't do it without His help, but maybe with God's direction, we could solve these murders.

While I wanted to solve the murders, I kept realizing that at least the world didn't lose two pillars in the community. They say that everyone has some good in them. I had yet to find the good in either of the departed. Plus, if anyone missed either of them, I had yet to find that person. Still, murder isn't right, even when it's nothing more than shutting a door on someone's life, so I had to see this through.

I fixed breakfast, let it settle, Wiied, and showered. I was amazed that I'd done all of that by 9:15. I'd just finished dressing when the phone rang. I hoped it was the department telling me that someone had confessed. Actually, I was hoping it was Jennifer, but the department ran a close second. Okay, a distant second, but second.

I answered the phone to hear the voice of someone from desire number two.

"Lt. Dekker, I'm calling to let you know that McPeak's Funeral Home called to say they didn't find what you want, but they have something else and want to know if you might be interested in that."

I thanked my caller and reflected on what she had to say. What did it mean? McPeak's didn't know what happened to Miriam Van Meter, but if I'd be interested in another body that was shipped to Tanzania by UPS Air they would be glad to fill me in. Why would I be interested in someone else? As far as I knew, Jimmy Conkwright had killed only one girl by driving drunk.

I called Lou to let him know that McPeak's called with a message in code and that we would run by there to see what the coded message meant.

"I got a coded message, too, Cy."

"Oh?"

"Well, I have our message of the day, and I don't understand what it means. You might want it now, Cy. This one's a message you might want to Google."

"Well, let me have it."

"Cy, why can't you say that when I'm standing beside you, and you've just done something to irritate me?"

"Lou, you know I never do anything irritating, but you have, so let me have it."

"Mark Dinning."

"That name sounds familiar. How do you spell it, Lou?"

"I T."

"Lou, how about when I see you, you say let me have it?"

"M A R K."

"That's enough, Lou."

"Okay, goodbye, Cy."

"Just spell the last name."

I wrote down the name as he spelled it, and then realized he was merely guessing since God hadn't written it down for him.

"I'll give this Dinning guy a quick glance. Then, I'll come on over and we'll beat it to McPeak's."

"I don't figure this one will take you as long, Cy."

"Why's that?"

"It's a guy. You won't click on all the swimsuit pictures."

"You know me. Now, I only have eyes for Jennifer Sparks."

+++

I Googled "Mark Dinning." It didn't take me long. Lou even spelled it right. As soon as I read it, I knew why his name sounded familiar. He was a singer. His one big hit was *Teen Angel*. It came out a little before my time, but I'd heard the sad song many times, about the girl who was hit by a train because she went back to get her honey's ring. Another reference to a dead teenage girl. I turned off the computer and dashed for Lightning. I wanted to know what McPeak's had for us.

+++

I filled in Lou on he way to McPeak's.

"Well, it seems like God keeps hitting us over the head with a dead teenage girl. Maybe Miriam Van Meter has more to do with this case than it seems."

I pulled up in front of McPeak's. Lightning could park herself. I wasn't blocking anyone, and with today's clue, I was anxious to hear what McPeak's had to say.

"Oh, hello. Lieutenant. Did you get my message?"

"I did, but I didn't understand it."

"Well, you asked for bodies shipped out of town. Would you be interested in a teenage girl that wasn't shipped out of town?"

"I've already checked with the cemetery. No teenage girls were buried there in May twenty years ago. You are talking about May twenty years, aren't you?"

"Yes, and while we do have only one cemetery in Hilldale, occasionally we have someone, particularly in a rural area, who has some acreage, who wants to bury their loved one on their own property, and also some rural churches have their own cemeteries. It's just that neither of these is a common practice anymore."

"And you say that you have a teenager who died in May of that year who was buried somewhere here other than at the cemetery?"

"That's right. Let me get the name. Let's see. Here it is. It's Sarah Jane Spickard. Mrs. Elizabeth Spickard signed for the body. We even delivered it and buried her. She was buried on Mrs. Spickard's property on Flat Rock Road. It says here that Mrs. Spickard was Sarah Jane's mother and her father was Earl Spickard. The ceremony was private. The family wanted all the particulars kept quiet. It says the victim died in a car crash."

Lou and I turned to leave. As we walked out, I realized that Earl Spickard was near the bottom of those I would have suspected, but suddenly he had rushed to the top. That meant we needed to talk to him. Would we get a confession? Was our ordeal almost at an end?

29

Lou and I talked as we drove out to Spickard's place.

"I have to admit, Lou, that retired janitor was near the bottom of my list of those who I thought might have done it."

"Same here, Cy. But it seems that now he has to be the one."

"I know. That's what bothers me. Nothing is ever as hard or as easy as it seems."

+++

As I drove out into the country, I hoped that there was some other explanation. I didn't want Earl Spickard to be our killer. I wasn't sure who I wanted instead of him, but for some reason, I didn't want it to be him. And yet, it looked like he had to be the one.

We pulled up to the dead end. I parked and locked Lightning, and we got out with heavy hearts. Maybe it was the grimness of the occasion, but I felt like we were being watched as we made our way through the trees to Spickard's cabin. Was Spickard sitting there somewhere in the trees, aware of why we'd come back, with a rifle aimed at us? I listened for banjo music but heard nothing.

Sometimes, it's worse to hear nothing than to hear something. Before long, we would realize that this was one of those times. But not yet.

We walked slowly, carefully. Our heads darted from left to right, scanning the forested area, looking for someone who might not be our friend. While there wasn't that much of a clearing, only a few feet on each side of us, and sometimes not that much, I hated being out in the open where someone could pick us off one at a time. I motioned for Lou to move as close to the tree line as possible. That way, maybe someone would pull one of us into the trees instead of shooting us. I figured if someone was out to get us, it was only one someone. I thought that two fat boys who had started working out could handle one person who put his gun down, especially if that one person was an old man. While I didn't want to be shot at, I didn't want Earl Spickard to get away, either. He knew the woods and the river better than we did. There's no telling how long it would take us to find him if he went into hiding. Considering how everyone else felt about the deceased, I was sure that others would be willing to help him, and not us. At least so far no one seemed eager to help us.

A couple of minutes later, I could see the cabin through the trees. I had no idea if Spencer was in there, out in the woods, down by the river, or if he had left town. I would soon find out. As quietly as possible, Lou and I walked up to the cabin. We reached the door, listened for a moment, and then knocked. I heard footsteps walking toward the door. Spickard was home.

Spickard opened the door and looked at us. He had no weapon.

"We're back, Mr. Spickard. May we come in?"

"Shore. I told you boys to come back anytime. Make yourselves at home."

We sat. I paused for a moment, decided to hit him with it right away.

"Mr. Spickard, we know about Sarah Jane."

"I was hoping you wouldn't find out."

"Tell me about it."

"Well, for years, her momma, who's been dead nigh on fifteen years now, kept her as close to her apron strings as she could. Nobody knowed 'bout us. We live so far out and all. So, her momma kept her at home for years, did all of her school learning here. Sarah Jane done all her work, and she was a right smart little girl if I do say so myself. Only Sarah Jane growed up and wanted to go to school with other boys and girls. This didn't set well with her momma, and they argued a might about it, but in the end, Sarah Jane won out. Only, as it turned out, she lost."

A lump formed in Spickard's throat, and tears formed in his eyes.

"If Sarah Jane was gonna go to school, she had to go to the county school. Only Sarah Jane had a problem with that. Her daddy was the jan-e-tor. She didn't want anybody to know that the fella who cleaned the toilets and swept the floors was her daddy. So, she changed her name. Her momma, who was right smart too, came up with some paper that made it look like Sarah Jane was transferring in from some school in Tennessee. Got away with it, too. She passed herself off as that Miriam girl you asked me about before. She wouldn't even look at me if'n she saw me when she was walking down the hall. She was ashamed of her own daddy. Then I seen it. She tried to impress everybody, make them think she was somebody. She took the rowboat to school, so nobody'd know where she come from. I don't think nobody ever found out until you come here today. She just got too big for her britches, and it ended up costing her her life. I didn't like that Conkwright boy before it happened, but I've hated him ever since."

Cops are supposed to remain impartial, unemotional. But sometimes that's hard. I sat there, trying my best to stay composed, when I wanted to get up and put my arm around that man and tell him that he was somebody, no matter what his daughter thought.

I gave him a second to compose himself, and then did what I had to do.

"Mr. Spickard, I have to ask you this. Did you know that woman was with him when you locked him in the freezer?"

He looked at me dumbfounded.

"What woman with who? In what freezer?"

I'd never thought of Earl Spickard as someone who could be a good actor. His incredulous look seemed so genuine.

"Jimmy Conkwright."

"I didn't know how he died. I didn't care how he died. I'm just glad he's dead, after what he done to my Sarah Jane."

"So, you're saying that you weren't the one who closed the freezer door and locked Conkwright and Betty Gail Spencer inside?"

"I didn't lock nobody nowhere."

"Do you have anyone who can verify that, Mr. Spickard?"

"I don't know. I just know I took Duck to the school. He goes in ahead of me. I walk in, go to the restroom and find my friend Walter Gillis. Walter and I was together the whole time I was in that school until I left to come home. I never seen Conkwright or Duck's wife neither one."

"And you don't know who locked those two people in the freezer?"

"I don't know and I don't care."

He showed no animosity toward me. While his whole declaration was full of emotion, he didn't come across as a murderer. I wondered if I was any closer to finding the murderer than I was the day before. Of course, I would check on Spickard's alibi, but I knew I couldn't arrest him yet, if at all, and I had to talk to other people. We visited with Earl Spickard a few more minutes, tried to calm him before we left. I mentioned that we might come out sometime and let him show us where the fish were biting. He said he'd enjoy that.

+++

We excused ourselves and headed back to Lightning, relieved that that much was over. There was still a murderer to catch, whether that murderer was the man we'd just left, or someone else.

We walked through the trees a little faster. I thought of all the people I planned to talk to in order to check up on Spickard's alibi. I would talk to most of them. Maybe if one of them wasn't willing to give Spickard an alibi, that one might actually be our murderer.

+++

We continued to walk until we neared the road. I looked over at Lou and noticed the incredulous look on his face. I turned from looking at Lou to looking in the direction Lou had been looking, which caused my look to match his.

"Where's Lightning?"

My yellow VW beetle, my other trusted companion, was nowhere to be seen. It wasn't like Lightning to take off without me.

I didn't know what to do. It wasn't like a missing kid, where I could look behind each tree until I spotted him or her. Cars don't hide behind trees. Even intelligent cars like Lightning.

"What do we do, Cy?"

"I don't know. What do people usually do in a situation like this?"

"Call the police."

I refrained from uttering the obvious.

I stood there, thinking of my options. My pride and joy was missing. I wasn't thinking on all cylinders. Some of them were working, however. I knew that even though I'd become a stud on the Wii, there was no way Lou and I were in shape to walk to town.

Earl Spickard's place was closer than the house where Duck Spencer lived. I didn't notice on the way out if Spencer was home or not, but I knew the old man was. I also knew that Earl Spickard hadn't taken Lightning. He was with us the whole time. Well, not the whole time. But I doubted that he could have stolen Lightning, taken a roundabout path through the trees, and still beat us to his cabin, even if we were walking slowly.

I also knew that Spickard didn't have a phone, and Duck Spencer did. If I'd been thinking clearly, I would've gone to Duck Spencer's place, instead. If I'd done so, I'd found my trusted companion much quicker, but I wasn't thinking clearly, so I hollered, "Come on, Lou," and took off running as fast as I could to Spickard's cabin.

He was standing in the door as we came to a stop, out of breath.

"Why are you boys in such a gosh darn hurry? Oh, I get it. The facilities are out back."

I shook my head "no" that that wasn't it.

"Well, I don't expect you are wanting to fish so soon. Think of another question?"

By this time, I was starting to breathe normally again.

"Someone stole our car."

"You're kidding."

"I wish I were."

"Must be those Clough boys. Orneriest dadblamed boys. I've had to run 'em off from here from time to time. Live up in them hills somewhere. Meaner'n snakes."

"I suppose you boys need a ride to town. Got my boat out back. You boys are pretty good size boys. I'm not sure the boat would hold all of us, but I'd be glad to loan her to you as long as you bring her back in a couple of days."

I was not ready for another boat ride, but I figured riding in Spickard's boat was better than walking. Or was it? I looked at Lou. He wasn't happy with our choices, either. But then we didn't want Spickard to think we were afraid of riding in his boat.

"Okay, Mr. Spickard. But are you sure it will hold both of us?"

"There's only one way to find out. Come on, boys."

30

We arrived at the river and looked at the skimpy craft that would soon hold my body, but hopefully not my dead body. It looked a little better than the rowboat I was in before but was far from the cabin cruiser I hoped he had. And, the boat had more amenities than my previous craft. I was thankful for those amenities, even if all they were were two paddles. But I wasn't thankful for much else about my upcoming trip upstream.

Spickard gave us instructions on how to paddle, recommended that we start with one of us paddling on the left side and the other on the right, and then switch sides periodically. He refrained from laughing at how gingerly we stepped into his boat. In a few frantic seconds, both of us were seated, and while water didn't come pouring into the boat, the aluminum antique did set lower in the water than it did before we boarded. Spickard could see our consternation and shouted a few words of encouragement as he pushed us out into the flowing river and told us which direction to head.

I knew that Spickard was standing there watching us. I reprimanded Lou once for turning around to check. As soon as Lou realized we were out of Spickard's sight and hearing, he began.

235

"Row, row, row, your boat."

"I'll row your boat if you don't stop."

"I sure hope so, Cy. After all, isn't that what we're both supposed to be doing?"

I frowned at him and then realized that he couldn't see my frown.

"Say, Cy, did you ever see the movie *Titanic?*"

"No, and you didn't either."

"But I know the ship sank."

"Yeah, but that was a long time ago, and that ship was in a lot more water."

"And it was a lot bigger boat, too."

"That's enough, Lou."

"Just remember, Cy, I'm in front. That means I'll be on the lookout for icebergs, at least until dark. How many days do you think it will take us to get back?"

The thought of icebergs did little to improve the sweltering heat. August 1 was almost upon us. It seemed to get hotter every day. I seemed to get smellier every day. Well, at least the days I spent on the water. I was interrupted by Lou's most recent ejaculation.

"Land ahoy!"

"Lou, do you see anyone on the shore anywhere?"

"No."

"Remember that. And remember the guy in the back can swing his paddle better than the guy in front, allowing him to hit the guy in front."

"But if the guy in the back knocks out the guy in the front, the guy in the back has to do all the rowing."

"That might be the only thing saving you at this point."

"Yes, Your Majesty. Does that mean I'm in the galley and you're cracking the whip?"

"Absolutely!"

Lou shut up and I was able to hear the birds, what ones were out on that hot day. I wondered if most of them were buzzards and vultures. The whole experience had an Alfred

Hitchcock feel to it, which was okay if I were sitting in a recliner, watching, but not so good if I'm one of the two doofuses in a small boat. I was alone with my thoughts until an approaching land mass loomed just ahead.

I looked at Lou, who had stopped paddling and seemed to be in a battle with his face. Evidently, the circumstances had already begun to affect his brain. Mine, too. I'd begun to think of Lou as someone who could paddle, or, if not, ballast that must be thrown overboard to lighten my load.

"Lou, paddle, paddle, paddle."

"Sorry, Cy. A mosquito landed on my nose."

"Well, the next time it lands let it feast for a while."

"I'll send it your way next time."

"Listen, Lou, since you're in such a mood to talk, why don't we discuss the case?"

"What case?"

"You're testing my patience."

"Yes, Doctor. Okay, shoot."

"I've been thinking about doing just that."

"I meant with your mouth."

"Enough already. What do you think of what the old man had to say? Obviously, he's strong enough to shut that door, but he said he was with someone all the time he was at the school."

"So, you think they did it together?"

"Sort of a bizarre type of male bonding. I never thought of that. So, what do you think?"

"Unlike most of these people, he looked like he was telling the truth."

"That does it! I'll snap the cuffs on him when we return his boat."

"What if we don't make it back, Cy? Can you write out a note while you paddle this boat?"

"That reminds me, Lou. Did you ever get a paddling in school?"

"No."

"That's why you're so obstinate."

"Oh, Cy, you're just upset because neither of the two who mean the most to you is here with you."

"You think Jennifer has been kidnapped too?"

"It depends on how smart the guys are wherever she is. No other guy can have all of her, though. She's already given her heart to you. Say, Cy, where do you plan to put ashore?"

"I hear Tahiti is nice this time of year."

"A lot of places are nice this time of year, but where do you plan to take one giant step for mankind?"

"Depends on whether or not we see any cars in the school parking lot. If so, we'll stop there. If not, I guess we have no options except to go on and land just outside of town. I just know that I'm anxious to get there, find Lightning, and check old man Spickard's alibi."

My stomach growled. I kicked myself for forgetting to bring my morning snack again but then realized that even if we had, we wouldn't have taken it in Spickard's cabin with us. At any rate, hunger had set in. Surely, it was getting close to noon. But were we close to any place I might call civilization?

+++

I bit my tongue when Lou started singing *Paddlin' Madeleine Home*. Several more minutes passed, and then things started looking familiar. If I remembered correctly, the school was just around the next bend. If Walter Gillis was there, I'd ask him if Spickard left him at any time that night. Spickard didn't have a phone, and only a boat for transportation, so there wouldn't be any way he would've been able to let Gillis know he needed him to substantiate his story.

We rounded the bend and neared the school. My consternation dropped when I saw there were no cars or trucks in the parking lot.

"Well, Lou, it looks like we're in this thing for the long haul."

"At least we're not being charged by the mile. By the way, do you have any idea how many miles we've come?"

"I'd say over a hundred, give or take a few."

+++

We continued to paddle, sometimes in silence, sometimes in conversation. Once, when we both admitted to having aching arms and backs, we stopped paddling for a couple of minutes. I wanted to get out and stretch my legs, but doing so meant a whole afternoon of wet socks, and possibly wet everything.

Even though there were two of us, I noticed how much harder it was to row upstream than downstream. Of course, I never rowed downstream. I just went with the flow.

It must have been 2:00 or later when I heard the first noise of civilization. When we rounded the last bend, almost to town, and saw where some of those noises were coming from, I wanted to hide under the boat. There, waiting at the landing, were my friends and colleagues Lt. George Michaelson, medical examiner Frank Harris, and officers Heather Ambrose and Dan Davis. When they saw us, they broke into thunderous applause and high-pitched whistles.

+++

I looked up at the coagulated mass cheering us on. Well, cheering until we got close enough to hear what they had to say.

239

"From the looks of them, I'd say this must be steerage class."

"Which one's the coxswain anyway?"

"Isn't that the guy who doesn't row and runs his mouth telling everyone else to row?"

"That's right."

"Then it's the one in the back."

"Okay, okay, enough already. How did you guys know we were lost at sea?"

"A call came in that some guy who looked very much like a dumb cop had traded his toy car for a rowboat. Hmm! Looks like you traded up, Cy."

"I'll trade up you, George. Say, Frank, what are you doing here?"

"I got a call, too. Two behemoths on the brink of death were seen traveling upstream in a runaway canoe."

"Heather, Officer Davis, what are you two doing hanging out with all this riffraff?"

The two merely laughed.

"They weren't hanging out with riffraff until you two showed up. Show me that old rowing stroke again, Cy."

"So, the ticker-tape parade starts here. Any word on Lightning?"

"No storms expected before sometime next week."

"You guys had better hope that you never lose your job because you'll never make it at a comedy club. Now, how about my car?"

"Only that an insect resembling yours was seen heading toward Key West."

"I mean it."

"Yeah, yeah, no one's spotted it that I know of. Why? Did someone steal it?"

"I'm afraid so."

"I thought we got a call that said someone had seen it and it now has purple spots."

"I heard orange spots."

"Sounds bad. Looks like we'll have to put it in quarantine."

"You mean driving through a car wash won't do the trick."

"Okay, guys. I mean it. Lightning means a lot to me."

"More than I do?"

"Heather, dear, you're the only one here who might mean as much to me as my car. How about the three of us going off somewhere together?"

"You mean you, me, and Dan?"

"I mean you, me, and Lightning."

"How about him?" she asked, pointing at Lou.

"Lou. He's already got a car."

"And Dan? Weren't you mainly responsible for getting the two of us together?"

"Yeah, I'm sorry that didn't work out."

"Oh, it's working out great."

I turned and looked up at Officer Dan Davis just as his face turned to crimson.

"Go easy on him, Heather. He's not ready to see you in that cute little number I saw you in. Now, is anyone willing to help us out of the floating bathtub?"

George and Frank reached down and each took one of Lou's arms and hoisted him up onto the dock, then looked at me.

"What about him?" Frank asked George, as he pointed in my direction.

"Might as well. I'm all for ridding the river of as much pollution as possible."

As two arms reached down to pull me up I briefly thought of yanking them off the dock and into the river, but then I figured it would be hard for me to do that and not fall in with them, so I let them pull me up to the hard ground.

"I'm serious now, guys, have you heard anything about Lightning?"

"Sorry, Cy."

"Then how did you know that we were in a canoe?"

"Some kid called in said that someone had stolen old man Spickard's boat. When he described the two criminals as too big to be in that canoe, we knew it had to be the two of you. Actually, the kid said that he thought he'd seen those same two guys driving a little, yellow car down Thornapple River Road. We knew that the two of you were out that way working on those murders that took place at the high school, but we couldn't figure out why in the world you'd be in a rowboat. We thought maybe old Tweetie Pie had broken down. We knew that neither of you carries a phone, and we know that parts of that road are very remote. While none of us could see you in a rowboat, all of us could see you in a rowboat if hoofing it was your only other option. So, what happened to Tweetie Pie?"

"Her name is Lightning, and we left her at the dead-end of Flat Rock Road when we went to interrogate a suspect. When we went back, Lightning was gone. The suspect owned a boat, but, as you can see, it's not big enough for three. He agreed to loan it to us. By the way, we would've called, but the suspect doesn't have a phone."

"You say this guy is one of your suspects?"

"That's right."

"I'm surprised he didn't give you a boat that would sink as soon as you got to water that was over your head."

"Let's stop wasting time. We need to report Lightning being stolen before whoever took her gets out of the state. Whoever it is has already had enough time to get out of the county."

"Are you sure it was stolen, Cy?"

"You think Lightning wandered off on her own?"

"No, but I can't picture anyone other than the two of you who'd want to be caught dead in that thing, other than some college girl."

242

"Very funny! And I wouldn't want to be caught dead in Lightning, either. I wouldn't want to be caught dead anywhere, at least not for a while. Now, can we get this reported, and can someone give Lou and me a ride to his place?"

+++

We called in and reported Lightning missing. It was the first anyone downtown had heard of it. We were assured that Lightning would be easy to spot since there were few yellow VWs in Hilldale. George offered to drive us to Lou's place, but I asked Heather to take us instead. She informed me that she and Dan had come together and that Lou and I would have to ride in the back. I suggested that Lou could drive and she and I could ride in the back. About that time, Lou leaned over and whispered the name "Jennifer" in my ear.

+++

While I was worried about Lightning, I was also starved, since it was after 2:30 and we hadn't eaten anything since breakfast. I informed Heather of this and asked her if she could stop somewhere quick, so we could grab something.

She pulled in at the first place we came to, which wasn't any place I was familiar with, but I wasn't picky at that point. She and Dan got out the front and opened the back doors of the cruiser to let Lou and me out. The people inside the restaurant noticed this and seemed to fidget. Heather took all this in, too. I could tell that by what she said as soon as we entered the restaurant.

"Don't be alarmed, folks! They are merely escaped prisoners we caught trying to get away upriver. They

243

promised they wouldn't try anything if we let them come inside to eat."

"See," I said. "They even gave us our guns back."

At that point, a couple of parties got up to beat a hasty retreat. Even when Heather told them we were kidding and all of us were cops, many of the restaurant's patrons remained on edge.

+++

All the way to Lou's place my thoughts were about Lightning. Who could have stolen her? After all, as George said, out where we were is a very remote region. It couldn't have been Earl Spickard. There was no way he could've outrun us, driven Lightning off, and got back to his place before we did. And he didn't have time to do it before we talked to him. It had to be someone else, but who? The only other person who lived close to where we were was Duck Spencer. Why would he have stolen Lightning?

+++

Lou could tell that I was despondent over Lightning's disappearance, so, when Heather and Dan dropped us off, he invited me inside so he could cheer me up. He tried to get me on the Wii, but I wasn't in the mood. He offered to take me out looking for Lightning, but I figured that it wouldn't do any good. Besides, I had no idea where to look, and all officers had been alerted as to Lightning's disappearance, and her license plate number. I told him that if we didn't hear anything by the next morning, we'd drive out to where we left her and see if anyone out that way saw someone in a yellow VW. We would kill two birds with one stone. While we were out that way, we planned to check with Duck Spencer and Walter Gillis to see if either of them saw Lightning. Then I remembered that no one was at the school when we floated by, so, more than likely, Walter Gillis wasn't a witness to anything.

+++

I went home and tried to read, but I couldn't concentrate, so I did what I did best. I lay down and took a nap. I was fine until I woke up again and remembered the circumstances.

I was a basket case for the rest of the day and night. I tried to focus on the case, but my mind kept wandering back to Lightning. Finally, it came time to go to bed. Before I retired for the night I called downtown to see if they'd heard anything about my car. Nothing.

31

I woke up the next morning and a few seconds later I remembered my dilemma. I sprang from the bed and hurried to the phone. Still no word on Lightning. Dejectedly, I went about my routine, but my heart wasn't in it. After I'd checked everything off my list and figured we'd arrived at a decent hour, I called Lou and told him the bad news.

"Maybe something will turn up today, Cy. You still want to drive out in the country and talk to Spencer?"

"Life goes on, my friend. Maybe if I'm busy, things will get better."

"Well, let me give you a chance to be busy while I'm on my way to pick you up. I have today's message. It's 'Verbal Kint'."

"Verbal Kent. Who or what's verbal kent?"

"Do I look like Google to you?"

"No, Google is smarter."

"If you weren't under duress, Cy, I might have a comeback to that."

I knew it wouldn't do me any good to ask Lou how to spell Verbal Kint because God never writes down his messages for Lou. And that's a good thing because the one guy God did write a message down for died that same day.

I prefer my messages verbally. I had to laugh. Verbal Kint. Verbal messages. Was there a connection?

I hurried to the computer, typed in Verbal Kent. I soon found out that there was a Verbal Kent, but there was also a Verbal Kint. I read about both. I was still studying them when Lou pulled up. I went to the door and motioned for Lou to come in and help me decide which one of these guys was our guy.

"What's wrong, Cy?"

"Nothing, Lou. It's just that there are two Verbal Kents, of some spelling or another. I wanted you to look them over and see which one you think is our clue."

"So, you think that a whole brain is better than a half?"

"Something like that."

Lou looked over the first guy, the one spelled with an "e". Chicago, music, and emcee. We didn't see what any of those had to do with our case. So, I clicked on the second guy.

"I knew I'd heard that name somewhere, Cy. One night Thelma Lou and I were alone and she wanted to rent a movie. My being a cop and all, we were fascinated by the title *The Usual Suspects*. This guy Verbal Kint is one of the characters in that movie."

"You remember a character from a movie?"

"Well, he was kind of the Scarlett O'Hara of the movie."

"Since you said 'he', I can't see the connection to Scarlett O'Hara. Do you mean he made his own clothes out of drapes?"

"No, I mean his character is the one who sticks with you. The best I can remember, he was a witness to something. At least, I remember the cops were interrogating him. Supposedly, he had some disease and walked with a limp. Actually, that wasn't true, and he was really the bad guy."

My eyes lit up.

247

"So, are you telling me that the guy who walks with the limp is the bad guy?"

"He is in the movie. I don't know who the bad guy is in our case."

"I think this is the Verbal Kint we want, and I know which one of our suspects walks with a limp, Jim Bob Gibbons."

Lou and I wondered if Jim Bob Gibbons was our murderer, or if there was something to the clue we were missing.

We realized that we were getting nowhere fast, or was it slowly. At any rate, we left my place and headed toward Flat Rock Road, both to look for tire tracks and to check on Earl Spickard's alibi.

+++

Since Lou was driving for a change, I got to look at the scenery. I have always enjoyed a drive in the country, although I preferred different circumstances than the ones that surrounded me that day. Lou turned off the main road out of town onto Thornapple River Road. He drove a while until I spotted the school up ahead on the right.

"Pull in here, Lou."

While there were no vehicles in the parking lot when we passed the school the day before, there were three vehicles in the parking lot that day. I recognized one of those as Walter Gillis's truck.

Lou pulled in and parked away from the other vehicles. I hoped that whoever had stolen Lightning didn't swoop down and take our last mode of transportation. We decided to chance it. Well, I decided to chance it. I was hoping Lou never gave it a thought. I knew what he thought of his red, classic, 1957 Chevy. He loved that thing as much as I loved Lightning, always kept it polished.

I didn't expect to be in the school long. We jogged up the steps and into the school. Walter Gillis' door was closed. I knocked, but no one answered. As we turned away, a woman popped around the corner, curious as to who was knocking at the janitor's door.

"Hi, I'm Lt. Dekker. This is Sgt. Murdock. We're the ones investigating the bodies found here at the school. Walter Gillis found those bodies, and we have another question for him."

"Oh, sure, Lieutenant. Walter is upstairs cleaning classrooms. I'm not sure which room he's in, but you shouldn't have any trouble finding him."

I thanked her and Lou and I took off for the steps. We climbed them in better time than I'd remembered climbing steps in a while, and looked down the hall. I heard a faint noise, but couldn't tell which room it was coming from. We walked past all the closed doors until we found an open one. We walked in and spotted the janitor moving desks. He looked up and saw us.

"Oh, hi, Lieutenant, what brings you back?"

"As a matter of fact, it's the sergeant's car this time, which reminds me. Were you here at the school yesterday?"

"No, with school starting next week, yesterday was my last day off for a while. Well, other than weekends. The teachers will be back Monday. That's means I have to get all these here rooms cleaned by Friday. The students come back next Wednesday."

"Well, I guess I just have one question for you, about the night of the reunion. What can you tell me about Earl Spickard after he got here that night?"

He smiled.

"Well, old Earl is the only one I can tell you about, except for myself. He was with me the whole time."

"So tell me your whereabouts after he got here."

249

"Well, I was in the restroom when somebody comes in. I didn't know at first it was my friend Earl. As a matter of fact, I was surprised to see him. Anyway, Earl took a seat in the next stall, and we ended up coming out at the same time. That's the first I knowed it was him. Before, I figured it was one of them guys from the reunion. I was so glad to see Earl. We hadn't seen each other in a while. We slapped each other on the back, and I asked him what in tarnation he was doing at the school. He told me about bringing some guy there in his boat. When I found out he didn't have to hang out with the guy that come with him, I invited him to my office, his old office, to catch up on things. He was with me 'til he left."

"And were you in the office the whole time?"

"No, Lieutenant, I thought I told you he wanted to walk the halls of the school again."

"How long was this after he arrived?"

"Oh, I don't know, maybe a half-hour, forty-five minutes. I checked with that woman in charge of the reunion to make sure everything was okay before we took off, and let her know we was going in case she needed me. I might've told you that things got a little rowdy a couple of times earlier in the night. That guy who got killed was responsible for the ruckus."

"At any time that night, did you see someone headed for the kitchen, or coming out of the kitchen?"

"I was in my office most of the time. I didn't see much of nothing, but I heered a couple of things, but all that stuff was before Earl and that other guy got here."

I thanked Gillis for his time and wished him luck getting everything ready for the start of school.

"Oh, I'll get 'er done all right, otherwise I'll have to come back this weekend and do it, 'cause it needs to be done before Monday. Well, this here second floor does. The other stuff I can do on Monday and Tuesday."

32

Lou and I walked out the door. I looked quickly to see if Lou's car was still there. It was. Evidently, his car isn't as desirable as Lightning. A tear came to my eye as I thought about my companion. Lou broke the silence.

"What do you think, Cy?"

"About what?"

"Well, if he's telling the truth, there's no way the retired janitor could have done it unless they did it together."

"I'm just wondering why no one saw Conkwright and Mrs. Spencer come back into the school."

"Well, I think that part is obvious. When they came back in they came in through the kitchen door, and they never made it past the kitchen. I doubt if they ever intended to go anywhere but the kitchen. Maybe they went to the freezer to get some ice for what they were drinking, or for Conkwright's face. Remember, he had lacerations on his face when the guys threw him out. Might have had some swelling, too."

"I think you might be right there, Lou. Remember, there were at least a couple of people in that kitchen that we know of."

"Yeah, the two that inherited."

"Yeah, and somebody said that they saw Duck Spencer coming out of there. I'd say that whoever shut that freezer door just missed getting caught, with all the traffic that was in and out of the cafeteria, up and down the hall."

+++

Lou turned right out of the school parking lot and headed on out Thornapple Road. He continued down the road until he came to the turnoff for Flat Rock Road. He turned left and we headed up the rollercoaster hill until the road leveled out. At least we didn't start dropping when we got to the top.

I knew we were getting close to Duck Spencer's place when I heard an exclamation come out of Lou's mouth. I looked ahead and saw what he saw. There, off in the distance, was a yellow spot. From what I could tell, the spot was on the road. As we drew closer, the spot began to look familiar, and my seatbelt was the only thing that kept me from jumping out of my seat.

There, facing me, in the other lane of traffic, one hundred feet or so past the entrance to Spencer's place, sat Lightning. Lou pulled up past Spencer's driveway and stopped. I'm not sure if I hopped out before or after he stopped, but it was close.

I expected Lightning to start tooting her horn at me, but the closer I got, the more I could see the shame she felt. Her headlights seemed to look down as if she was embarrassed. Lightning had never been violated before and didn't know how to handle it.

I ran up beside her, yanked on the door. It was locked. Whoever had driven her there relocked the door when they left. I took out my key and opened the door. The stench was too much for me. Cigarette smoke and far worse odors wafted from Lightning. I looked her over and then walked all the way around her outside. Other than the smell she had had to endure, I could see nothing else that would tell someone that she had had a frightening experience.

I got in long enough to see if she would start. She started right up as if nothing had happened. The smell was too much for me, so I got out quickly, told Lightning I'd be back in a few minutes. I noticed that Lou had remained in his car. He knew that Lightning and I needed a little time alone.

As soon as I got out, I walked toward Lou's car. As I walked, I looked over at Duck Spencer's place. His truck was there, so he was probably home. I would check to see what he knew of this. I walked around to the passenger side of Lou's car and opened the door. I got in and told Lou what I had in mind. He shifted his car into reverse and backed it up until he had passed Spencer's driveway. Then, he drove up and parked behind Spencer's truck. Spencer was just coming out of his garage when he heard us.

"Now this is a fine set of wheels. Nothing like that one you drove out here the other day, Lieutenant. By the way, did you see there's one like yours parked out on the road?"

"That one is mine, Mr. Spencer. What do you know about how it got there?"

"As a matter of fact, I know quite a bit. I was out bush hogging my property out near the road yesterday when I seen this little car like yours coming down the road. It surprised me to see any kinda car comin' down the road from that direction, 'cause nobody lives down there except Earl Spickard, and he ain't got no car. Anyways, right after I seen 'em, they seen me. They stopped that car so fast and took off running down the road back the way they come from. It was them Clough boys. Meaner'n snakes, them boys is. Well, I knowed that car wasn't theirs, but since I didn't see no one drive it past my house on the way to Earl's place, I had no idea it was yours. I went up to check on it, locked it up, figured the owner would miss it and come 'long shortly. I was out there another hour and still, no one

253

come along. I was gonna call and report it this afternoon if nobody claimed it by then."

"You say it was some boys named Clough."

"That's right. Ever' now and again, they come out of them hills and cause trouble. They live back in there somewhere," he said, as he pointed across the road and down. "People's gone in looking for 'em before, but they never found 'em. I ain't sure if they's in this county or the next 'en."

I wondered if it would do any good to try to find them and prosecute. Mr. Spencer let me use his phone and I called downtown and had them send out a print crew just in case. I would use some of the time we had to wait on them to ask Spencer some questions.

"Mr. Spencer, I have a question about the night of the reunion."

"Like I told you before, I weren't there long."

"That's okay. Just tell me this. You said that Earl Spickard took you there in his boat. Did you go into the school together?"

"No, I ran on ahead. He come in a minute or two later."

"You came to the kitchen door first. Why didn't you use it?"

"I figured it was locked. I figured the front door was the only one unlocked."

"So, you didn't try the kitchen door?"

He looked at me like I was crazy.

"Did you notice if it was shut?"

"Of course, it was shut. If it was open, I would've gone in that way."

"So, what happened when you walked into the school?"

"George was standing there, leaning against the cafeteria door. I'd called him and told him we was almost there."

"And what about Mr. Spickard? Did he come in and join you?"

"Naw, I seen him walk in, out of the corner of my eye. He motioned to me that he was going to the restroom."

"And did you see if he stopped somewhere on the way to the restroom?"

"Well, my mind was on my wife and where she might be, but I'm pretty sure he went on in the restroom. Anyways, he come out of there a couple of minutes later, and there was this here other guy with him. I found out that the other guy was the janitor who took his place when he retired."

"Did you see Mr. Spickard any time after that that night?"

"Yep. I stopped off and told him I had a way home. Course, when we was running back and forth trying to find my wife, I heard the two of 'em in the janitor's cubbyhole talking."

Well, two people had backed up Earl Spickard's alibi. Unless someone was lying, I couldn't see where the old man would have had an opportunity to lock the freezer door.

Just as I was about to end our conversation, I thought of Lightning.

"Oh, Mr. Spencer, one other thing. Do you have any air freshener?"

The look on his face said it all. Spencer was not the type of person to use an air freshener.

I thanked Spencer for his time and Lou and I turned to leave.

+++

It was about a quarter of a mile from Spencer's house to where Lightning was parked. Lou drove back toward the road and we sat at the end of the driveway until the print crew arrived. A half-hour or so later, they had finished and had lifted several prints, not all of them mine or Lou's.

255

+++

The print crew drove off and Lou and I talked about what was next. I knew what was next for me. Lightning needed a bath, a good scrubbing, inside and out. I told Lou I needed to take Lightning to the car wash and would call him when I got home. There were a few other people I wanted to check with, just in case someone saw Earl Spickard where he shouldn't have been.

"Cy, why don't you go first on the way to town? That way, if something happens on the way back in you won't be stranded."

33

Lightning received a good scrubbing, inside and out, including washing behind her taillights, and the car wash sprayed something inside to take the smell out of the air. I wasn't too crazy about the smell, but it was better than what was there before.

+++

Anyone else I needed to talk to that day wouldn't be home until after 5:00. It was time to head home, take a nap, and maybe read for a few minutes.

+++

As I drove to pick up Lou so that we could question people who were at the reunion about the retired janitor's nocturnal wanderings or lack thereof, I hoped that we could soon file this case in the finished drawer.

It was almost 5:30 when I pulled up in front of Lou's apartment building. He was watching for me, and bounced down the walkway toward Lightning. I noticed that he patted Lightning as he rounded her front on his way to get in.

257

"So, Lou, are you ready to wrap this up?"

"A lot more eager than I am to wrap your Christmas presents. Of course, then, as you know, most of the time I use bags."

"And maybe we are well on our way to bagging someone in this case."

"Who do you want to bag, Cy?"

"At this point, I'll take almost anybody."

It didn't take us long to get to Rose Ellen Calvert's house, and as we pulled up we saw her outside watering her flowers. She turned as we shut Lightning's doors, and the look she gave me made me think I had an overdue book.

"Hello, Miss Calvert. Good to see you again."

"I wish I could say the same, Lieutenant. What do you want this time? You have a witness who saw me standing over the deceased?"

"I was hoping you could be my witness."

"Oh? In what way?"

"I want to know what you saw Earl Spickard doing on the night of the reunion."

"That's the old janitor? Right?"

I nodded that it was.

"I saw him standing, but he wasn't standing over any bodies."

"Did you at any time see him by himself, in the hall, or any of the rooms of the school?"

"I saw him only once, and that time he was with the current janitor. There were other people around, too."

"Did you see anyone heading toward the stairs leading to the second floor?"

"Only when we were up there before dinner."

"What about the kitchen?"

"Only what I've already told you. I think Jim Bob Gibbons headed in there just after I headed out. At least, he looked in the kitchen. Whether or not he spent any time in there I couldn't tell you. I have no idea if he used the kitchen door to leave the school. He's the only one I can remember seeing in the kitchen, but the whole thing is starting to get a little fuzzy."

I thanked her for her time. I think she was relieved to get off so easily, and she never mentioned anything about Lou.

+++

Trips to the Korleins, Justices, and Jim Bob Gibbons didn't give me any incriminating evidence against Earl Spickard. Those who saw him at all that night, and most people saw him at least once, never saw him by himself.

+++

"You know, Lou, it would really help if we knew when those two were locked inside the freezer."

"Especially if they were locked in there before Duck Spencer and Earl Spickard got there."

"Right! The best we have to go on is what Rose Ellen Calvert said. She saw them heading toward the kitchen door a few minutes before Spencer got there. What if they stumbled around outside long enough that Spencer saw them heading to the kitchen?"

"But if he saw them, wouldn't old man Spickard have seen them, too?"

"You would think. Unless he was too busy tying up his rowboat."

"But even if he was, George Justice said he saw Spencer come in through the front door. That means Spencer would have had to have gone back out the kitchen door, and I would think that by that time Spickard would have seen him."

"I wonder if someone, Spickard or otherwise, saw someone go in the kitchen and isn't telling us. Everyone hated Conkwright. Could it be that someone saw the whole thing or suspected what happened and is keeping quiet? Or did someone do it, and then confess what he or she did to someone else?"

"I don't know. I think at least two of our suspects are lying about something or other, but I'm not sure they are lying about that. Someone would have to be awfully good not to have been the murderer, but still be able to lie in order to protect someone else."

+++

It was late when we finished questioning all those involved. I didn't want to go home and fix something to eat. Lou didn't either. So, we opted to cheat, sort of. We stopped off at a new pizza joint that opened recently, A Slice of the Pie, in order to find out if they were any good. Lou and I split a thin, medium pizza, with sausage, pepperoni, green peppers, black olives, and onions, and between the two of us, we ate only half. We had them box up the rest of it so that we could have it the next day for either lunch or supper. Surely, two pieces of thin-crust pizza each wouldn't cause us to go off the wagon.

+++

It felt good to be able to drop Lou off at his place again. I was sure that Lightning had some after-effects of what had happened, but she was a trooper and was handling it as well as could be expected.

I returned to my place, grateful that my next-door neighbor had not invaded my space since she was arrested. I liked being able to enter my house by whichever door suited me and to do it at whatever pace I wanted.

I was tired when I got home, but I wasn't ready to fall into bed. It had been a few weeks since I had gotten together with my friends from *Hogan's Heroes*. I felt that a few weeks were long enough. I put the DVD in, sat back in my recliner, and watched three episodes of Hogan getting the best of Sgt. Schultz and Col. Klink. When I ejected the DVD and turned off my TV, I had the feeling I always have after watching some classic comedy TV shows. They don't make them like they used to. At least modern technology allows me to go back in time anytime I want.

+++

I was trying to decide whether or not to go to bed when the phone rang.

"I didn't wake you, did I, Cy?"

"If you had, it would have been more than all right. So, how's my Jennifer?"

"Missing her Cy."

"That's good to know. I guess you know the feeling is mutual."

"So what were you doing, if I may ask?"

"Would you believe sitting in front of the computer looking at your picture?"

"No."

"Okay, I was unwinding."

"And how were you doing that?"

"*Hogan's Heroes.*"

I heard a chuckle on the other end of the phone.

"I went back farther than that yesterday, Cy. I found an old episode of *The Danny Thomas Show*. True, it was on long before I was born, but I saw a few episodes years ago and liked them, particularly the ones where someone is getting the best of Danny. So, are you still working on the same case?"

"That's why I needed to unwind. I had another busy day today. I'm hoping we can put an end to this soon."

"Well, I'll let you go get ready for tomorrow. I just wanted to hear the sound of your voice."

"That's not good enough for me. I'd rather see your smile."

"Well, you can always go to Facebook. Since the charade is over, I changed the picture back to my real one. As a matter of fact, I have several pictures of me on there."

"Any bikini shots?"

"One. I was two at the time."

This time it was my turn to laugh. We said goodbye, and I went to bed with a smile on my face.

34

Like the week before, that week seemed to be speeding by, speeding by with no conclusion. I didn't want to have to go through another weekend on the same case. After breakfast, I took my frustrations out on the Wii Fit board without breaking it. Even inside an air-conditioned house, the July morning heat is enough to make me sweat when I exercise. Actually, July had gone and August had replaced it, without my realizing it.

I don't like for my body to smell, so after sitting for five minutes, relaxing, I hurried to the shower, just in case Jennifer paid me a surprise visit. My workout and shower hadn't eliminated all my frustrations, so I dressed and sat down to spend time alone with God. I read my devotionals and I prayed. Once again I prayed for the wisdom, strength, courage, and desire of God's will. When I'd finished, I still had no idea what course of action we were to take that day, but I felt calmer about the whole ordeal. I called Lou and told him that I was on my way to pick him up. He answered by telling me that if that was the case he was glad he'd lost a lot of weight. At least he still had his sense of humor.

+++

Lou opened the car door, smiled, and sat down.

"Cy, a friend is closer than a brother."

"Why thank you, Lou. I didn't know you felt that way."

"I don't. Well, maybe I do. But I was letting you know what God thinks."

"So, you think God thinks of me as His brother?"

"Somehow, I don't think so, Cy. More like a son. An imperfect son."

"Lou, let's refrain from throwing in all the adjectives."

"I was just giving you our message of the day."

"So this friend-brother thing doesn't have to do with me or you. It's one of our suspects."

"From the way the thing is worded, I'd say two of our suspects, Cy."

"Any idea which two, Lou?"

He gave me the look he always gives me when I asked him to interpret the clue of the day.

"Well, let's see who we can eliminate. Well, I think Rose Ellen Calvert is out. I don't see her having any friends. At least not any friends that we've met, and I think we should limit this to the people we've met. I tell you what, Lou. Let's mull."

He nodded, and we began our period of silence. I didn't care how many people strolled by walking their dogs, and how stupid we looked sitting there in front of God and everybody with pensive looks on our faces. Actually, it didn't take long. A couple of minutes later, a light bulb went off in my head. Yes, it was possible. It wasn't anyone I'd considered before, but it was possible. I hoped I was wrong, but I did want to solve the case and solve it as soon as I could.

"Lou, I've got an idea. I think it's time to bluff. I'm going to see someone who definitely doesn't fit the role of a murderer, but is still someone who might allow us to put an end to the festivities."

"I'm all for that, Cy."

+++

I smiled at the little old lady who had stopped to look at us, and then started the car, and took off. We were on our way back to the country.

A few minutes later, I pulled into the school parking lot. Walter Gillis' truck was there, as were a few cars.

I jumped out of the car and headed for the school. I looked inside Gillis's office, but he wasn't there. I needed to use the facilities, so I opted to do so before I hunted for Gillis. No woman hurried around the corner to see if she could help us, and I encountered no one on the way to the men's restroom.

As I came out, I glanced across the hall to the right. It was the first time I noticed that if you moved a couple of steps to the right, you could see into the kitchen from the restroom. I made a note of that. I was sure that Gillis had heard and seen someone in that kitchen, on his way to the restroom that night.

We walked down the hall until the same woman we'd seen the other day stuck her head out of a doorway.

"Here to see Walter again?"

"That's right."

"He's on break. I think he stepped out back."

Lou and I retraced our footsteps, walked out the front door and around the school until we arrived at the back, not far from the riverbank, and the tree root Lou fell over on the day I was kidnapped by that rowboat. There, several feet away, seated on the grass in the shade, we found Walter Gillis.

"Back again so soon, Lieutenant. I can't think of any way I can help you."

"Oh, I think you're being modest, Mr. Gillis. I think you could have helped us from the beginning. Tell us about the night of the reunion. I believe you said you went to the restroom that night and that was where you first saw your good friend Earl Spickard."

"That's right. Earl come in while I was in there. We left at the same time."

"And you were seen together by several members of the search party. That's not the part I want to cover. I want to know about before you went to the restroom."

"I was in my office before I went to the restroom. I was there pretty much the whole time."

"I don't dispute that either, Mr. Gillis. But I want to know about just before you went into the restroom. You heard a noise, didn't you? Tell me, who did you see in the kitchen?"

For the first time, the man seemed unnerved.

"Why, uh, no one."

"Let's digress for a moment, Mr. Gillis. Tell me about what you know about Sarah Jane Spickard."

"Sarah Jane Spickard. Was that Earl's mother?"

"Come on, Mr. Gillis. You can do better than that. I'll tell you what. I'll tell the story. You can just tell me if I get anything wrong. You and Earl Spickard got to be good friends the year you worked together. How good? Good enough that you were one of the few people, and maybe the only person, that Earl Spickard told about having a daughter. Not only did he tell you he had a daughter, but he told you all the gory details about how he came to lose that daughter. He talked about her from time to time, and evidently, he talked enough about her that not only did you remember her name, but you remembered the name of the man who took her life. It must have been hard on you that night when you were sitting in your office and you overheard someone mention the name Jimmy Conkwright, and that Conkwright, the man who took your friend's daughter's life, was there that night, in the school.

266

"Later, you realized that everyone there hated Conkwright almost as much as your friend Earl hated him. And by listening, you realized that the drunk who took one young woman's life was drunk again and running around with another man's wife. Maybe you'd decided to stay out of it, but when you headed to the restroom and heard a noise coming from the kitchen, the kitchen where no one was supposed to be, you were curious as to who was in there. I'm sure you only planned to run that someone off, but then either you saw Conkwright go into the freezer, or you saw the freezer door open and was curious as to who was inside. When you saw Conkwright, you shut and locked the door. Maybe you saw the woman with him. Maybe you didn't. Maybe at first, you planned to let them out after a while. Why don't you take up from here? Tell me if I missed anything."

"That's quite a story you got there, Lieutenant. How long did it take you to make it up?"

"Actually it took up until now to realize how two people came to be locked in the freezer."

"Lieutenant, I didn't even know them people."

"Oh, from all the conversations you and Earl Spickard had, it must have seemed like you knew one of them. And knew him well enough to hate him for what he did to Earl's daughter, and to Earl. Maybe I should talk to Earl, see what he can tell me about it?"

"He don't know nothing about this. I mean, if it happened like you say."

"So, you didn't tell him the favor you did for him?"

"Lieutenant, you go tellin' this tale and I'll deny it."

"Mr. Gillis, Walter, I understand how you felt. Who knows? I might have done the same thing myself if I were in your shoes. You like Earl Spickard a lot, don't you?"

"The best friend I ever had."

"I'm sorry, Walter, but I have to let my superiors know about this."

267

"Like I said, accuse me of it and I'll deny it ever happened."

"Walter, I don't know what's going to come of this. Under the circumstances, you might get off with a lesser sentence, but I have to report it. What you did was wrong."

He looked at me with tears in his eyes.

"I'm not saying who did it or didn't do it, but I'm not so sure that it was wrong. That varmint deserved what he got, and from what I heard, that woman with him wasn't no saint, neither."

"That doesn't matter. There are laws against taking someone's life."

"I'd say that whoever done it just saw a door open and shut and locked it. I don't think nobody tried to murder nobody."

35

"So, Cy, what're you going to do?"

"Just what I told him. I can't be judge and jury here. I'm going to tell the chief just what we know and let him and the DA get their heads together and decide where we go from here."

"But you got a confession, sort of. I mean he did slip up enough that we know he's our man."

"And I don't think that will mean a lot in a court of law, but then I'm not the lawyer, the DA is. We'll just tell them what we know and let them decide."

"You know, Cy, in a way I feel sorry for the guy. He didn't even know these people."

"You know, Lou, sometimes right and wrong suck."

+++

We headed back to town, to the place that we rarely go, and have no desire to go to any more than we do. Police headquarters.

While Hilldale is larger than many towns in our state, it's not a large city, and our police department isn't a large one. But unlike some small towns, we are large enough that we have two full-time homicide detectives. Well, at least we used to, even though there were lots of times when we had no murders to investigate.

We parked in the lot and headed inside and back to the Chief's office.

"Is he in?"

"He is. Just a second and let me see if he has a minute."

"Tell him it's important."

"I figured that, Cy. We all know that you don't come here to have a good time."

A few seconds later, the Chief's secretary returned and motioned for us to go on in.

"Cy, Lou. Good to see you. I assume this has to do with the case you've been working on."

"That's right."

I spent the next ten minutes filling the Chief in on what had transpired over the last couple of weeks, and as best I could, a verbatim account of what had happened that morning. He whistled at the end.

"I guess the best thing to do at this point is to call the DA in. I'll try to get him in here this afternoon. Call me back around 1:00. If he's free, if he's not in court, I want you to tell him exactly what you told me."

It wasn't what I wanted to hear, but it was exactly what I expected. I could tell that, once again, Lou was glad I was the spokesman for our duo.

+++

There was no reason to linger there. The Chief excused us and we beat a hasty retreat to Lightning.

"So, what do we do now, Cy?"

"Well, it's just a little after 11:00. What say we hang out at my house? Remember, we have half of a pizza there with our names on it."

"Yeah, and the best thing is that after eating it last night when I weighed this morning I hadn't gained any weight."

"Me, either, Lou. It's okay to cheat every now and then. What's not okay is to revert back to the way we were."

Lou smiled.

"What's so funny, Lou?"

"I never thought I'd hear you say that, Cy?"

"Me, either, Lou. Me, either."

+++

Having leftover pizza was new to me. Because of the places Lou and I hung out, we seldom ate pizza, although we like it. But wherever we hung out, we seldom had leftover anything.

"You know, Cy, there's not a lot of drop off from the way this thing tasted last night and the way it tastes today."

"That's the way I feel, Lou. However, I wonder how much of that is how it tastes and how much of it is that we're eating something that most people would consider taboo on a diet."

"We're not really on a diet, Cy. This is a lifestyle change. Whether we change what we're eating or not, we're definitely changing how much we eat of whatever it is we're eating."

+++

Right at 1:00, the phone rang. I looked at my watch, figured it was someone from downtown. It was. We were to meet the DA in the Chief's office at 2:00.

It would take us only a few minutes to get downtown from my place, so we sat around for a few more minutes, then looked in the mirror to make sure we looked presentable. Considering who we were, I thought we looked pretty good.

+++

"Cy, Lou, I think you know the DA. I want you to tell him everything you told me this morning."

I tried to repeat everything just as I told it to the Chief. Since the Chief didn't interrupt, I figured I must have done a good job.

"So, Lt. Dekker, tell me. What's your gut feeling? Do you think we have a chance of cracking this guy?"

"My gut feeling is no, and I don't think we're going to pick up any witnesses against him. One of the two deceased was hated by everyone who knew him. The other one was merely tolerated by most, but I haven't found anyone who would say that she had impeccable character. Maybe the dead woman's husband mourns her a little, but he's not so broken up about this that he'd be willing to testify about anyone if he did know the facts. At least that's my opinion."

"I'll tell you what. Give me the weekend to think about this. By the first of the week, I'll have a feel for whether or not I think we should proceed."

Lou and I were dismissed, and the Chief and the DA waited until Lou had closed the door to continue their conversation.

Once we were outside, Lou popped the question.

"So, what are we going to do now, Cy?"

"Well, you heard the DA. It doesn't look like we have anything else to do before Monday, if then. I don't know about you, but I have a book at my house that's calling me."

"I think I know the one you mean. I think its twin will be calling me, as soon as I unlock my door."

"Just in case, it will probably be good to hang out at home until we know any more."

"I've got no problem with that."

Little did I know, but it was a good thing that I hadn't planned on going anywhere the next day. The case might be nearing completion in some form or another, but that didn't mean our work was over.

+++

I unlocked my door, stepped inside the house, and looked at my watch. It was not quite 3:00. I had grown fond of the retired aspect of semi-retirement, and I missed getting to be lazy every day. Between working out and working outside, in the real world, I was a little more tired than usual, so I opted to take a nap before picking up my book.

+++

While I wasn't sure about the final outcome of the case, I felt that I'd done all I could and that one way or another, my work on the case was at or was almost at an end. Because of that, I felt relief, and I sat down to read with a smile on my face.

For years, I never read. It had been only a couple of years or so since Lou and I opted to take up a hobby of reading. When we retired, semi-retired, or whatever you want to call it, we wanted something fun to occupy our time without exerting much energy to have this fun. One of us came up with the idea of reading about fictional characters who did what we did each day, or at least each time someone committed a murder in or around Hilldale. While solving the murder before getting to the end of the book is the most fun thing about reading murder mysteries, another fun thing is reading different authors, who have various types of sleuths with many different personalities. When the murderers of Hilldale are chilling,

273

which means they aren't causing problems for the two of us, Lou and I can read four or five mysteries over a two week period. While both Lou and I have shelled out a lot of money on books in the last couple of years, both of us think that buying books is one of the best values for our entertainment dollar.

+++

I had no problem finishing my book that night. If things worked out right, I figured before the weekend was over I could read another book or two. I was pretty sure that Lou would finish reading the book, too, so sometime the next day I planned to call him to see what he thought of the book. In the meantime, I would excel at something I'd mastered over the years, being lazy.

36

I awoke the next morning, realized that I had nothing I had to do that day, and contemplated staying in bed, but the new me wouldn't let me. I sprang from the bed in a manner I wouldn't have attempted three weeks before and greeted the world. I fixed and ate breakfast, Wiied with newfound vigor, and relished the time I spent with God.

I planned my day. My only pressing engagement was that I needed to change my calendar from July to August. With my busy schedule, I'd forgotten to do so. I dreaded doing that each month. I was always afraid I'd tear the place where the hole was, and it had been years since I'd seen any of those sticky reinforcements I used in my notebook in high school. I completed that task in record time and stood and looked at the new calendar picture for a couple of minutes. I'd always wondered why calendar companies didn't put snowy scenes on their summer month pictures and bright sunshiny pictures when we had to endure six months of winter. But then I realized that they'd never gone along with my suggestion of having winter start on December 1, when it should begin.

I had nowhere to which I had to rush, so I sat down in front of the computer, and visited my new friend Google. I found an article titled *Six Powerful Health-Boosting*

Foods and scanned the list to see if I could stomach any of them. In a matter of seconds, I realized that I was already eating four of those six foods; tomatoes, kale and spinach, blueberries, and sweet potatoes, and liked one of the other two, walnuts. I looked at the last one, pomegranates. I wasn't sure what they were, but I suspected they were something closely related to figs or dates, something else I wasn't sure if I had eaten.

I studied the list. I'd been eating walnuts on my ice cream sundaes for quite a while, but I was quite surprised I had managed to choke down some of those others, particularly kale. I was about to Google pomegranates, to see what they were when the phone rang. I figured it was Lou, calling me to see if I had finished the book. I figured wrong.

+++

"Lt. Dekker, I have a message for you."

I assumed that the message was from the DA and had to do with whether or not they planned to prosecute Walter Gillis. Again, I assumed wrong.

"Lt. Dekker, a man called here this morning. An Earl Spickard. He wants you to come to his place. He says it's urgent. It has to do with those murders you've been working on."

"Does the Chief know about this call?"

"The Chief is the one he insisted on talking to. At first, the man wanted to talk to you, but when we told him that wasn't possible, he insisted on talking to the Chief. That was about ten minutes ago. Anyway, the Chief wants you and Sgt. Murdock to go out there as soon as possible, and to report to him as soon as you return. Mr. Spickard wouldn't tell the Chief what he wanted with you, just that it was very important, and that it has to do with the deaths at the high school."

"I'll get right on it."

My day of leisure was no more. I couldn't figure out what old man Spickard wanted. I didn't even know he had a phone. I had one though, and I used it to call Lou to let him know that he too was no longer a man of leisure.

"I'll be ready when you get here, Cy. I was going to call you in a few minutes anyway, to make sure you finished your book. We can talk about that on our way out to the country."

+++

I made a clean getaway, sort of. I walked out the door and saw my next-door neighbor and her mutt in her front yard. When they saw me, both of them turned around to face the other direction. The mutt promptly squatted to do her business. I bet she wanted to do it in my yard but feared incarceration.

As I neared Lou's place I saw he was already standing at the curb. I pulled up, and he quickly got in and buckled as I sped away.

"So, what's our message of the day, Lou?"

"Don't have one."

"Don't have one?"

"Is there an echo in here?"

"Is there an echo in here? I wonder if this means that we are about to become free men again."

"We're already free, Cy. At least I'm not married. You didn't happen to tie the knot last night, did you?"

"No, remember, I was never a boy scout. I'm not any good at tying knots. So, enough of this fiddle-faddle. What did you think of the book?"

"Of course I enjoyed it. I figured out who did it, too."

"So, did I, but then I usually do."

"Me, too."

"So, Lou, we've been at this for a couple of years now."

"Has it been that long? It seems like we only discovered the bodies months ago."

"I'm talking about reading mysteries and you know it. Now, tell me, have you got any favorite authors?"

"Well, there are some I prefer to others, but I can't say I have one or two favorites. It's more like favorite books. Most of my favorites of the books I've read are classic mysteries."

"Me, too. Which ones?"

"Well, let's see. I really like *The Murder of Roger Ackroyd* and *Death on the Nile* by Agatha Christie, *Green For Danger* by Christianna Brand, and *The Red House Mystery* by A.A. Milne. You know, the guy who's famous for writing about Winnie the Pooh."

"I know. I love that book, too. It's a shame it's the only mystery he ever wrote."

"So, how about you, Cy? Do you have any favorite authors?"

"Well, as far as classics are concerned, I like Christie, Erle Stanley Gardner, and S.S. Van Dine. My favorite current authors are Mary Higgins Clark, Carolyn Hart, and Martha Grimes. Of course, there are several others I like a lot."

I thought about who some of those other authors are until I realized we were getting close to the school. While I didn't plan to stop at the school, I wanted to see if our conversation yesterday had frightened Walter Gillis away. A couple of minutes later, I realized that I was no spider and he was no Miss Muffet. Evidently, he really felt we didn't have a case against him.

We passed the school. I was beginning to get the lay of the land. As we neared Flat Rock Road, I slowed Lightning down and flicked Lightning's left turn signal, even though more than likely there wasn't another vehicle for miles. As always, the incline pushed us against the back of the seat, until we leveled out. I was thankful that I didn't have to attempt that incline in the winter, but then coming back down would have been even worse. I could see us sliding through the stop sign and Lightning ending up in the trees across the way, with her body full of lacerations.

We passed Duck Spencer's place, saw him out front near the road, appearing not to notice us. He seemed to be mowing grass that didn't need mowing. I wondered if he knew of our visit.

As we neared the dead-end near old man Spickard's place, I sensed that Lightning had begun to tense up. I too wondered if it was safe to leave Lightning alone. I decided to do so, because I wanted Lou with me, in case Spickard tried to fill me with lead.

I parked and we got out. I walked across the road and looked through the trees, trying to see if riffraff were afoot. I saw or heard nothing. When I had satisfied my feelings as much as was possible considering the situation, I moved back over to Lightning, whispered some comforting parting words, and headed off with Lou to Spickard's cabin. Every few feet, I stopped and turned around, checking on Lightning. Halfway there, I was surprised to see Spickard approaching.

"I heard you coming, so I decided to come to meet you. I remember last time you was here, those juvenile delinquents stole your whatchamacallit."

He laughed before continuing.

"Though, Duck Spencer said if he had one of them things you drive, he'd put it out on the road and hope somebody stole it."

This time he stopped, laughed and slapped both knees. I didn't share his humor. I wanted to tell him that a Whatchamacallit is a candy bar, and it might have been the name of one of Volkswagen's cars at some point, but my Lightning wasn't one of them.

When Spickard didn't slow down when he got to us, I realized that he really was going to stage this to do out by

Lightning. Lou and I turned around and followed him back to where my pride and joy was waiting.

After what Spickard called my baby, I was a little perturbed when he leaned up against her.

"Mr. Spickard, what's so important that we had to come all the way out here today?"

"Walter Gillis is what's so all-important. I heard you thinking of arresting him for these here murders. I just want you to know it ain't gonna do you no good."

"Oh?"

"If'n you arrest him, I'm gonna say that it was me that done it."

"But you have an alibi for the whole time you were at the school that night."

"Them there alibis have a way of appearing and disappearing whenever they's convenient."

"How did you hear this, Mr. Spickard? And how did you call us? I was under the impression you don't have a phone."

"I was under the same impression, but I got legs, and Duck Spencer's got a phone. He let me use his'n."

"And how did you hear this news, anyway?"

"That's not important. What's important is that I'm gonna do what I have to do. Now, it'd be best for you city boys to forget all about these here murders and go about more important things. I'm serious about what I say. You ain't gonna convict my friend, so there's no need of you stirring stuff up."

I told Spickard I'd pass his message on to the Chief and the DA, but I had no voice in the matter. He said he understood that, but just to let them know that they can't win this time.

We thanked him and I headed around to Lightning's driver's side. Lou said, "excuse me," and Spickard moved from near the door. I stood at the door, thanked Spickard for calling, and got in and started the car. Spickard backed up a little but stood there until we turned around and headed back toward town.

We seemed to be popular that morning because we'd gone only a quarter of a mile when I looked up and saw Duck Spencer standing in the middle of the road with his hand up. I guess he wanted a few minutes with us, too.

I rolled down the window but refrained from turning the air conditioner off.

"Mr. Spencer. So, what can I do for you today? I can't help you with your grass cutting. I don't even mow my own."

"That don't surprise me, Lieutenant. I seen you on your way to see Earl Spickard. I didn't figure you'd be there long, so I just come out to put my two cents worth in. Just in case you's planning on charging either of 'em janitors with them murders, I want you to know that there's some of us who is willing to say that them janitors never went near that kitchen that night."

"Is that right? Do any of you plan to claim responsibility for shutting the freezer door?"

"Nope. We figured it was Conkwright and my wife that shut theirselves in that freezer."

"And it doesn't bother you that someone ended your wife's life?"

"Didn't nobody end it but her. Just remember, Lieutenant, you ain't gonna win this one. You might as well give up."

I thanked Spencer for his contribution and he stepped back. I rolled up the window and Lightning puttered on toward home. I took in the sights on the way back, figuring that I wouldn't be making any more trips out that way.

+++

Luckily, it was not yet noon, so the Chief wouldn't be keeping us from lunch. At least, I hoped he wouldn't be.

For the second day in a row, Lou and I headed to the police station, parked, and walked in to see the Chief. He had alerted his secretary that Lou and I were his top priority, and she got up to knock on his office door as soon as she saw us coming down the hall.

"Well, Cy, what did the old man want?"

I filled the Chief in on what Spickard and Spencer had to say to us and he wasted no time calling the DA. This time he relayed the message to the DA over the phone, which kept us from having to make a second trip to headquarters or a trip to the DA's office. A decision was arrived at quickly. A story would be released to the newspaper that the two people died accidentally. Everyone hoped that the paper wouldn't pry for more information. The Chief thanked the two of us for all the work we did on the case and hoped we weren't disappointed.

+++

"So, Cy, what are you planning on doing?"

"I think I'll go home and see what pomegranates are."

"Cy, I think the sun's getting to you. Want me to go with you to the hospital and see if you're suffering from heatstroke."

I filled Lou in about pomegranates being good for us, and I was curious as to what they are. Then, he understood.

"But Cy, I don't think that'll take long. What do you plan to do after that?"

"Well, I'm thinking about taking a little trip."

"You? Take a trip? And without me?"

"It's not that I don't like having you around, Lou. It's just that the last time you were around when she was, I felt like you were cramping my style."

"Oh, I see now. So, do you plan to surprise her?"

"No, I want to make sure I'm wanted."

"Well, unless things have changed considerably, I'd say you're very much wanted. Do you want me to call you at her place the next time someone's murdered?"

"I'm not planning on moving in with her. I just thought it'd be nice to drive down and see her for a couple of days."

+++

I went home and Googled pomegranates. I had no idea what they taste like, but they looked like red lemons. I guess I could try one. If I didn't like them, I'd give the rest of them to Lou, and go with the other five food groups.

I didn't want to become an expert on pomegranates, so I moved on to Google maps. After checking out a couple of things, it was time to make my phone call.

In a few seconds, that beautiful creature answered the phone. She sounded out of breath. She must have Caller ID.

"Did I catch you at a bad time?"

"Cy, you can catch me anytime you want. As it turns out, I just got through with a five-mile run on the beach."

"I didn't realize there's a beach anywhere near where you live."

"There's not. But there's one on my Wii."

" I see. Say, I was thinking. I've been looking at that place where you live and did you know there's a Holiday Inn Express not too far from your house?"

"I've seen it many times. Are you trying to tell me you've finished with your case?"

"We have. And I thought this might be a good time to take Lightning for a long drive, see what she can do. She's never been too far away from home."

"Well, I think this would be about the right distance to check her out, see what she can do."

"Actually, I was thinking about checking someone else out. That is if you can spare a couple of days for a cop who has nothing to do."

"I think I can arrange it. When are you coming?"

"Well, if Scotty were around to beam me up, I'd say in a few minutes, but I need to pack some things. Would it be okay if I left in the morning?"

"I'll dream of you all night long."

"I'll try to wait until tomorrow to dream of you. I've heard dreaming about that special someone makes a long trip seem not quite so long."

We talked for another half hour, and then I hung up. It was time to think about what I planned to take with me and to print directions to her place. But before I did anything else, I went over and turned on the Wii. It was time to find out if old Cy could make it all the way through the Ten Minute Run.

Author's Note: Ready for another Dekker mystery? Only a couple of detectives can attend an art and craft fair and find a dead body. Murder at the Art & Craft Fair is the next book in the Dekker Cozy Mystery Series. Click below to download it now.

Made in the USA
Columbia, SC
28 April 2023